CHEMSWORTH HALL
BOOK ONE: VIOLET

Lady Mulholland is Up to Something

Chapter One

Chemsworth Hall was rather more a castle than a hall, with all the associated crumbling walls and cold rooms that one expects in the best old castles. The great hall was large enough to accommodate a half-dozen horses riding abreast, though nobody had tried such a feat in the past hundred years. There was even the remnant of a moat just outside the doors, filled in after the need for moats had come and gone. The house sat on a hill overlooking miles of rolling countryside, a veritable stone sentry surveying its land with a satisfied eye. It was the seat of Viscount Mulholland and the scene of the ever-expanding Granger family.

The Viscountess, Elspeth Granger, known in society as Lady Mulholland, was a tall and regal-looking woman. Her blond hair was generally swept up into a complicated style that only her lady's maid understood and she was in the habit of wearing her best jewels as a regular occurrence. Lady Mulholland did not don her emeralds to impress others, but rather to impress herself. She generally viewed her own opinion as being paramount to everybody else's opinion, as her opinion could be counted upon to be right.

Lady Mulholland ruled her kingdom with a friendly fist, though that fist being composed of a material as strong as iron. It was well that she ruled over her family so firmly, as the lady was in the habit of producing children with a gusto that surprised her neighbors. She was also in the habit of naming those children with systematic rigor and she had early become enamored with the idea of naming one's daughters after the flora that might be found in one's garden.

As Lady Mulholland had delivered more daughters than was generally expected of a viscount's wife, by the time she had delivered number seven, flower names had begun to run a bit thin on the ground.

Over the course of twelve years, the female side of the Granger household had expanded to include Violet, Rose, Daisy, Lily, Marigold and, finally, the twins—Poppy and Pansy. The girls joked that if there were one more daughter brought into the world by Lady Mulholland, that child should be named Feverfew or Foxglove. Lady Mulholland, herself, was rather relieved that her remarkable run of daughters had come to an end, the twins now having been in residence for eight years. The only offspring to escape this naming frenzy was the Granger's only son, who was very sensibly named Henry.

Lord Mulholland, having been well-pleased after his wife had produced an heir during their first year of marriage, was vastly good-humored regarding the alarming string of daughters that followed. And, as he knew his wife to be fond of patterns and regular order, he thought it just as well that she had chosen flowers to guide her. Had the tea things caught Lady Mulholland's eye while she mulled over the question of baby names, Lord Mulholland may have looked down a dining table at the likes of Charlotte and Madeleine, only to sadly end with the twins—seed cake and clotted cream.

On this day, Lady Mulholland had seated herself in the drawing room, having requested an interview with her son. The room was cavernous and the heat from the fire made its way up into the rafters with hardly a pause to warm its inhabitants. Since the fireplace could not be convinced to do its work properly, there were various throws covered in beaver, fox and marten strewn about to assist in the endeavor. She pulled just such an item over her lap and regarded her son.

"The whole scheme hangs on you, my love."

Henry stood in front of the fire, warming his hands. He was relieved that his mother had not heard some report from his term at Oxford, as he had perhaps had occasion to drink too much and he always found that pranks and hi-jinx seemed a good idea when he drank too much. However, that relief only lasted a moment as he considered her actual directive.

"I do not see how I am to be responsible for getting all these girls married," he said, vaguely uncomfortable in the knowledge that once his mother determined that something must be done, that thing was inevitably done—whether or not anybody agreed to it, or even understood it.

"Of course, you are responsible," Lady Mulholland said. "Just think, Henry. You shall wish to marry someday and then how shall it be? You will become the next Viscount and shall you expect your wife to share the house with seven spinster sisters? The notion is absurd."

That notion *was* absurd, though Henry did not see what he was to do about it. Why should not his sisters go out and find their own husbands? Could they not go to neighborhood balls and scrounge somebody up?

"You cannot expect your sisters, daughters of a respected viscount, to go round the neighborhood gathering up likely-looking fellows," Lady Mulholland said.

Henry once again cursed the Gods that his mother had been given the gift of being able to read his thoughts. That was *precisely* what he had hoped. Somehow, she always seemed to know what he hoped, and then cheerfully explained to him why his hope was wrong.

"My darling," Lady Mulholland said, "the thing is simple enough. We shall have house parties. The bird shooting is excellent, there are foxes everywhere, your father has been breeding and fussing over those hounds of his for years and we've plenty of horses to spare for those who arrive un-equipped. When it is not the right season for hunting, we shall devise some other way to amuse. You shall review your Oxford friends and invite down the most eligible. Nobody shall turn their nose up at an invitation from Viscount Mulholland—we are too renowned for our hospitality and our guests always do find our ancient dwelling so very interesting."

Henry sighed. It appeared his mother wished to line up his friends as so many sacrifices to the altar of the Granger girls. "But why should they not just have a season in town?" he asked. "That is what everybody else does."

"Because there are seven of them," Lady Mulholland said. "I should have to spend half my life and half of your father's money to get the job done. Further, I despise town and most of the people who live in it—one woman is more falsely delicate than the next. I cannot live amongst ladies who wave their smelling salts like so many white flags. No, we Grangers are far more sensible people. *We* shall have the gentlemen come to *us*."

Smuckers discreetly knocked and entered the room. The butler was tall and portly and his shirt was starched to such a degree that it was perfectly possible for that garment to walk off on its own if it had a mind to. His expression was grim, he being of the opinion that it suited the illustriousness of the house.

As was Smuckers' usual habit, he carried Dandy to his mistress, holding the dog in front of him as if it were a dangerous predator intent on overpowering him. The Pomeranian had the heart of a lion, but had been saddled with the body of an overfed cotton ball. For that reason, Dandy did not care to walk great distances. Or any distances.

Lady Mulholland took Dandy onto her lap. "Thank you, Smuckers. Would you be so kind as to send in tea for our returning academic? He shall have a lot to think of when I am through and tea always does help, I find."

Smuckers nodded and walked out, picking off the white Pomeranian hairs that now clung to his black coat. It was a useless effort in Henry's mind; as soon as Smuckers got them all off, it would be time to pick up Dandy once again and move him to another room in the house.

Lady Mulholland cupped Dandy's face, appearing to talk to the dog, though Henry was well aware she was still talking to him.

"Do not for a moment rule out anybody who cannot shoot. These days there are such gentlemen, so Mrs. Dallway tells me, and I will not allow myself to be prejudiced against them. If the gentleman's family and money are up to snuff, I shouldn't care if he'd never picked up a gun in his life. Though it might be the sort of thing best left unmentioned to the Viscount."

Henry fairly recoiled at the idea. What sort of man did not shoot? Certainly not any of his own friends. His father would think a man who did not shoot completely mad.

"Your father and I knew we should send you to Oxford for this very purpose once we noticed how many daughters were to be had. Or, at least, *I* knew. I apprised your father of the idea some time ago, but one never knows precisely what he's heard—he was entirely engrossed in a plan to rehabilitate a tenant cottage at the time."

His whole education had been predicated on how many sisters were roaming the grounds? He supposed he should rejoice that there were seven. If he had only one sister he might be educating *himself* in his own library.

"Fortunately, we are but two hours from Oxford, that great eternal spring of eligible young gentlemen," Lady Mulholland said, kissing the top of Dandy's head. "We are blessed, indeed."

Though it might be close, Oxford had opened a whole new world to Henry. He had stumbled around when he'd arrived for his first term, taken slightly aback at finding himself not very important. He had thought, wearing a gold tuft on his cap, that he would be afforded all the respect that he received from his neighbors at home. He quickly became apprised that he had left his own neighborhood entirely and was now thrust into the wider world. This wider world contained a large number of gentlemen who held rank above him. He was no longer the most important man in the room and he had stumbled along until Smythesdon had taken him under his experienced wing. *Lord* Smythesdon to those not on intimate terms with the man.

Smythesdon had opened doors. Smythesdon had taken him to *The Queen's Lane*, that esteemed coffee house where the intellects of England debated the issues of the day. Or, if not all the intellects of England, then surely some of them. Smythesdon was determined to become a leading intellect himself. Henry had, at first, joined in on the idea, but in the end he had decided it might be more work than he liked. He was content to step back and merely admire Smythesdon's intellect.

"Now who do you suppose would do for Violet?" Lady Mulholland inquired.

"I have no idea," Henry said. "She's comely enough, but she's a bit of a know-all, in case you haven't noticed."

"Henry," Lady Mulholland said, in that tone that was friendly on the surface, but which Henry knew to be an iron fist poised above his head, "do not become too important for your own family simply because you now find yourself an Oxford man. I would also caution you not to forget that your sisters bring ten thousand apiece. Naturally, it would have been more had there not been quite so many of them, but it is still a respectable sum. They are attractive, with the exception of Marigold who no doubt shall grow into her looks any day now. They are accomplished in every feminine art, with the exception of Marigold who no doubt will settle down any day now and learn how to sew. Any gentleman would be fortunate to win Violet as his own. Further, you have no higher responsibility or purpose than to help your family. And do see that you bring me somebody likely to favor Violet rather than Rose or Daisy. I have a mind to go in strict order. Write your letters and I shall expect at least one likely somebody to arrive in all haste."

Lady Mulholland stood and plunked Dandy onto her chair. As she swept from the room, she said, "And do not mention a word of this to the girls. Love is best sowed in an air of mystery and mention of practicalities is rarely helpful." The Pomeranian watched his mistress go, then it turned its scowl on Henry.

Henry sat down. It was the most ridiculous scheme he had ever heard. He could not very well ask a friend if he should like to come to Chemsworth Hall so that his sister could have a look at him. What should he say? And by the way, my good man, if you would not mind proposing to Violet, and it must be Violet, that would be jolly decent of you.

He had not invited any friends home for the term break because he thought any gentleman his own age would be alarmed at so many females wandering around. Especially females like Violet and Rose. Violet knew enough information to be a Vice Chancellor and did not hesitate to inform all and sundry of that fact. Rose was to be counted on to say anything that came to mind, and what went on in Rose's mind could be frightening. Why they could not be like Daisy, he could not understand. Daisy was what one would expect from a young lady—kind, cheerful and never holding a grudge against anybody.

Now, he was to lead some innocent victim into a veritable lion's den of females.

Still, his mother had issued a directive and so he must produce somebody. He decided he'd better consult Smythesdon on the matter. Smythesdon knew what to do about everything. If there was a right way and wrong way to go about the thing, Smythesdon would know it.

Smuckers brought in the tea and set it down. He handed Henry a letter from the post, then stared glumly at Dandy. He picked the dog up and muttered, "Lady Mulholland requests Dandy's presence in her sitting room."

Henry took the letter. He knew from the handwriting that the letter was from Smythesdon. He was beyond pleased that his friend had written him so promptly. It showed that Smythesdon had not forgotten about him and it gave him the perfect opportunity to write his friend back and get some much-needed advice. He tore open the letter.

Hello chap—

How are things at Chemsworth? Your dear old family rejoicing at the return of the prodigal son? Things are a right mess at Donneville at the moment. My father has got some harebrained idea that I ought to marry soon and has inflicted more than a few unwelcome conversations upon me. Dash it, I hate to disappoint the old soldier, but what can I do? For now, at least, my studies must be my only passion or I do not see how I shall become a leading intellect. I've explained the thing backwards and forwards but he says it's all stuff and nonsense and he did not send me to Oxford to turn myself into a handkerchief-waving intellectual. I'm tempted to run off to Brighton or some such place until he's cooled his heels on the topic.

Send me cheerful news as there is no cheer here. I am just now going to the stables as I know he is in the house looking for me.

Smythesdon

Henry laid the letter down. He knew what he would do, he would invite Smythesdon. Smythesdon would thank him for sending out the life boat. At the same time, he would satisfy his mother's demands, and then prove to her that the whole idea was ridiculous. Smythesdon was eminently eligible, but he would not be caught. He most certainly would not be caught by Violet Granger. Once Lady Mulholland was convinced that such a scheme could not find success, she would do something sensible like take the eldest girls to town for a season. There would, of course, be no need to mention any of this nonsense to Smythesdon.

Chapter Two

V iolet Granger's bedchamber was a study in blues and purples. She did not particularly care for the color and would have much preferred a sunny yellow, but her mother had insisted that each girl's room be the color of the flower she was named after. Fortunately, Lady Mulholland was also of the opinion that all her girls should be comfortable and so the room was well-appointed with heavy carpets and curtains to keep out the cold, a large- bedstead piled high with goose down covers, a dressing table with a looking glass, and a cozy collection of overstuffed chairs in front of the fire. Two of those chairs were currently occupied by her sisters, Rose and Daisy.

Violet fussed with a ribbon. "She is up to something," she said.

It was an unspoken understanding between the three eldest Granger females that when *she* was the subject of a conversation, *she* was Lady Mulholland. They had various code words for this gale wind that directed their lives—Lady Mulholland was also known as the ODM, short for Our Dear Mother, and the TFD short for The Friendly Dragon.

"How can you know it?" Rose asked.

"I just know it," Violet said.

Daisy twirled a blond curl around her finger. "Come now, Miss Grim Granger," she said teasingly to her eldest sister, "You always think the ODM is up to something."

"And I am always right," Violet said. "Do you not recall my last alarm on the subject? Do you not remember her lamenting that none of us could sketch sufficiently despite years of tutoring? I *knew* she was up to something. And then what do you suppose happened? We spent the entire month of April under the tutelage of that horrible Mr. Jenkins. We were veritable slaves to charcoal and paint, traipsing around in cold rain to locate his idea of inspiring vistas. By the end of it, I could hardly feel my legs."

"Of course," Rose said, "it was only I who told Jenkins that he was horrible. The rest of you pretended that he was not horrible. It seems to me that if a man is horrible, he ought to be told it."

"You tell people far too much," Violet said. "A very bad habit that will get you into trouble one of these days."

"Now Rose," Daisy said, "Marigold did tell him that she much preferred her horse, so you were not alone in your insults. And, for all your complaints, we are ever so much more accomplished in drawing now. Can you deny it? Mr. Jenkins would certainly not be liked by all the world, his scowl would prevent it, but I always suspected he had a rather soft heart underneath all that bluster."

Rose slumped in her chair. "Daisy, why must you insist on liking absolutely everybody?"

"Because it is far more pleasant to like everybody than it is to dislike everybody," Daisy said.

"I do not dislike *everybody*," Rose said.

"We are veering away from the matter at hand," Violet said. "I say once again, she is up to something."

"And what if she is?" Rose said. "We could no more stop her than tell the stars to stop shining in the sky. Once the ODM has decided upon something, we must all just duck for cover and hope to be passed by unnoticed."

Mr. Smuckers was in the habit of taking his tea with the housekeeper, Mrs. Featherstone. They took this tea in his butler's closet, that room having a desk where he might view accounts and two comfortable chairs placed in front of a small fireplace. It was not large by anybody's standards, but he could not envy those above stairs in their elegantly drafty rooms. *They* might have space, but *he* had warmth. That was no small thing in a house like Chemsworth.

He was comfortable in taking tea with Mrs. Featherstone, as it gave him a half hour to relieve his feelings regarding whatever he had witnessed upstairs. Smuckers witnessed quite a lot upstairs, as he took some amount of pride in his lurking capabilities. Should there ever be an emergency of any sort, Smuckers was invariably nearby and could step into it in a thrice. That there had not, as of yet, been any sort of emergency only convinced him that one might very well be looming on the horizon and poised to strike. While he was happy to lurk at the ready, and heard quite a lot while he was at it, he would not for the world be known as a gossip. Mrs. Featherstone could be counted on to keep information close. Smuckers could discuss various happenings with all confidence that nothing he said would be repeated by that good lady. He had been complaining of Dandy and the white hairs on his coat for above two years to her sympathetic ear and yet nobody knew a thing about it.

"You shall never guess what our good Lady is up to now," he said, pouring a cup of tea for Mrs. Featherstone.

"I shan't never guess, no more than guess the weather for a fortnight from now," Mrs. Featherstone said. "So you'd best tell me."

"It seems," Smuckers said, relishing the originality of the news he was to impart, "that Lady Mulholland has directed Mr. Granger to begin bringing home friends from Oxford. *And*, he is to bring them as suitors. The first is to court Miss Violet Granger."

Mrs. Featherstone sipped her tea and stared at the fire with a thoughtful expression. She was a woman of unknown years, though one could reasonably speculate that she had left her youth behind some time ago. The fact that *'feather'* and *'stone'* comprised her surname was of great amusement to the maids of the house, as she was as thin as a post and might be in some danger of blowing away like a feather in a strong wind unless she were secured to the ground with a stone. Her lips were usually pursed, as the lady liked to look upon the world with a certain air of suspicion.

13

Mrs. Featherstone considered herself the more practical of the two senior servants ruling Chemsworth Hall, and she prided herself in bringing a hefty dose of commonsense to Mr. Smuckers' attention. After having considered the matter from every angle, she set her cup down and said, "It don't make a lick of sense. What's to say that any of these fellows is looking for a bride or, if he is, that he be looking for such a one as Miss Violet? What's to say he comes here and finds he fancies Miss Rose, or Miss Daisy?"

"Lady Mulholland is far ahead of you on that point," Smuckers said. "Mr. Granger has been given strict instructions that any gentleman coming must court only the eldest. You know how she prefers order, she will not be thwarted in it."

"And there's the rub," Mrs. Featherstone said, triumphant. "Lady Mulholland is a marvel, I'll not deny it. But even *she* cannot rule a gentleman's heart. A man's heart is a wild and unpredictable thing and why I never thought to chain myself to one in holy matrimony. A person cannot guess what will be in the confounded thing next. An uncomfortable state of affairs, but there you have it."

Smuckers was disturbed at this assessment. For one thing, he was certain his own heart was not wild and unpredictable. It was steady and dignified, if it was to have the audacity to be anything at all. For another, after twenty years of service, he knew his mistress well. He had been an observer from the very beginning and, from the beginning, Lady Mulholland had ruled the roost. That lady was seldom disappointed in a scheme and he could not look with complacence upon the possibility of some gentleman's wild and unpredictable heart thwarting her.

"And what's to say," Mrs. Featherstone continued, "that Miss Violet will favor the gentleman that's been dragged in?"

"*Dragged* in?" Smuckers said, mortified that Lady Mulholland should be associated with any sort of dragging.

Yet, despite his disapprobation at the housekeeper's phrasings, Mrs. Featherstone had broached yet another complication. The eldest Miss Granger *could* be headstrong. She was very much in the habit of having her own opinions. He would even go so far to say that she could be, at times, contrary.

Still, if Lady Mulholland was determined to enact such a plan, he could only carry on with it in supreme confidence. To do anything less would be to let down the house. Smuckers was not the sort of butler that let down the house. The very idea was anathema to him.

What his own role in the scheme would be, he did not yet know. All he did know was that he would be lurking in anticipation of it. While he waited, he had formulated a few ideas.

"We must do our bit in this campaign, Mrs. Featherstone," Smuckers said gravely. "We shall subtly hint to Victorine that she is to take special care with Miss Violet's person. She shall employ all of her lady's maid skills to present the eldest Miss Granger in the best light possible and that will intrigue the visiting gentleman. As for Miss Violet herself, we shall direct Mr. Moreau to see to it that there are almond biscuits at tea. We know them to be a favorite of Miss Granger's and that shall dispose her to kind feelings. We can only hope those kind feelings may extend to any nearby gentleman. Then we shall standby for further orders—we shall be as ready as troops in his majesty's army."

"Or," Mrs. Featherstone said, "we can just let them all sort themselves out however they might."

The dining room of Chemsworth Hall was a cavernous affair—long enough to have been built with six fireplaces to warm it, two on either side and one at each end. That these fireplaces did not particularly warm it should have surprised nobody, as Chemsworth's fireplaces were known to be lackadaisical and wholly unsympathetic to the inmates of the house. The candles on the table provided better warmth to the diners and Lady Mulholland was in the habit of ordering the table to be lit as if it were noon-time so that her family might experience a slight warming of air. Braziers were placed underneath the table and it was generally the one time of day that the family's feet were not cold. The table of the room was, in fact, many tables and could be pulled apart to make a small and cozy space for the family or put together all the way up to a formal dinner for sixty.

The Viscount sat at the head of the family's small table, just then waxing on about hay or sheep or cattle. It was unlikely that anybody knew which he waxed on about, as they had all given up attempting to keep track of the doings of the estate. If the Viscount were not hunting, he spent his days with his steward—he was keenly interested in the workings of the home farm and the health and welfare of his various tenants. He could not be particularly blamed for failing to notice that the rest of his family was not so enamored with the subject, as he never inquired into their opinions. Eyes gazing and heads nodding in his direction were deemed entirely sufficient.

Lord Mulholland finally came to the conclusion of a rousing tale of an escaped pig and the methods and trickery employed to get it back. Lady Mulholland, as she did every evening at this exact moment of the family dinner, said, "My darling, you are so very clever. It gives me great comfort that Chemsworth is in your capable hands."

There was always some slight variation to the compliment, but it was generally well received by Lord Mulholland. That gentleman knew that Lady Mulholland meant what she said. It *did* give the lady comfort to know that her family was secure of their estate. If he were the captain of the ship, she was its surgeon, keeping a hawk's eye on Chemsworth's inhabitants to assure herself of their good health and prosperity.

Having accomplished her duty to her husband, Lady Mulholland looked meaningfully at her son. "I believe Henry has news?" she said.

"Do you?" the Viscount said, peering at Henry. "Good news, I hope? I have little patience for bad news, it generally benefits nobody."

"Yes, I believe it is good news," Henry said, knowing he was already coloring at the idea of finding himself in the middle of this farce. "I shall have a friend visit. Lord Smythesdon. Bertram Smythesdon."

Henry could feel his sisters' eyes boring into him, all ten eyes from five sisters. Had Poppy and Pansy been old enough to sit at table, he was certain he would feel seven pairs of eyes. His sisters, especially Violet, were particularly good at noticing when something was not quite up to snuff.

Marigold said, "Can this Smythesdon sit a horse creditably? And you know what I mean by creditably, he is not to be hanging on like a fool. He must be in full control of his animal. If he cannot ride creditably, we should not allow him through the doors."

Henry suppressed a sigh. Marigold was obsessed with horses. She was even more obsessed with who rode well and who did not. Those that did not ride well, in her opinion, were some sort of traitors to all that England stood for. Those that did not ride well also happened to include her younger sister Lily, who was rather frightened of the beasts.

Lily looked to Lady Mulholland to counter this attack on her character, which Lady Mulholland promptly did. She stared gravely at Marigold and shook her head. Marigold slumped in her chair—her own particular style of protest, as she knew perfectly well that her mother frowned on slumping.

"Smythesdon?" Lord Mulholland said. "Never heard of the fellow."

This was not surprising to Henry. His father owned no copy of Debrett's and, had he owned one, he would never have cracked it open. Lord Mulholland only concerned himself with his own county and, for all he cared about it, the rest of the counties in England might drop off the map. Henry could only be grateful that he need not announce that his friend kept a house in London, as that town, in the Viscount's opinion, should fling itself off the map with vigor and haste. He had heard the story of his father and mother's courtship many times—they had fallen in love while commiserating with each other at a London ball about how much they despised the town and everybody in it. Lord Mulholland had asked Lady Mulholland for a dance, as she had appeared just as disgusted with the evening as he had himself. The first words she uttered during the Quadrille were, "This town is tiresome and these people are a bore." He had proceeded to escort the lady into dinner and was in her father's library requesting her hand within the month.

Loathing for a place and its people was not generally thought to be a promising beginning to romance, but it had seemed to be just the thing for Lord and Lady Mulholland.

"Smythesdon is from Hampshire," Henry said, knowing he'd better get that bit of unwelcome news out at once.

"Hampshire?" Lord Mulholland asked, as if that place were no closer than the Americas.

"His father is the Earl of Ainsworth," Henry said, mainly for the benefit of his sisters, as Smythesdon's father might be the Earl of Timbuktu for all his father would care about it.

"Is he the eldest?" Lord Mulholland asked.

"He is," Henry said. "He is the only son."

"Very respectable," Lord Mulholland said.

Henry had known that Smythesdon being an only son was the one point that would find favor with his father. Lord Mulholland had an aversion to second and third sons. He often noted that nobody knew what to do with them and what sort of man would want to be born if he knew he would be forced to become a vicar or join the army? The Viscount counted himself lucky that he had not that particular problem to sort out. He had evidently forgotten that he had the problem of seven daughters to sort out.

"He arrives in two days' time," Henry said.

"Well," Lord Mulholland said, appearing resigned to the notion that a gentleman he'd never heard of, from the far-off land of Hampshire, should soon be one among them, "I suppose we shall keep this foreigner entertained as best we might."

Somebody, and it might very well have been Daisy Granger, giggled into her napkin. She found her father deliciously eccentric and would not change him for the world.

"Do you suppose he's a pheasant man or a fox man?" The Viscount asked. Viscount Mulholland was disposed to a fox man, as that required horsemanship. When one had beaters for pheasant, a hunter might stand around and shoot at his leisure. Even an idiot might hit something if he stood around long enough.

Smythesdon, according to what he had told Henry, was an excellent shot and an experienced horseman. However, Henry knew his father's views on the subject. "Fox hunting will surely suit," he said.

There was a silence at table and Henry dared broach the detail that had weighed on his mind ever since he had imagined Smythesdon walking through the doors of Chemsworth Hall. "Perhaps," he said softly, "it would be just the men going out to a hunt this time."

"What?" the Viscount said from his end of the table. "I could not hear a word of that."

Marigold, though, had heard Henry quite clearly. As he feared, a look of fury settled over her features.

"I just say, father," Henry pressed on, "that it's not so usual for women to go foxhunting."

"You can hardly expect a foxhunt to go out from this house without Marigold," the Viscount said. "She sits a horse better than you do."

Marigold nodded her assent at this assessment. "I do not hang on like a fool," she said.

Henry sighed. He would have to explain to Smythesdon how it was that one of his sisters would not only accompany them, but would likely shame them with her skill.

"I do not see why Rose and I should not go," Violet said. She did not, perhaps, love foxhunting, but she could sit a horse and it irked her that this Smythesdon should prefer the females left behind.

"I do not see why either," the Viscount said. "I do not suppose our Daisy can be persuaded?"

"Dear me, no, papa," Daisy said. "I would sooner stab myself in the eye than kill a poor little animal."

19

The Viscount sighed and waved his hand over the table. "Everything you see here once walked on two legs or four. What do you suppose they did, jumped into the pot with no assistance? Furthermore, your beloved foxes would take all the small game if we let them—they have a particular penchant for young chickens."

This turned Daisy a bit green, as she was one of those individuals who could eat a chicken with gusto and then sob inconsolably over a dead chick found in the yard.

Henry felt greenish himself. He would have three sisters on the hunt and he was certain such a thing had never occurred at Donneville.

"Bah, Daisy," Marigold said. "We do not always kill a fox. That is the fun of it, the chase. It is a thousand times more interesting than shooting at birds."

Despite Marigold's assurance that Daisy would much prefer running down a fox to shooting a bird, her sister would not be moved.

The house had fallen into its nightly silence, the family having gone up. Smuckers, never entirely allowing himself to be off duty, kept one ear open for the sound of intruders. That there had not been any intruders since the unrest of 1530 only convinced him that their luck would soon run out. He intended to die a glorious death at the front door to keep them out.

He set down his tea. "The campaign begins, Mrs. Featherstone," he said. "A gentleman by the name of Lord Bertram Smythesdon arrives in two days' time. I cannot say that him being from Hampshire particularly weighed in his favor. However, the Viscount appears resigned to having him in the house and Lady Mulholland was pleased. For our own part, we shall shortly have the son of an Earl in the house, the only and eldest son of that particular Earl and so to be an Earl himself someday, and I am determined he shall find everything up to his own standards."

"You know me, Mr. Smuckers," Mrs. Featherstone said, "I like to put a bright face on things and walk on the sunny side of the road. But as much as I'm searchin' for the sunshine in this, all I see is disaster racing round the corner. Disaster is racing round the corner fast and hard."

Smuckers had heard of this allusion to walking on the sunny side of the road many times from Mrs. Featherstone. He was sure she was mistaken, as she generally predicted disasters that made him shudder.

"How did Miss Violet appear to take the news?" Mrs. Featherstone asked.

Smuckers shifted uncomfortably in his chair. He had watched the eldest Miss Granger's expressions closely while the announcement had been made. She had first stared at Lady Mulholland with a grim expression. Then she had turned and stared at Henry, then she had given a meaningful look to Rose Granger.

"I cannot say for certain," Smuckers said, "but I may have noted the slightest hint of suspicion."

"I knew it," Mrs. Featherstone said, appearing satisfied that things had gone wrong once again, just as she had predicted.

Smuckers was not to be so easily defeated. "Mrs. Featherstone, as the two senior members of the below-stairs household, we must hold our heads high and charge forward for the glory of the house."

Mrs. Featherstone snorted.

If there were anything Smuckers would complain of when it came to Mrs. Featherstone, it would be her lack of enthusiasm for his finer feelings of honor. He felt such things deeply and, had he ever had the chance to prove himself on the battlefield, he was convinced he would have died for King and country. As it was, his own battlefield was Chemsworth Hall and he was determined to bring his troops through to a triumphant victory.

Violet, Rose and Daisy were sprawled on Violet's bed. They had gone up early after Violet had given the signal. They had quite a number of signals, but the one for going up early was "Heavens, I *am* tired." For it to be understood as a signal, it was necessary to include 'heavens' and for the emphasis to be on 'am.' One by one they had excused themselves. Henry had seemed uncomfortable, Violet thought, and she often wondered if he had somehow figured out the meaning of their various signals.

"Did I not say the ODM was up to something?" Violet asked.

"Your imagination runs away from you," Daisy said. "What on earth gives you the idea that some plot is in the works just because we are to have a visitor?"

"Henry's face," Violet said. "Did you not note that he blushed when he announced the arrival of his friend?"

"I did note it," Rose said. "But I rather thought it was the schoolboy in him. You know, bringing a schoolmate home from Oxford for the first time and having the fun of saying he was *Lord* whoever. Young men are like that—to wrangle in a gentleman above their own rank is rather like they had caught the biggest trout in the stream. Though he dare not brag of it, I suppose Henry must be quite pleased with himself."

"Poor Henry," Daisy said, "to be so unmercifully teased by his own sisters."

"As he is not in the room to hear it, I do not see why you should pity him," Rose said. "He hasn't heard a word about it."

"But were he to," Daisy said, "I imagine he would be quite put out about it."

"And yet again," Violet said, "we digress. Why was the TFD so eager to encourage Henry to announce his news? Why was Henry seemingly mortified?"

"Why does father think that Lord Smythesdon is a foreigner because he is from Hampshire?" Daisy said, giggling.

"If she *is* up to something," Violet said, "we've got to discover it."

"If she *is* up to something," Rose said, "it is easy enough to divine what it is. A young gentleman come to stay? Think, Violet.

She wishes to unload one of us. And, if I know our dear mother, she means to go in order."

"Oh," Daisy said, "That would be you, Violet."

Violet had been on the verge of dismissing that speculation as ridiculous, until it occurred to her that it was not so very ridiculous. Her mother had, of late, begun vaguely referring to her children's future. How many of their own children would they have? Would they find the same happiness that she had found with the Viscount? Violet had taken these nebulous questions directed at nobody in particular as a pointed message to Henry—he had best begin considering his future after Oxford.

The idea that her mother had been addressing her eldest daughter...could that be right? After all she was only...well she was just...eighteen.

Violet had been in the habit of ignoring the birthdays that came and went, she had far too much to accomplish. She did not have the time to marry. At least, not just yet.

"Do not be silly," she said. "I have not even completed my studies."

"You will never complete your studies," Rose said. "You just go on and on with it."

"Our Violet *is* terribly clever," Daisy said to Rose.

"I would be further along in those studies," Violet said, "if I had not lost the entire month of April to Mr. Jenkins and his charcoals. In any case, as daring as the ODM can be, not even she can imagine she can manage me in such a fashion. Whoever this Smythesdon character is, I do not like him."

"Violet," Daisy said, "that is hardly fair. Poor Lord Smythesdon has not done a thing you can complain of. Further, he is a friend of Henry's and so I am sure we shall like him."

"Daisy," Rose said, "if, sometime far in the future, you should ever run across somebody you do not like, assure me that you will put pen to paper and alert me to this development. I do not care what distance separates us. I cannot rest easy until you positively dislike at least one individual who walks this earth."

"If we have surmised correctly," Violet said, ignoring Rose's constant irritation over Daisy's lack of discrimination on who ought to be liked and who ought to be despised, "our mother shall find herself disappointed. However, if I am to look on the bright side, this scheme may prove diverting. It should be quite entertaining to observe her machinations and thwart her at every turn."

Chapter Three

Henry lay in bed, a sense of unease settling over him. He had, for some days, felt rather sanguine about his situation. He had been directed to invite somebody to the house and had accomplished his task. Lady Mulholland had been well-pleased. His friend, Smythesdon, had written him back and called him a brick for coming to the rescue. Everybody approved of him and it had all been very comfortable. He had even thought of a way to prevent Marigold from going on the hunt—he would pay her. He still had some of his allowance saved away and he would give her all of it. Violet and Rose might not have really meant to go at all, that had just been Violet's contrariness. It was really only Marigold that would have to be bought off.

But then, Marigold had refused to be paid. She had said that nothing, not even ten thousand pounds, would keep her off her horse on a hunt day. Henry, in a fit of desperation, had claimed that the future Earl would find her silly for going. As it turned out, Marigold did not care who was to be an Earl and who was not and if such persons could not ride creditably they would earn no respect from her.

Now, he felt his steady nerves giving way. The future would come at him at an alarming pace. Smythesdon would actually arrive. What then? What would he make of Violet? He was certain to dislike her—Smythesdon had a very low opinion of know-all females. He said no fact was ruined faster than having a woman spout off about it.

The hunt would be an embarrassment. The sort of thing Smythesdon might mention to everybody when they went back for the term.

And what of his mother, who was certain to not so subtly push his friend and Violet together? What would Smythesdon say if he were to discover that he had been lured to Chemsworth Hall under false pretenses? He was supposed to be helping Smythesdon outwit his father by making the Earl think that his son came to visit with an eye toward a betrothal with one of his sisters. It was all supposed to be a ruse, when in truth Lady Mulholland and the Earl were in unknowing league with each other.

Somehow, he had to ensure that Smythesdon never did discover the truth. If it were known that he had treated his friend in such a manner he would not just lose *that* friendship. He might well be ostracized by all of Oxford. Smythesdon had been his sponsor of sorts—Hemmins, Galbreath, Kingston, all of them, had taken him on like a pet. They were older and more worldly and seemed to like to guide him along. Good grief, Hemmins was to be a Duke. These were the connections he would wish to have for the rest of his life and he may have thrown it all away.

He could not even be sure if his sisters remained in the dark about the whole scheme. They had signaled each other—for years he had noted their glances at one another and then somebody would say, "Heavens, I *am* tired." And then off they would go, one by one. Or one of them would say, "My goodness, that *is* edifying" and then they would wink at each other. He was certain they used these communications as some secret language. He knew they often used them so that they might run up the stairs and congregate in one or the other's bedchambers. He had even once seen Rose and Daisy leave Violet's room long after midnight. What in the world did they talk about? What did they know?

They had signaled each other and fled the drawing room and Lady Mulholland had sent Marigold and Lily up to their beds shortly after. Poppy and Pansy had long since made their appearance and been taken up under the watchful eye of Miss Millthorpe. His father was half asleep near the fire. Lady

Mulholland had leaned over to Henry and said, "We shall seize the day, my darling son, and that will leave us just six more to go."

Henry had been so fixated on his current problem that he had not even considered the future. Poppy and Pansy were only eight! He would be tricking gentlemen into coming to Chemsworth for the rest of his life! It would become known, if not this time, then another of the times. He would become notorious and they would speak of him in London drawing rooms. Be careful of an invitation to Chemsworth Hall, they would say, unless you have a mind to marry a Granger girl.

Then, once the word got out, he would have every adventurer in England angling to visit. He would have to be shrewd in fighting them off. If one were to slip through and cause one of his sisters to marry injudiciously, he would be blamed.

Just a week ago, he had been happy-go-lucky with not a care in the world. What had happened to him?

Of course, he knew what had happened to him. Elspeth Granger, the fourteenth Viscountess Mulholland, had happened to him.

The day had dawned bright and Violet had woken early. A maid had been in to build up the fire and she had leapt out of her bed as soon as the air had warmed. Victorine had interrupted her reading in front of the fire earlier than was her habit, though the lady's maid pretended there was no reason for it. Moments later, Lady Mulholland had arrived. Violet would have been surprised to see her mother in her bedchamber, as that lady was seldom found there or anywhere else so early in the day, had it not been the precise day that Lord Smythesdon was set to arrive. Victorine fussed with Violet's hair, while Lady Mulholland oversaw the whole operation.

"I wonder, mama," Violet said, "that you take such an interest in my hair on this day."

"Why should you wonder?" Lady Mulholland said. "You are my very first daughter and I take an interest in everything about you."

"And yet," Violet pressed on, "there was not such an interest yesterday."

"Yesterday," Lady Mulholland said, "I did not even rise until eleven. Dandy and I were having a marvelous time lying abed. There is nothing so delicious as finding it too cold to rise and deciding not to rise at all. Though heaven help your father, he was up with the roosters and gone out with Mr. Tidewater to see about some broken fence or other. He looked in before he left and called us a couple of layabouts. I replied that nobody could lay about as creditably as his Viscountess and her beloved Dandy when we had a mind to do it. Then he very sensibly agreed with me. He is a very practical man, your father, as he never bothers to disagree when the outcome of the argument means little."

Violet narrowed her eyes. She knew perfectly well this strategy of dodge the subject. Lady Mulholland had befuddled her children more than once by taking the conversation in an entirely different direction. Only a month ago, Violet had asked to take the carriage to town and, somehow, by the end of it she was reciting the Latin names of plants and never did get anywhere near town.

"Anyway, my love," she said, fussing with a strand of Violet's dark hair, "I must be off to confer with Smuckers and Mrs. Featherstone. Henry's friend, Lord Smythesdon, arrives in time for dinner."

Violet took this opportunity to launch the first salvo in the war to be waged against The Friendly Dragon's scheme. "Smythesdon seems a stupid name for one to have," she said, just as Victorine set the last curl around her face. "And then to make it entirely worse, he has the nerve to carry around a name like Bertram." Violet heaved a long and disgusted sigh. "I suppose they call him Bertie at home, nothing could be more ridiculous."

Lady Mulholland paused in her departure. "What could be stupid about Smythesdon? No, Violet, you have got it all wrong— the name Smythesdon fairly drips with dignity."

Violet suppressed a snort. Drip with dignity, indeed.

"In any case, he only carries the Viscount title until he is the Earl."

"And what is the family name?" Violet asked, hoping it was something suitably absurd.

"Battleboro," Lady Mulholland said.

"Battleboro?" Violet asked with glee. "Bertie Battleboro? It sounds like something one would find in a silly children's rhyme."

"Bertram Battleboro is a perfectly respectable name," Lady Mulholland said.

Violet sat looking at her mother's reflection in the glass. That lady heaved a sigh and said, "Withhold your judgment until you have at least laid eyes on him. You may find the name becomes more pleasant upon knowing the owner of it."

Lady Mulholland strode from the room. Violet smiled. "She is a crafty one, Victorine."

"Femme diabolique," Victorine said.

That afternoon, Violet was determined to focus on her studies. She was just then reviewing a paper from the *Philosophical Transactions of the Royal Society,* her opinion being that one ought to know a good deal about the natural world since one was living in it. She found herself re-reading whole paragraphs as her mind drifted this way and that way. It was an unusual sensation, for she generally found that once she began her studies, she became completely lost in them and had to be called away.

This day, the visit of Lord Smythesdon would keep interrupting her thoughts. She was not at all concerned with any danger to herself and she felt well-equipped to outwit the ODM. However, it made her uneasy that she would be the focus of so many different individual's attention. Her mother would stare at her all the day long, Daisy and Rose would too, to see how she conducted herself. Then there was Henry, who was surely in on the scheme. And what of the Lord himself? Was he apprised of it? Was he some sort of bride hunter poised to descend upon Chemsworth Hall to collect his ten thousand pounds of dowry?

It aggravated her in the extreme that others should see fit to attempt to manage her in such a manner. She was a woman of intelligence and she would not submit to this sort of wrangling. Naturally, she would marry someday. What else could she do? Hang about Chemsworth as a spinster sister? Certainly not.

But she would marry *when* she decided to do so, to *who* she decided upon. She did not yet know who this lucky gentleman would be, but she had fully determined that he must be at least as intelligent as herself and interested in her mind, rather than her sewing or playing.

Lord Smythesdon leaned back in his carriage, happy to watch the countryside go by outside the window. The whole scheme had come off. His father, the Earl of Ainsworth, had quite suddenly determined that his son must think of marrying. Or, perhaps it was not suddenly, but merely more forceful than it had been. The Earl had pointed out his age, his gout, his intemperate drinking of port, all to convince his son that he might expire at any moment. The Earl could not comfortably slip into his grave until he knew his son had produced an heir to the line. Had he more than one son, he might be content to wait. Had he multiple sons, one might crack his head open in an overturned carriage and, while it would sadden the Earl in the extreme, there would be no danger to the line. But with just one son, a grandson or two must be got in all haste. If he were to lose his only son now, the estate would go to his brother. That gentleman was a ship's captain and an irresponsible layabout who would run the thing into the ground just as he done with his last ship.

Smythesdon had spent a week as a virtual ghost at Donneville. His father would be reported in one room and he would run to another on the opposite side of the house. His father would look for him in the stables, and he would ride out the back way. The Earl could not be dodged for dinner, however. It was in those after-dinner moments that he was caught. His mother and sister retired to the drawing room and there he was, left with a bottle of port and his grim-faced father.

But then good old Granger had come through. Granger had pointed out in his letter that he had an abundance of sisters decorating Chemsworth Hall. Why should not Smythesdon pretend to agree to his father's wishes and claim he would visit the Grangers with an eye toward a betrothal?

It had been the work of a moment. The Earl, having become acquainted with the fact that there were three ladies of good family, all with a respectable dowry and all of marriageable age, to be found under one convenient roof, had wished him Godspeed.

For now, at least, he was free.

The door to the library swung open. Violet fully expected to see Smuckers with tea or Smuckers looking for Dandy, or Smuckers just generally lurking about. Instead, it was Henry.

"Oh!" Henry said. "I did not realize anybody was in here."

Violet did not answer, since it was an entirely silly statement. Henry knew perfectly well that she studied in that room every day but Sunday.

"I just thought I'd come in for a book," Henry said.

Violet waved her arm around. "Well," she said, "here they are. It is the library, after all."

Henry walked along the shelves. Violet remained unconvinced that he really sought out a book. For all his bragging about Oxford, he was only rarely spied with a book in hand. She was even more unconvinced when he selected a book of sermons. She was certain he had not even noted the title he took, as if there were one thing her brother despised, it was a sermon. Poor Henry. Whatever he had really come in for, he was now saddled with pretending to be interested in Fordyce.

Henry sat down in a chair and cleared his throat once or twice. Then he said, "I suppose you remember my friend Smythesdon comes this day?"

Violet supposed she did remember. There was not much chance of her not remembering it. "Does he?" she answered.

"He does. Yes, he does," Henry said.

There was a long silence as Henry cracked his book open and thumbed through the pages. "The thing is," Henry said, "he has this very particular opinion regarding a woman's education."

"Does he?" Violet asked, entirely unwilling to help her brother say whatever it was that he had come to say.

"And I think, well we have become particular friends and I, for one, would like to keep it that way."

"Friends are so necessary to happiness," Violet said, narrowing her eyes at her brother.

"So I think," Henry said, his voice faltering a bit, "that perhaps it would be best, since he will be our guest after all, to keep certain things under wraps."

Violet was not at all certain of what her brother meaned to say, but she was very certain she should not like it. "What things shall we keep under wraps, Henry?" she asked, in as sweet a tone as she could muster.

"Your knowledge," Henry said in a rush. "Keep all of that under wraps."

Her knowledge? She was to keep her knowledge under wraps to appease the great Lord Smythesdon? The last thing she had ever done with her knowledge was keep it hidden, now she was to do so for a stranger named Bertie Battleboro?

"Is Lord Smythesdon temperamentally opposed to knowledge?" Violet asked, careful to keep her tone neutral.

"Opposed? No, of course not. He plans on being a leading intellect. He just feels it should be, well, that it is really...a gentleman's purview."

"Ah," Violet said, "and so he does not approve of scholarly women?"

"That's it," Henry said, sounding relieved that his sister had finally caught on. "That is it exactly."

She was to appear the mindless female to avoid disturbing the considered opinions of this Smythesdon person? This leading intellect in the making found he disapproved of women becoming too educated?

"After all," Henry said, seeming to gain in confidence, "you *can* be a bit of a know-all."

A know-all?

Violet did not immediately answer. Henry took that to be an acquiescence to his wishes and visibly relaxed. "He is a jolly fellow, in any case."

Was he a jolly fellow? Violet supposed Bertie Battleboro might well be jolly if everybody was to go round careful not to upset his narrow views on life.

She rose and leaned over the desk toward her brother. "I would no sooner keep my intelligence *under wraps*, as you call it, then I would howl at the moon. The other thing I find I cannot keep *under wraps* at this moment, is my fury. So my advice to you, brother, is to run from this room before I begin hurling books at your head. I am not only well-educated—I am also a very good shot."

Henry had run from the library, unwilling to be hit in the head by flying books. He reached his bedchamber and shut the door behind him. His sister was a menace! Her name should be Violence, not Violet. He had thought it wise to subtly hint to her that she ought not to go parading all her knowledge in front of Smythesdon, but now he could see he had made things worse, rather than better. She was so irate that she would no doubt make the attempt to tell Smythesdon everything she had learned in her entire life.

Henry found himself torn in all directions. He was fond of his sisters and did not care one bit that Violet fashioned herself a scholar. At least, usually he did not care. He had occasionally had a debate on some subject with his eldest sister and, finding himself bested, was rather less fond of her intelligence. Still, for all that, he and Violet usually got on well enough.

Then there was his mother. He would also wish to please Lady Mulholland. It was true, she could be a tyrant, but she was an affectionate tyrant and only wished the best for her brood. Further, he knew it entirely pointless to refuse her, as once his mother decided on a course of action, she was a regular Hun in pursuit of it.

But then there was Smythesdon! He valued Smythesdon's opinions very much and wished to appear in a good light to his friend. His whole society at school revolved around Smythesdon's patronage. Henry was much admired by the other first term gentlemen on account of his being connected with Smythesdon and his friends. And Smythesdon had been so kind to him, he would not for the world wish that his friend look with disapproval upon his family. But how would his friend approve if Violet was to go round showing off her scholarship? How would his friend approve of wild Marigold, riding out to the hunt? How would his friend approve if he were to discover Lady Mulholland's scheme to throw him together with Violet?

How was he to please everybody? It seemed nothing he could do would make everybody happy.

Smuckers had gathered the staff in the servants' dining hall for the momentous announcement. He had spent a half-hour pacing his bedchamber, seeking out just the right words to convey the gravity of the moment.

"As you may have heard," he began, "we are to be graced with the presence of Lord Bertram Smythesdon. He is the only son and heir of the Earl of Ainsworth. I cannot stress what an honor this is to the house. The Earldom is a jewel in our majesty's crown, an ancient and cultured jewel. Our young Mr. Granger has befriended this eminent individual while at Oxford, that place being our finest institution of higher learning. We are to be *surrounded* by, and I might even say *steeped* in, the illustrious history of England."

"Surrounded and steeped in potatoes, more like it," Peggy said. "Them nobs can eat plenty, for all their fancy ways."

Smuckers frowned at the kitchen maid. The chef, Mr. Moreau, snapped out his dishrag and smacked her on the back of her head with it. Peggy did not seem at all perturbed by this assault, as Mr. Moreau attempted to knock sense into his kitchen maid's head via dishrag at least twice a day with little success.

Smuckers continued. "The standards of this house are high," he said. "They have always been high, and always will remain high. And yet, we find ourselves in such a circumstance that those standards must go higher still. We must gird ourselves to reach for the heavens."

He paused to gauge the effect of that noble sentiment. Peggy appeared dubious, but then she always did appear dubious. Mr. Moreau had straightened his back, as if somebody had insulted his cooking, and Smuckers dearly wished he were not on the verge of another lecture about the superiority of French cuisine. Victorine seemed bored, but the butler supposed that was an improvement on Lady Mulholland's maid, Fleur, who had not even bothered to answer his summons. Mrs. Featherstone just shook her head sadly, as if she were perfectly aware of the various disasters that were poised to strike Chemsworth Hall.

"I expect each and every one of you to exceed your own standards during this visit." Mr. Smuckers said. He paused dramatically, then pointed skyward and said, "For the glory of the house!"

There was much shuffling and nodding and then everybody went back to their work.

Smuckers, as he always did at times like this, felt there was beginning to be an erosion of the proper awe for rank and title in his beloved country.

Chapter Four

Most unwillingly, Violet stood outside with the rest of the house to meet this Smythesdon individual. The family was lined up on one side of the drive and the servants on the other. The order in which they were lined up was by rank and strictly observed, as Lady Mulholland could not abide disorder on display.

There was always ample time to see that everybody was in their proper place, as Chemsworth Hall was rarely surprised by the arrival of a visitor. The house sat atop a hill with a good view of the Viscount's land, all the way to the crossroads that led to London in one direction and the village of Swarston in the other. A carriage might be seen before it had come within a mile of the house.

Poppy and Pansy had spent the morning eagerly manning the lookout on a third-floor balcony. That particular balcony was generally where they could be found in any case as they had last year set up their 'inviolate kingdom where no person might enter without invitation' in the room connected to it. The kingdom itself was comprised of three pillows and an old blanket. The twins regularly used the balcony to spy out intruders to the kingdom, by way of evil knight or frightful dragon or Cassie, the neighboring farmer's daughter, bringing cheese. They had accepted this latest call to arms with all the bravery and stout hearts of knights of the round table and were thoroughly prepared to race through the house shouting the alarm once the carriage had been spotted. Race they had, shouting rather more loudly than had absolutely been necessary.

Violet had thought she might be able to stay above stairs, pretending she had not heard Poppy and Pansy's mayhem, but Lady Mulholland had seen fit to personally escort her down with her usual Friendly Dragon finesse.

As they waited for the carriage, Violet noted with some amusement that Smuckers was at his most dignified. He picked Dandy's hairs off his coat with an air of self-possession, all the while keeping a sharp eye on his staff. Mrs. Featherstone had a satisfied look about her, as if she could not help being found out to be right about something. Victorine looked slightly bored, but smiled at Violet when she caught her lady's eye. Lady Mulholland's maid, Fleur, looked as she always did—a mixture of contempt for everybody in England except Lady Mulholland, and admiration of her own person. The footmen, Jimmy, Johnny, Charlie and Oscar stood ramrod straight, making the most of their good heights. At least, Jimmy, Johnny and Charlie did, poor Oscar was rather shorter and should never have been hired had he not been Mrs. Featherstone's nephew.

Her own family were as to be expected. Lady Mulholland and her Viscount stood at the head of the line. The lady from time to time bent toward her husband's ear to assure him that Hampshire was not so very foreign and Lord Smythesdon, after all, *did* have the good sense to be an only son and he *was* a fox man and he *did* have the fine discernment to befriend Henry and whatever other facts she might pull from the air to make the Viscount comfortable in receiving this stranger from another county.

On Violet's right, Henry was pale. She thought she had done a creditable job of scaring the wits from him in the library the day before. She could not say for certain whether or not she would have hurled books at his head, but he'd had the great good sense not to remain and find out.

Rose and Daisy were on her left, both silent but stalwart soldiers. Marigold was still in her riding habit, that particular item of clothing being preferred whether she would ride or no. Lily was blushing furiously, though one could not guess at what. Poppy and

Pansy pinched each other and made faces and generally did everything in their power to make the other laugh or cry.

Horses trotted around a bend in the drive and the carriage was soon seen. Violet noted at once that it was not a hired chaise, but rather a private carriage replete with the Earl's coat of arms. She might have admired such a thing, had the carriage not carried the ridiculous Smythesdon.

Two of the Viscount's grooms stepped forward, ready to hold the horses while Lord Smythesdon made his descent to the drive. Jimmy, being the first footman and proud of it, stepped to the carriage door and opened it with all the pomp one could hope for in a sixteen-year-old.

Smythesdon leapt down from the carriage without waiting for the steps to be brought out. He was all smiles as he viewed the whole house out to meet him.

Violet, though she would admit it to nobody, was rather incensed that the Lord had the ill-manners to be good-looking. He was tall and, though he had hair as dark as midnight, his eyes were very blue. His face was tanned, as if he spent a deal of time out of doors, and his features were annoyingly regular. She had been much better pleased if the lord's features had been as ridiculous as his name. This was not at all how a Bertie Battleboro should look.

"Lord Smythesdon," Lady Mulholland said.

"My Lady Mulholland," Smythesdon said, gallantly bowing, "I thank you for receiving me to your house."

"Any friend of Henry's must always be welcome to Chemsworth Hall," Lady Mulholland said graciously.

"Indeed," the Viscount said. "Though how the boy finds friends as far away as Hampshire, I am sure I do not know."

Smythesdon seemed entirely amused at this pronouncement and Violet knew this would cement him forever into Daisy's good graces.

Smythesdon was speedily introduced to the rest of the family. Violet was coolly civil, her curtsy just low enough, but no lower than necessary. Smythesdon was to know she was not awed by his title or his looks. She was not at all perturbed to find a gentleman visiting. Her good breeding and manners were impeccable. She was, in short, unflappable. At least, she wished to appear so.

Henry and Smythesdon greeted each other as old friends. Henry hurriedly escorted him into the house and requested Smuckers to direct Smythesdon's valet to his bedchamber.

Violet was thankful that there would be no awkward standing around in the drawing room, as it was late enough for the ladies to change for dinner. Let Henry show his friend about the downstairs and then lead him above stairs with no help from her.

The gong sounded and Lady Mulholland said, "Smuckers, do bring tea for Lord Smythesdon. He shall have it with Henry in the drawing room. The ladies will retire to change while Lord Mulholland meets with Mr. Tidewater in the library."

Lord Smythesdon bowed low, as if he had just been knighted by the king.

Violet stepped up the stairs in what she hoped was a regal manner, quite sure The Friendly Dragon's eyes followed her. She intended to give the impression of having no impression made upon her at all. Smythesdon, or *Bertie*, as she was sure he was known, was just one more person within the confines of Chemsworth Hall. It was of no concern to Violet Granger.

But why should he be so handsome? That was what she would like to know. Why should he not be some short and fat individual with a pockmarked face and swinging jowls? Why should he not be balding or hunched or frail or with a limp? Why should he be some sort of dashing individual, leaping down from his carriage without the use of its steps? He was entirely too energetic.

Victorine knocked and entered the bedchamber. She skipped to Violet's closet and said, "Which shall be? Très belle robe formelle for the important man? These yellow silk, crème satin, or maybe bleu silk?"

"Which do you think I look terrible in, Victorine?" Violet asked.

Victorine laughed her pretty little laugh, like a series of bells. "Une femme qui ne cherche pas à faire de son mieux est un imbécile."

"I am not an imbecile for not wishing to appear my best," Violet said. She was certain her maid was in the habit of forgetting that she was fluent in French. Or else, she was the sauciest girl alive.

Victorine seemed entirely unconvinced. Violet sighed. "Never mind, I do not care. Whichever is closest to your hand."

Victorine reached and rummaged and moved various boxes and emerged triumphant with the cream silk.

"That one was closest to your hand?" Violet asked, knowing it was no such thing.

"Not so to my hand," Victorine said pertly, "but to my heart."

Smythesdon had tea in the drawing room with Granger, the ladies having gone up to change and the Viscount closeting himself away with his steward. Granger had been nearly jumping out of his skin and had fired one question after another at him. He must have been asked about his journey three times.

He could not fault his friend, after all Granger was only to be a Viscount and the poor old sot had very little life experience. When Smythesdon had found him at Oxford, he had been as unsteady as a newborn foal. He had been delighted to take the fellow under his wing, there was nothing he liked better than a bit of noblesse oblige. And Granger was such a grateful chap, too. He supposed it could be no wonder that Granger should feel his nerves now, having brought a Lord home to his family.

Granger did have such very comely sisters, though. If Smythesdon *had* been looking for a wife, he might very well have looked here. The eldest Miss Granger, in particular, was rather smashing. That cool reserve he found so alluring in a woman, as if nothing would impress her so much that she would reveal it. Then, she had that heap of dark curls set against alabaster skin and those very interesting hazel eyes. Miss Violet Granger was just the type he should seek out in that far distant future when he would take a wife. Whoever she may be, Lady Ainsworth would be serene and gracious, her various emotions never revealed on her features. *That* was what was required of an Earl's wife. Of course, he had no need to leap into the marriage mart this instant, regardless of what his father thought about it.

Smythesdon gazed around his bedchamber. What a funny place Chemsworth Hall turned out to be. It was as if one had dropped oneself into medieval times. His own estate having been rebuilt in his grandfather's time in the Palladian style, he was quite unaccustomed to this sort of heavy and looming structure capped with turrets. When he had entered the house, he had even noted the markings of chains having been removed on either side of the doors, which meant a drawbridge had once stood there. The great hall was one that would be admired in Henry Tudor's court. It would be marvelous to explore this old pile of stones.

And thanks to Granger, he was out of his father's grips and could enjoy his holiday. He would be sure to tell all of his Oxford friends that Granger had been an absolute brick. While he was here, he would be all condescension to the house, he would not for the world make the Grangers feel the honor of his visit. He would even go so far as to hide his superior knowledge, lest it made them feel ill at ease. These were not the inhabitants of the *Queen's Lane*, but simple country people. The Viscount did not strike him as a scholar, but rather one of those fellows who lives delightfully eccentric in the countryside. They had their own such gentlemen in the neighborhood of Donneville. Was not Squire Newtown known to consider learning an activity best suited for those gentlemen who had not the energy to go about doing manly things like castrating pigs? Did not Mr. Mantone and Sir John conduct a running feud of decades duration over a fence, though the land disputed was less than a half-yard wide?

Then, of course, he must give all consideration to the Granger women. Their simple educations could not allow them to understand half of what he said were he to unleash the full power of his intellect. He supposed they could all speak French, play the pianoforte, sew and draw and be content to consider themselves well accomplished. He would not wish to disabuse them of that sentiment. He certainly would not wish for Miss Violet Granger to feel it. In any case, they were only achieving what women were meant to achieve and they should not be caused to feel small over it. He had learned that lesson from his mother who had told him, in no uncertain terms, that he was never to disparage any of his sister's embroidering attempts again.

Smythesdon allowed his man to remove his coat. He heaved a contented sigh. Yes, it would be a very pleasant visit to Chemsworth Hall.

Victorine had finished with Violet's hair and had moved down the hall to Rose. As was her habit, Violet had followed the maid to Rose's room and now sat on a footstool next to her sister's dressing table.

"I did not see at all why he must go leaping from his carriage like a hound to the hunt. Why should not he wait one moment for the steps?" Violet said. "It was very showy, I thought."

When Rose did not second her in that condemnation, Violet said, "Poor Johnny did not know what to do, having his work taken from him like that. Most inconsiderate to our second footman."

Rose watched Victorine in the glass as the maid unwrapped her curl papers. Rose's hair was a beautiful light auburn, but it was straight as an arrow and could only be convinced to curl by being wetted down, generously coated with pomade and set by the heat of the fire. "I cannot think Johnny cared much about it," she said. "I always do get the impression that he does not care for much, except only to moon over a certain lady's maid."

Victorine, being French, did not even blush at this accusation. "He is idiot," she said.

"Of course, you will not approve of anything Lord Smythesdon says or does. He was doomed from the start," Rose said.

"Why should he not be doomed?" Violet asked. "According to Henry, the man would prefer that we women keep our knowledge to ourselves."

"Actually, it was only that *you* should keep your knowledge to yourself. Daisy and I do not have enough of that commodity to pose a danger. Perhaps you should consider, though," Rose said, "that the opinion is, indeed, *according* to Henry. There have been many things *according* to Henry that have been proved wildly false. Remember what we heard from the wood that very first night that we were moved from the nursery to this side of the house? How we trembled at the screams outside our window? He said it was the cry of unsettled souls trying to claw their way out of their graves, when it was only a fox."

Of course, Violet did remember that. The nursery's windows had long ago been bricked up to keep out the cold. It had been a dark set of apartments, but cozy and warm—the womb of the house. The sounds of the nighttime had been entirely unknown to them and so, while foxes had let out their unearthly screams into the darkness from time immemorial, Violet had first heard such a sound on the very night they had moved into a regular bedchamber. The bedchamber had been fitted out with three beds and Rose and Daisy had flown from theirs and into hers at the sound of it. Then Henry had come in and gravely explained about the unsettled souls. They had been up half the night in fright.

"We were just children then," Violet said.

"Henry has always had a penchant for stories. Remember Lady Mary? The unhappy ghost of the third floor? When it was only Henry up there knocking on the floor. Or the legend of the Padfoot, the black dog who hunted innocent souls at the full moon? For all we know," Rose said, "it is just Henry's own opinion that you should hide your scholarly tendencies. It would not surprise me at all to find that he had decided upon that course all on his own."

Violet was thoughtful. Could that be right? It might be right, Henry could be a callow young man and he *was* in the habit of inventing stories. It was plausible that he might be so intimidated by this Lord that he would seek to show him only the dullest of households. That might be, in Henry's small mind, the safest course.

"Perhaps," Violet said. "But then, I have another cause to dislike Lord Smythesdon. He comes here as part of a dastardly plot engineered by the ODM. For that alone, I must despise him."

"Mon dieu," Victorine said softly, fixing the last of Rose's curls and wagging her finger at it, lest it dare move.

Without further conversation, they moved down the hall to Daisy's bedchamber. Their procession from Violet to Rose to Daisy had gone on as long as they had been old enough to have a maid. It was necessary that Daisy be the last, not only because she was the youngest of the three, but because she was generally the most problematic.

As usual, Daisy's room appeared as if a great north wind had come through. Gowns of every color and description were piled upon the bed. Shoes were strewn across the floor. Bonnets were scattered upon the landscape. A single glove had somehow landed atop the rod that held up pale yellow velvet curtains.

Victorine stood looking at the carnage with disapproval, though she could not have expected anything else.

"Do not be cross with me, my darling Victorine," Daisy said, twirling in her dressing gown. "At first I thought the peach gown, I was very sure of it, but then I thought, what about the sky blue, and then, of course, I could not decide and thought I had better pull them all out and have a look."

"And here we is," Victorine said, "looking."

"Violet, Rose?" Daisy said, looking at them enquiringly. "What do you think?"

Both sisters knew that if they did not agree which gown would be best, it would be a further half hour of Daisy debating herself, and so had long ago decided on the general rule that they were to pick whichever Daisy had first mentioned.

"The peach," they said together.

"Goodness," Daisy said. "I was right the first time. I really should learn to trust my own instinct, as I seem to always be right the first time."

As Victorine helped her into the peach gown, Daisy said, "So? What do we think of Lord Smythesdon? I thought he was awfully dashing, jumping down from the carriage as he did. He was just like a hero in a novel...had there been anybody to save from imminent disaster."

"You make it sound as if he had leapt from one galloping horse to another in pursuit of a damsel kidnapped by highwaymen. There is nothing heroic about jumping out of a standing carriage onto a perfectly immobile drive," Rose said.

"Nothing at all heroic," Violet confirmed. "It was showy, if it was anything at all."

"But he does seem a pleasant fellow, does he not?" Daisy asked, looking through her various necklaces and shoes and gloves while Victorine followed her around attempting to do up her dress.

"Perhaps the TFD has missed her mark," Violet said. "Perhaps it is Daisy Granger who will fall hopelessly in love with her prospect."

Daisy fell into a fit of giggles. "Me? Me for Lord Smythesdon? Certainly not. I know just the sort of gentleman I shall fall in love with. I will know him instantly."

"Let me guess," Rose said. "He shall be that sort who goes along, happy-go-lucky, and liking absolutely everybody. If he is faced with a thief, he will assume the man had good reason to steal. There shall be nobody at all he does not approve of and he shall perpetually wear a smile upon his face like a great grinning buffoon. Have I got it right?"

Victorine had finally wrangled Daisy into her chair in front of the looking glass and began the work of sorting out her wild blond curls.

"He is to perpetually wear a smile? That is what you think?" Daisy asked. "Dear me, no. Smiling is for *me* to do. My one true love is a brooding sort and will need much cheering up. He is

46

devilishly handsome, and yet no woman has ever been able to touch his feelings. He has suffered some terrible tragedy in his past, perhaps his whole family was burned up in a fire, and he goes about scowling and being unpleasant to absolutely everybody. But then, he sees me at a ball and is overcome and declares I am the only woman in the world who can heal his bruised heart. And so I do, of course. I very cheerfully heal his bruised heart and he is in love with me and happy forevermore."

Rose stared at Daisy. "You have read entirely too many French novels," she said.

"No blame French for this," Victorine muttered.

"The wonderful thing about novels," Daisy said, "and you would both know this if you read them, is that they show you the possibilities of love. It can be very grand, and I intend to have a very grand love all my own."

Rose laughed. "We must alert the ODM that if she thinks to unburden herself of Daisy, she had best tell Henry to bring back some sulking young gentleman who is in the habit of reciting poetry while standing alone atop the cliffs of Dover in a cold rain."

"Goodness," Daisy breathed, "that *does* sound romantic. Is he pining after me, do you think? For if he were, I would ride horseback through that rain to tell him his love has been requited. Any self-respecting heroine would."

The second gong sounded and, while Violet was not so terribly anxious to go down, she *was* terribly anxious to escape Daisy's imaginings of the Dover cliffs. It was time to repair to the drawing room.

"To battle, my sisters," Violet said. "The Friendly Dragon is a worthy opponent, but we shall ride to victory."

"Bonne chance," Victorine said cheerfully, as the three sisters made their way to the door.

"It will not be luck, Victorine," Violet said. "It will be cleverness and determination."

Chapter Five

The three eldest Granger sisters, now dressed and primped to Victorine's high standards, glided from Daisy's room to the top of the stairs. There, they met with Marigold, still in her riding habit.

"Marigold," Violet said, "why have you not yet changed? You are running very late."

"I will not change," Marigold said. "I have decided that dresses are silly and frivolous and I shall no longer wear them. I shall only, from this day forward, wear my riding habit. I shall always be at the ready, should I need to set off in a moment." Marigold cast a derisive glance over her sister's finery. "Just look at you, you could not climb onto a horse if you tried."

Violet and Rose frowned, though Daisy seemed amused.

"You shall thank me," Marigold said, "when you are dying of something and I am ready to gallop through the night to fetch the doctor at a moment's notice."

"Mama shall not approve," Violet said.

"Mama has not forbidden me," Marigold said, jutting her chin out.

"Has she seen you?" Rose asked.

"No," Marigold said, rather less boldly.

Rose and Violet quietly stared at their sister, while Daisy covered her mouth to stifle her laughter.

"Oh bother!" Marigold cried, and ran to her room to change.

Smuckers lingered in the hall, supervising the comings and goings of all in the house. He looked approvingly at Violet, Rose and Daisy skipping down the stairs.

"Lady Mulholland is already in the drawing room," he said, as if this very news had caused him to wait in the hall.

"You are looking in fine fettle, Smuckers," Violet said teasingly. "I suppose you like having a Lord in the house?"

Smuckers nodded and said gravely, "Those of us who proudly serve Chemsworth Hall remain fully prepared to bring honor upon the house."

"You are a darling, Smuckers," Daisy said, patting his cheek as she passed by him.

Upon entering the drawing room, Violet saw at once that Lady Mulholland had been at work to transform it from its usual frigid expanse into a somewhat warmer environment. This had necessitated the lady to order the fire built up to roaring proportions and dozens of candles placed throughout. A half-dozen were lined up with precision on each window sill and Violet only hoped that the curtains would not go up in flames as a fiery tribute to Lady Mulholland's determination.

Lord Smythesdon stood near the fire, speaking to the Viscount. Violet noted immediately that her father spoke of crop rotation and that Smythesdon, though he no doubt did not know a thing about it, was heartily agreeing. This had the effect of soothing Lord Mulholland's feelings upon finding a foreigner within the confines of Chemsworth Hall. Talk of crop rotation, for reasons Violet could not fathom, was like a soothing draught upon the Viscount.

"Here are my daughters," Lady Mulholland said, rushing at them as if they had just returned from a long sea voyage.

"Violet, Rose, Daisy," she said, steering her daughters toward the hearth.

Violet had no choice but to be led, but she made it a point to be led regally. Disdainfully. Looking bored, perhaps. Decidedly cool.

"Ah, girls," the Viscount said. "I was just telling Smythesdon here about our plans for the spring. He finds the idea intriguing and will inform his own father of it. Funny, that," Lord Mulholland mused. "To think I should have some effect on Hampshire farming. Most unexpected."

"Unexpected, indeed," Violet said, quite sure that Lord Smythesdon would not know how to plant a single turnip if his very life depended upon it.

Smythesdon did not answer and Violet could see perfectly well that he had no wish to continue a conversation about farming as he was bound to be caught out in his ignorance sooner or later.

"Do you have many conferences with your own steward, Lord Smythesdon?" Violet asked. "Father and Mr. Tidewater meet most days to discuss matters."

"Oh, well, I," Lord Smythesdon stuttered.

Violet smiled at Henry's glare.

"Of course, he must, Violet," the Viscount said. "No self-respecting landowner would allow a steward to go off and manage things as he might. A very bad business, that."

"My husband is supremely clever about managing the estate," Lady Mulholland said, "and I am always very grateful for it. Now, tell me Lord Smythesdon, how do you find Oxford?"

"It is the finest institution of higher learning, ma'am," Lord Smythesdon said, "and, therefore, I feel as if I had encountered a right proper home."

"I am delighted to hear it," Lady Mulholland replied. "I did so wish that Henry find it as a second home. One does fret at having a son away from the house for the first time."

"What makes it so home-like, if I may inquire?" Violet asked. She was not sure why she was still talking, she could just as well have remained silent now that the ODM had rescued Lord Smythesdon from any more talk of farming.

Smythesdon was for a moment silent, as if considering his words. Then he said, "To find oneself amongst those men who would seek to improve and expand their own intellects is what is most gratifying. After all, except our own thoughts, there is nothing absolutely in our power."

"Descartes," Violet said with a smile.

The Viscount did not respond to this statement, as he assumed it was French for he knew not what and did not speak a word of that or any other foreign language. Lady Mulholland stood with a frozen smile on her face. Rose pressed her lips together and Daisy looked away and covered her mouth. Henry paled. Lord Smythesdon looked as if he had not heard Violet correctly.

"You said, except our own thoughts, there is nothing absolutely in our power," Violet repeated. "That is a quote from Descartes, is it not?"

"Yes," Lord Smythesdon said. "Yes, it is."

"You have an interesting way of expressing it, Lord Smythesdon," Violet continued, rather feeling as if she were a fox slyly circling a henhouse. "In the usual way, one might introduce the quote in some manner such as '*Descartes was known to say,*' or '*I believe Descartes said,*' or some other sort of attribution. But you have so cleverly, even seamlessly I would venture, woven it into your speech."

The Viscount, not having long patience for conversation on subjects he knew nothing about, said, "And where is this Descartes fellow? Not in Oxfordshire, I do not think. I ought to have heard of him if people are going about quoting him."

Marigold and Lilly entered the room, thereby providing a life boat to the sinking Lord Smythesdon. He was re-introduced to these two young ladies and then appeared greatly relieved to hear from Marigold, quite extensively, that she had absolutely decided that when she was eighteen she would don a riding habit and never take it off. When she was eighteen, nobody should tell her otherwise and she would not even take it off for the Christmas holidays. Not if she were hard pressed on all sides. She was only inspired to cease her diatribe on her future wardrobe plans when Lady Mulholland laid a hand on her arm.

Lily hung back, as she always did, and only very reluctantly spoke to the Lord. He asked her how she did and she said, "Very well." Then, apparently deciding that 'Very well' was not sufficient, she complimented his coat and said that it also looked very well.

While Lord Smythesdon was engaged with the two younger, Henry approached Violet. "Descartes? Truly?"

"I am not the one who so proudly quoted him," Violet said.

"But you insinuated, you hinted, you *implied* that he tried to make the quote his own," Henry said, his voice dropping to a hissing whisper.

"I did, did I not?" Violet said, looking pleased with herself. "He rather stepped into that."

"I shall not have you insult my friend. He is my guest in this house," Henry said.

"Your friend? Your guest? Do not you mean to say mama's guest?" Violet said.

Henry was silent and she continued. "Oh, I am in on your scheme with our mother. You cannot think I would not discover it. Well, I shall make short work of it. Lord Bertie will leave this house as unattached as he was when he came into it, while *I* do not bother to keep all of my knowledge *under wraps*."

Henry huffed and puffed himself up and reddened, but said nothing. He could not deny the charge.

The third gong sounded, Chemsworth Hall being fond of gongs to announce every happening in the house. The third in the evening signaled that Mr. Moreau had completed some culinary masterpiece in the kitchens, that masterpiece was even now making its way up the back stairs, and he would be in a very French temper if it were to go cold on account of dawdling.

"Shall we go in?" Lady Mulholland said.

The dining room was ablaze and Violet squinted against the light. The chandeliers up and down the room were lit, all six fires were stacked high and burning bright and candles ranged across the table and on every surface from the windowsills to the side boards.

Lady Mulholland took advantage of her daughter's momentary blindness to steer her to a chair beside Lord Smythesdon.

Violet cursed the woman's speed. She should have anticipated the move. It was like a chess match and whoever thought furthest ahead would come out the winner.

Violet sat down and pulled off her gloves. As she laid them in her lap, her hand grazed Lord Smythesdon's hand. She snatched her hand away and he did the same.

What was he thinking, to have his hand dangling in her way? Why should a man leave his hand in the way like that? Is that what was done at Donneville—hands just flailing about without a thought as to what other hands they might encounter? A man should keep his hands closer to his person so an innocent individual did not encounter them.

Smuckers led the footmen in with the soup, the butler seeming inches taller as he was so determined to present a formal figure to their guest. He directed the footmen in an intricate dance around the table. There might be some houses that would serve the soup concurrent with the meat dishes, but the Viscount could not abide meat growing cold while his family took their time over their soup. With the full backing of Mr. Moreau, who was quite passionate on the subject, the practice had been banned. The Viscount also did not see why he was to dole out the soup like a waiter at a posthouse, so rather than one large tureen, a series of smaller tureens were brought round the table and served according to rank. Smuckers, having accomplished this maneuver to the satisfaction of any tome on correctness of manners, surveyed the scene as if he had just served the king at his coronation.

"How do you find your soup, Lord Smythesdon?" Lady Mulholland asked.

"It is a delight," Lord Smythesdon answered. "There is nothing so good as white soup. I often wonder what the world did before La Varenne in 1653—I suppose they must have been relegated to *brown* soup."

Henry laughed overloud at this weak jest. Violet said, "You mean, Lord Smythesdon, 1651."

"I am sorry?" Lord Smythesdon said, a rather leery look on his face, as he had just narrowly escaped a Waterloo in the drawing room.

"It was in 1651 that La Varenne publicized his recipe for white soup," Violet said.

"It was?" Lord Smythesdon asked.

"It was," Violet said. "I suspect you confuse the date of origin with the date of translation to English, which was, indeed, 1653."

A pall settled over the dining table. Lady Mulholland smiled weakly but, for once, Violet noted with satisfaction, did not seem to have anything to say.

Finally, Marigold said, "My Lord, do you ride? And by ride, I mean ride creditably and not just foolishly hanging on."

Lord Smythesdon was able to recover himself from the white soup debacle and assure Marigold that he did ride creditably. She did not appear entirely convinced and Violet presumed that Marigold would need to see absolute proof before she would admit him into her special club for those who rode creditably.

"I would hope he could ride, my child," the Viscount said. "I was under the impression he was a fox man. We hunt on Wednesday."

Henry, thinking he had better translate the Viscount's unique phrasings for Smythesdon, said, "I told my father you are equally skilled at hunting fox or pheasant. He is of the opinion that there is more skill, and therefore more enjoyment, in hunting fox."

Smythesdon, appearing to have landed on a subject where he could not help but be the expert, said, "The wondrous early morning with the hounds milling about, anxious to begin their work. Then the fox is away and the chase is on, over hill and dale, fence and forest, all the day long until the men come home victorious."

"Ah," Violet said with a smile, "you meant to say, the men *and* women come home victorious."

Though Henry stared at her as if he wished he could hurl his soup at her head, Violet happily awaited the lord's answer.

Smythesdon seemed to examine that statement from a variety of angles. He suddenly smiled and said, "Of course, the ladies will have had a rough time of it in the carriages and so victory must also belong to them. I would even venture that the men would have no hope of success without the cheering on from the ladies."

Henry seemed to sink into his seat. Violet said, "There will be no carriages, my lord. With the exception of the footmen setting up a luncheon on Lookout Hill."

"No carriages?" Lord Smythesdon said, his voice seemed to have risen an octave higher. He looked at Violet as if she were some dangerous animal that must be carefully handled to avoid being bitten.

The Viscount said, "Good grief, man, how should anybody hunt from a carriage? Is that what they do in Hampshire? I'll wager they don't catch many foxes if they choose to go on like that. I suppose one could shoot pheasant from a carriage, though it seems a lackadaisical way of going on."

"You see, Lord Smythesdon," Violet said in a silky tone, "the ladies shall all be on horseback. Hunting."

Smythesdon paled and looked at Henry. Henry gave him a weak smile and shrugged.

"And we shall not be hanging on like fools, either," Marigold said.

"None of my daughters hang on like fools," the Viscount said. "With perhaps the exception of Lily, who has yet to be convinced to get on at all."

Lily, having been singled out once more for her terror of horses, looked to Lady Mulholland. Her mother gave her a sympathetic look that said, 'Never mind, you are perfect as you are.' Lilly dabbed her eyes and regained her composure.

Lord Smythesdon regained his footing and said, "I have heard of it done on occasion. I once heard that the Earl of

Darlington's daughters do hunt. Though I have never witnessed such a thing myself."

"There is nothing to fear, my lord," Violet said sweetly. "We shall not slow you down."

"I should think not," the Viscount said. "Does that fellow Darlington's daughters slow *him* down? If they do, then he is an idiot for allowing it."

The rest of the dinner went on without incident, though rather quietly. Violet was of the opinion that she had taken her stand and won the day and did not see the need to boast of her victory.

Smythesdon might not like to see a woman's knowledge on full view, but he *had* seen it and she doubted he would challenge her further after getting the dates wrong about the white soup. She had come across that particular piece of information entirely by accident and could not, for the life of her, work out how she had remembered such a thing. She was, however, inordinately good with dates—she could remember those various series of four numbers as well as Daisy could remember everybody's birthdays.

Smythesdon might not like that the ladies of the house were just as prepared to hunt a fox as the gentlemen, and yet he would witness it all the same. Violet would leave it to Marigold to determine if he could sit a horse creditably or only hung on like a fool.

Lady Mulholland had no doubt been convinced that her scheme was washed up on the rocks like a foundered ship. Violet need not worry how she might express her dislike of Lord Smythesdon, as she had made very sure that the lord did not like *her*.

At Lady Mulholland's signal, the ladies rose and left for the drawing room. Violet thought with some satisfaction that Lord Smythesdon could not very well avoid the subject of farming with just the three men left at table. Henry would need to do some very fast dancing to prevent the Viscount from returning to his beloved subject, especially now that he assumed he was on the verge of bringing the modern practice of crop rotation to the backward county of Hampshire.

In the drawing room, Lady Mulholland sent Marigold and Lily to bed and had Dandy brought in from nobody but Smuckers knew where. Violet thought it must be a credit to Smuckers that he always managed to find the white ball of fur when he was asked to. Lady Mulholland carried her puffball of a squire in her arms and circled her eldest daughters as if she were a high-flying hawk spying out a mouse crossing a field. Violet was entirely amused by it, as her mother could not scold her too much for putting off Lord Smythesdon because she would then have to admit why the gentleman had been brought to Chemsworth Hall to begin. Lady Mulholland, for all her daring, never owned to one of her schemes.

"Violet, dear," Lady Mulholland said, stroking Dandy's brow, "do not be so hard upon our guest. Not everybody can have a mind like a metal trap, slamming closed on facts and never allowing them to escape. Though why you should know anything about white soup is entirely beyond me. In any case, I find our Lord Smythesdon very charming."

Now he was *our* Lord Smythesdon?

"I understand from my cousin Harriet that Donneville is an elegant estate, with all the modern conveniences. She has been there, you know, and says the rooms are not nearly as drafty as ours."

Violet did not respond, but thought her mother was rather shortsighted to think that her daughter would become enamored of a man on account of his less drafty rooms.

"And Lord Ainsworth, I hear, is a genial individual. Harriet says he is an exquisite host."

Now Violet was certain that her mother fabricated the entirety of the information. Harriet Dunphy would not describe anybody as an exquisite host. Harriet was fortunate that she was very rich, as she was also very coarse. She was every bit the horsewoman that Marigold was and, therefore, did not spend any amount of time thinking up pretty phrases. She was just as likely, upon arriving as a guest to a house, to say, 'where's my bed and be sure to give my horse good oats' as she was to say hello. Exquisite host, indeed.

"I wonder though, mama," Violet said, "how exquisite a host Lord Ainsworth could be when he appears entirely unprepared for females on a fox hunt. Lord Smythesdon seemed wholly taken aback by the notion so certainly it is not done at Donneville."

Lady Mulholland appeared torn. Violet knew her mother to have been a skilled hunter in her youth. She knew the lady to be of the opinion that if one were young enough to join in on the hunt, one would be very silly to view the thing from a carriage. On the other hand, she was determined to paint Lord Smythesdon in the best possible light.

"Naturally," she said to Dandy, as if the Pomeranian awaited the answer to this conundrum, "one cannot count on finding progressive attitudes everywhere, my dear. It is our role as a leading family to bring such people round."

"Shall we write Lord Ainsworth a letter outlining the case?" Violet said, teasingly.

Lady Mulholland ignored that statement and said, "I suppose you will not mind showing him the library on the morrow?"

"He is Henry's guest," Violet said. "Let Henry show him the library. In any case, it would be quite improper of me to be alone with a strange gentleman. I would not, for the world, appear improper."

"Heavens," Lady Mulholland said. "It is only the library and you need not shut the door." Lady Mulholland looked over at Rose and Daisy and then shook her head as if it would not do. "But very well," she said, "I will indulge your sensibilities. I shall send Marigold to you."

"Marigold?" Violet asked, though as soon as she asked, she saw her mother's plotting on the subject. She was determined to marry her daughters off in strict order and would not wish Lord

Smythesdon to take a fancy to Rose or Daisy. Rose and Daisy were to be kept well away from the library.

Chapter Six

"Marigold shall be quite put out about it," Rose said to Lady Mulholland. "She had much rather be on her pony traipsing through the wood than in the library. I do not believe she has set foot in that room in months."

"Marigold shall be delighted," Lady Mulholland said with a finality that convinced Violet that however she might mean to avoid showing Lord Smythesdon the library, she most certainly would find herself showing that gentleman the library. And towing along an incensed Marigold.

As Victorine would say, femme diabolique.

Violet moved to the pianoforte in the corner of the room. She planned to seat herself and play until one of her sisters said, "Heavens, I *am* tired," and then make her escape up the stairs. The next days were certain to be tedious. On the morrow, she would be forced to show Lord Smythesdon her beloved library, and then on Wednesday she would be up with the chickens and riding through who knew what weather after an elusive fox, all to show the lord how entirely wrong he was about absolutely everything.

The men did not stay in the dining room long, and Violet assumed this was Henry's doing. Her father could be persuaded to sit over his port for an hour or more, debating with himself the right course of action for this or that problem with a field or a tenant. Henry, being the eldest and only son, was in the habit of listening dutifully, as he knew that someday he would be expected to manage it all. On this night, however, he could not wish for his friend to become ensnared in any further conversations about rotating crops. On the other hand, poor Henry could not wish to subject Smythesdon to any further abuse from Violet.

Violet presumed that if he could, Henry would keep his friend suspended in the hall between the dining room and drawing room, that being the only place he could be assured of finding peace.

As Henry could not keep Lord Smythesdon suspended in the hall, they entered the drawing room. Her brother appeared relieved to find Violet on the pianoforte, as if there was little harm she could do from that outpost.

Lady Mulholland approached Lord Smythesdon and said, "It has occurred to me, my lord, that as you have such a fine intellect, you will wish to see our library on the morrow. We have some very interesting collections, I think."

"Indeed, ma'am," Lord Smythesdon said, attempting to ignore Dandy's low growl and deadly stare. "Seeing a new library is one of the chief pleasures in visiting a house one has not been to before. Only last year I stayed at Magden Place and was delighted to find they had even employed a learned gentleman to keep things up to snuff."

"Fortunately," Lady Mulholland said smoothly, "we have our own resident expert. Nobody understands the contents of Chemsworth's library better than Violet."

Smythesdon may have slightly paled at this pronouncement, but only said, "Indeed?"

"My goodness," Lady Mulholland said, fairly gushing, "hear how prettily Violet does play."

"She ought to," the Viscount said, "I thought that music teacher should never leave the premises. I wondered if I were to pay the man for the rest of my life."

"Mr. Templeman is still with us, dear," Lady Mulholland said, leading her husband to the tea table. "He is teaching Poppy and Pansy now."

"Poppy and Pansy," the Viscount said, as if he had just remembered he was the father of those two individuals. "But nobody after that, eh? Templeman is done after those two?"

"I suspect so, my love," Lady Mulholland said.

Lady Mulholland poured the tea, while Violet determinedly worked her way through one ballad to the next. Her selections were all quiet and sad pieces meant to put everybody to sleep. This worked effectively on nobody quite as well as it did on the Viscount and he was soon dozing by the fire.

Lady Mulholland attempted various gambits to enact her scheme to bring Lord Smythesdon and Violet together. She suggested Rose take a turn at the pianoforte, but sadly Rose had a sore finger. She suggested Daisy have a turn, but Daisy was quickly developing a headache. She wondered if Lord Smythesdon might not wish to go over to the instrument and pick out some music, but Henry leapt up and insisted that he take on the onerous task.

Henry, for all his claim that he would wish to pick out music, merely bent over Violet and said, "You do not even like to hunt. You are being contrary just for the sake of it and it does not bring any credit to you. And, for the love of God, cease pontificating about soup."

He left her picking out a sad Irish air and stinging badly. Of course, Henry would know her soft spots, those areas where he might poke and bruise. Was she being contrary just to be contrary? As a young girl, it had been her greatest fault. She would be told she adored trifle and she, not liking to be told what she liked, would say that she was not so certain that she did. Somehow, as events unfolded, she would find herself the only one at table without trifle. The Friendly Dragon had counseled her that she ought not cut off her own nose to be revenged of her face and Violet had seen the wisdom in it, though she had found it hard to give the habit up. But she *had* given it up.

What else was she to do in this new circumstance? Her mother and brother had gone on a hunting expedition and brought back a gentleman who apparently did not think much of the fairer sex. Was she to be treated as if she were somehow inferior? Was she to pretend she liked being cast as a helpless individual who could not retain facts or hang on to a horse, but must sit pretty and empty-headed in a carriage while the men outside did great things? Perhaps this was what the world thought she should be, but it was not what she was. She would not give up her working, thinking mind in pursuit of some idea of feminine perfection. Not for anybody, and certainly not for the puffed-up Lord Smythesdon.

Rose and Daisy had drained their tea with a speed unprecedented. Daisy stifled a yawn and said, "Heavens, I *am* tired."

At the signal, Violet ceased her playing and Rose jumped up. "I fear we are all tired, and will bid you goodnight."

The three eldest Granger girls made their curtsies and left the drawing room, despite Lady Mulholland looking severely upon them. Violet knew that if the Friendly Dragon could have thought of a mannerly way to drag them back, she certainly would have.

"I shall find Smuckers and have tea sent up," Violet whispered to Daisy and Rose. "We shall convene in my room."

Daisy and Rose skipped up the stairs. Smuckers stepped out from behind a doorway and said, "You looked for me, Miss Violet?"

"Goodness, Smuckers," Violet said, laughing. "I never do know where I should find you hiding."

"Lurking, miss," Smuckers said with a dignified air. "I am lurking so that I shall always be at hand."

"And so you are always at hand most conveniently," Violet said.

"I trust the family experienced an enjoyable evening?" he said, not being able to resist his curiosity on how Lady Mulholland's plan had got on after the unfortunate dinner. He had only been able to hear bits and pieces from the drawing room as he brought in tea and walked out. Not enough to paint a clear picture.

"I cannot speak for all of the family," Violet said, "but between you and me, Lord Smythesdon is a bit of a ninny."

"A ninny, miss!" Smuckers said, a look of horror on his features.

"Truly," Violet said. "I know I can trust you with my secrets, you are my confidante only after Daisy and Rose, and you shan't repeat what I've said. He is a thorough ninny."

"He is to be an Earl," Smuckers said, as if that fact must preclude any sort of ninny-ish tendencies.

"He is to be a very silly Earl, then," Violet said. She paused as she noted Smuckers' crestfallen expression. "Do not be broken up over it, after all it is not as if anybody belonging to the house has been pronounced a ninny."

Smuckers was able to temporarily rally at this idea. He stood straighter at the very mention of the house.

"Now, Smuckers, do be a dear and send up a tea tray with nobody the wiser."

Smuckers had long been in the habit of sending up tea with nobody the wiser. He had been managing that particular operation since they had been girls just out of the nursery and had plied him with pretty cajoling to convince him to send up sweets. Tea may have taken the place of candied lemons and sugared nuts, but the operation remained the same—he would send the kitchen maid up the back stairs, quick and quiet. He had justified this maneuver long ago by reasoning that if Lady Mulholland had not wished him to send sweets or tea up the back stairs, she surely would have mentioned it.

Smuckers nodded to Violet, though he was not heartened by what he had heard of her opinion of Lord Smythesdon. The very idea of a lord being a ninny was anathema to his finer feelings. The man would be an Earl someday. What was happening to the respect for rank? He supposed he must only cling to the idea that Miss Violet Granger had acknowledged him as a special confidante. He had known it, of course, but there was always something gratifying in acknowledgment. It was not every butler who was in the habit of hearing secrets from the family he served.

"He is the most narrow-minded, unenlightened person I have ever met," Violet said. "Did you note the look of shock when he understood we would ride out on Wednesday?"

"Dear me," Daisy said, curled up on a large upholstered chair in front of the fire. She pulled her dressing gown tight around her and said, "He sounds dreadful. Are you certain you speak of Henry's little friend downstairs?"

"Little friend?" Rose asked, lounging on the chair opposite. "There is nothing little about him, he is taller than even Henry."

Violet poured the tea, having surreptitiously taken the tray from Peggy after she had knocked quietly on the door. Peggy had, as always, been all giggles and Violet thought the kitchen maid quite enjoyed these nocturnal outings full of danger and intrigue on the back stairs. Or, it might have been that she enjoyed the annual Christmas-time present she received from the three sisters as a token of appreciation for her tea-time valor.

"Perhaps he is tall in stature," Daisy said, "but he is little in temperament. He is nothing like my hero, who is all passion. Lord Smythesdon is too genial to be anything but regular. Regular is small."

"He is not meant to be *your* hero, Daisy," Rose said. "He is meant to be Violet's hero."

"Yes, that's true," Daisy said. "Do you find him little, Violet?"

"Little in mind and spirit," Violet said. "But what can you mean, he is too genial?"

"Well," Daisy said, "I suppose he did very well with all your teasing. A less genial man might have sunk into brooding and needed very much cheering up."

"I did not think he did very well at all," Violet said, unwilling to allow Lord Smythesdon to gain a single point, even if it were true.

"If you wish it," Rose said to Violet, "I shall tell him that he is horrible. Nobody else will do it, that burden always does fall to me."

"You had better not," Daisy said. "The ODM would be very cross with you."

"Only if he tattled on me," Rose said. "I shan't do it when she is nearby."

"But Violet, dear," Daisy said, "you were a bit hard on him, do not you think? After all, how many people really know anything about white soup?"

"Perhaps," Violet admitted. "Though white soup was not the point. The point was that Lord Smythesdon does not think a lady should know anything at all. So, I found I must cross him at the first opportunity. White soup was the first opportunity."

"Actually," Daisy said, "it was the second opportunity. Descartes, remember?"

"He is handsome, Violet," Rose said. "You cannot deny it."

"I'll not deny it," Violet said, "as it has so little effect upon me." As Violet said it, she knew that was not entirely true. When her hand had brushed the lord's hand at dinner, she had felt a light, prickly feeling, like the shock of a wool blanket unfolded in the midst of a dry winter. She was able to account for this feeling by noting that she had not, as of yet, had the opportunity to touch the bare hand of any other gentleman not related to her. No doubt other young gentlemen would produce more than tepid sparks and so Lord Smythesdon's hand must not be held up as remarkable.

Rather than mention that particular circumstance, she said, "Perhaps, Rose, Lord Smythesdon is *your* hero come to court."

"Do not be ridiculous," Rose said. "I shall marry a man who is all directness. For instance, after your white soup put down, had Lord Smythesdon risen from the table and cried, 'You are a horrible girl, Violet Granger,' and stalked out of the house, I should have fallen violently in love with him. But he did not, and I cannot respect him for it."

"And so I," Daisy said, "shall marry the passionate poet on the Dover cliffs and Rose shall marry a man cursing at all the world and throwing his napkin down at dinner. But Violet, for all your disdain for Lord Smythesdon, who will *you* marry? What sort of gentleman will sweep Violet Granger off her feet and make her swoon?"

"I shall never swoon," Violet said resolutely. "I am far too intelligent to swoon. As for who I shall marry, he will be as intelligent as I, and he will require a wife of intelligence. That combination, and that combination only, can lead to intelligent conversation. He shall inform me and I shall inform him and we shall have remarkable children. Our dinner conversation shall be riveting and I shouldn't be surprised to find that invitations are sought after. Our house will be a veritable intellectual salon."

"It sounds rather dull," Daisy said.

Violet tousled her hair. "It only sounds dull to you because you are intent on riding through the rain to locate your ridiculous poet, who is just now teetering on the Dover cliffs."

"I shall dream of him tonight," Daisy said softly.

Bertram Smythesdon had never encountered any lady like Violet Granger. He had only meant to make civil conversation about soup! How was he to know there were so many different dates associated with it? Then to actually call his mistake to his attention in front of all!

And why should the lady know anything of Descartes? That, surely, was a man's purview. She had even hinted that he ought to have given attribution to the author of the quote, as if he were guilty of some sort of plagiarism. That had not been at all what he had meant to do. He knew that Granger would understand the reference and that had seemed to be all that was needed. It was the common thing at Oxford. Had he not, just a fortnight ago, woken from a night of drinking and said, 'I think, therefore I am.' Nobody had expected him to say who had said it first.

Smythesdon had been pacing his bedchamber, relieved to be out from under the family's scrutiny. Now he paused. Did his own mother and sister know such things, but discreetly avoid correcting him? The thought was galling. He could not bear to entertain the idea that, while he pontificated at dinner on some subject for their elucidation, they might know something of the subject beforehand. That they might have been only smiling and nodding to humor him. He had gloried in his studies at Oxford and been careful to curate the information he chose to give them—it must not be overly complicated and must be of interest to them. What if, all that time that he assumed they were sewing or playing the pianoforte, they had been studying? What if drawing or netting a purse had only been a clever ruse? Who really knew how women spent their hours? Gentlemen *thought* they knew, but there could be no positive proof.

No, it could not be so. It must only be Miss Granger.

But what had Henry Granger been about, forgetting to mention such a person in his household? And forgetting to mention that his sisters would go on the hunt? Ladies, on a hunt? His own mother and sister very sensibly either stayed abed, or followed in late morning in a carriage to bring sustenance to the men.

This household was most strange. He could no more imagine his own sister riding to the hunt than imagine her conjugating Latin.

Still, he reasoned, for all that, he was away from his father's narrowed eyes. He was free and unencumbered. And Violet Granger, for all her knowledgeable ways, was very pretty. Her hand, for that brief moment that he had touched it, had felt very soft. She was to show him the library on the morrow and perhaps he would be inclined to show *her* the error of her ways. Miss Granger might have a passing interest in white soup and Descartes, but there were other subjects that he was certain she remained ignorant of. Showing himself an expert in one of those would restore the natural order of things. He rather felt she would admire him for it. If there was one thing he knew of women, it was that they liked the men around them to be superior, as it reflected well on their own worth. And, after all, it might be very pleasant to be admired by Miss Granger.

"I am afraid, Mrs. Featherstone, that the picture looks grim," Smuckers said, glumly staring into the fire and taking a sip of sherry from his private stock.

The two senior servants of Chemsworth Hall were in the habit of consuming a small glass of sherry, or Madeira on special occasions, before turning in for the night. They might have even been known to take two glasses, as Smuckers reasoned with himself that his glassware was unusually small to begin.

Mrs. Featherstone had drained her own glass, that lady not inclined to the delicate habit of sipping, and said, "Course it's grim. It was never going to be anything but grim."

Smuckers nodded and was silent. Mrs. Featherstone, not having been privy to what was said at dinner and not having the genial habit of lurking about the hall, could only wonder at what had gone on.

She said, "While I knew, all along, Mr. Smuckers, that it should be grim, my powers of prophecy don't go so far as to lay out the details of *how* it all went wrong."

"I shall tell you, Mrs. Featherstone," he said, refilling her glass. "It was one stumble after the next—white soup, Descartes, a foxhunt—they could not have got off on more mistaken footing."

Mrs. Featherstone, not one to show her lack of understanding on any matter, nodded sagely. "It is as I thought," she said. She allowed a long pause to fill the air, then she said, "Exactly how did white soup, Descartes and a foxhunt go wrong?"

Smuckers heaved a sigh. "There were two different dates on the white soup, or some such palaver. Then there was a contretemps over a fellow named Descartes, though I do not see why we should care about him, as he is not even from our county. And finally, there was the matter of hunting. I shall guess that the young gentleman's female relatives do not go out on a hunt. It was at that announcement that I observed him to be truly shocked."

Mrs. Featherstone had nodded through Smuckers' speech as if dates on white soup and disagreeing about people nobody knew and a disapprobation of ladies hunting were all too typical in cases such as the one they now faced. "And I suppose Miss Violet *will* go a-hunting, then? She's a contrary miss, she is. Though why it should matter to anybody *who* chooses to go galloping around the countryside in that ridiculous fashion I shall never know. They so rarely kill a fox and if they even spot a brush going to ground they come back victorious. It doesn't make a lick of sense."

Smuckers had wondered the same thing about the foxhunts at Chemsworth Hall, but would never speak such treachery out loud. It was an English tradition and, even if he did not understand the ins and outs of the thing, it must be respected. He rather thought the point of it was not so much to kill a fox, as they rarely did, but to send *all* of the foxes a message—careful where you tread, vermin, we know you are here and could catch you if we had a mind to.

"All it means to us, I suppose," Mrs. Featherstone continued, "is an early morning confusion in trying to serve champagne and brandy on the drive, dodging trays around those beastly barking hounds. Then we must rumble across hill and dale with refreshments in a carriage, all to be set up on Lookout Hill as elegant as if they were at their own table."

"Mrs. Featherstone," Smuckers said gravely, "a picnic is the least of our problems. What hangs in the balance is the very happiness of the family. If Lady Mulholland is not happy, nobody is happy. And, I am sorry to say, I have not yet told you the worst of it. Miss Violet pronounces Lord Smythesdon a ninny."

Mrs. Featherstone, knowing how the butler *did* worship a title and knowing that she *did* say it would all go wrong, bit down on her lip to stifle her laughter.

"I am sure," Smuckers said, "that I do not understand what we have come to when a man who is to be an Earl is called a ninny. What next, I wonder? Is a Marquess to be an imbecile? Is a Duke to be a numskull? It is as if the whole glorious structure of our beloved country is crumbling beneath our feet."

Chapter Seven

After Rose and Daisy had left her, Violet had lain awake for quite some time in the night, devising various plots to foil the ODM in her schemes. She could not outright say that she would not show Lord Bertie the library, but there were other ways to display her loathing of the project. She had finally settled on an idea. She had risen early and crept down the backstairs to the kitchens. There, she informed Mrs. Featherstone that she would take her breakfast in the library.

Mrs. Featherstone had seemed all trepidation upon hearing the idea, but Violet had assured her that Lady Mulholland was not against it. Of course, she did *not* mention that the only reason Lady Mulholland was not against it was that she had not yet heard of it. Her mother took her breakfast while still abed and would not discover the arrangement until she descended the stairs long after the meal time had passed.

The plan was simple. She would start her studies earlier that was her usual habit and that would accomplish much. She could avoid the lord at breakfast, and she would not lead the lord into the library, he must come to her. Further, when he arrived, he should find her surrounded by heavy tomes on serious subjects. Lord Smythesdon should find a female at work, acquiring knowledge faster than his valet could button his coat.

Having made the arrangements with Mrs. Featherstone, Violet had crept back up the stairs. She had rushed Victorine through her duties and then gone down the main stairs to the library to await her tea and toast. The library was as she had left it, the glorious smell of ink put to paper permeating the very air of it. A cheerful fire burned bright on the hearth and at least gave the illusion of warmth. Icy rain beat against the windows and Violet sighed as she contemplated the hunt on the morrow—it would be muddy, cold, and slippery, simply everything disagreeable. Apollo would be thoroughly disgusted with it and protest from the moment he was walked out of his stall to the moment he was put back into it. Despite her horse's protests, she would not sit it out. The lord would be made to understand that women were perfectly capable of charging over fences and crashing through streams and galloping across fields as madly as any man. Especially Marigold, who would no doubt leave the lord far behind in any race.

Violet thought, with further satisfaction, that the man might faint on the drive when he realized the ladies of Chemsworth Hall rode astride. Lady Mulholland had always been an excellent horsewoman and, upon their marriage, the Viscount and his wife were in the habit of flying across the countryside together. During one such flight, Lady Mulholland was thrown when her sidesaddle slipped underneath the horse's belly, as sidesaddles were so often prone to do. The Viscount, having never given much thought to sidesaddles, gave much thought to them after that accident. He examined the rogue saddle and pronounced it the silliest, most impractical item to ever have made its way into a stable. He'd had a fire built in the yard and threw the offending equipment into it. His lady, laid out on a sofa near the window with a sore leg, had approvingly viewed this decisive action and never rode sidesaddle again. It went without discussion that the Viscount would not like to see one of his daughters on such a stupid contraption. The Viscount, for all his eccentricities, was a practical man and, as he treated Chemsworth Hall as his own kingdom, was never concerned about what the rest of society might be doing.

The neighborhood had grown used to the sight of Granger females riding like men, and Marigold Granger riding like a one-girl Mongol horde, but Violet knew it would come as a great shock to Lord Smythesdon and his delicate sensibilities. For all Marigold's traipsing around the house in her habit, Violet was certain that the lord had failed to notice that her skirt had two drapes tied up instead of one.

A soft knock on the door alerted her to Smuckers bringing in the tea.

"Mrs. Featherstone mentioned you would prefer your breakfast in here?" he asked, in a tone that said he rather thought Mrs. Featherstone had gone mad and had been speaking to him in tongues.

"I did request it," Violet said, smiling at the shocked expression of the butler. "I am directed by my mother to show our esteemed guest the library this morning. I, and my poor sister Marigold. But you see, Smuckers, I am one step ahead. I shall not lead him in, he shall be led in to me. He shall find me sitting here. A woman. Reading. Learning. Acquiring knowledge."

There were so many parts to it that Smuckers was not certain where to begin. "Miss Marigold? In the library?" he said.

"If you can imagine," Violet said, "which I am certain *she* cannot. I suspect my sister shall have her revenge upon Lord Smythesdon on the morrow when she positions her horse to spray him with mud. An elusive fox shall be the least of his problems."

"But," Smuckers said, setting down the tea on the only table not covered by books, "he is to be an Earl! Certainly, nobody dares to spray the gentleman with mud?"

Violet laughed. "Marigold shall spray him with mud and I shall spray him with facts and between the two he shall be entirely undone. He shall run from Chemsworth like a scolded puppy."

"Is he truly that awful to you?" Smuckers asked. "Or perhaps you chafe because Lady Mulholland has directed you to show him your books and you do not like to be managed?"

Violet poured her tea. The lord was certainly not awful *looking*. However, she could not allow herself to give him any credit for it. To do so would be to betray her own worth. It was his opinions that were awful, and that made him, in his entirety, awful. She said, "You know me too well, Smuckers. Naturally, I do not care to be managed. However, what I have really got against the lord is that he thinks a female should not be an intellectual. You cannot expect me to give up that point?"

Smuckers was thoughtful, for indeed he would not expect her to give up such a point. Violet Granger's life had been dedicated to her studies and he was quite sure that not even the king himself could convince her to give it up. Lord Smythesdon, had he been older and wiser, might have realized it.

"I know you like him very well," Violet said, "as he is a lord and will one day be an Earl. But you cannot be on both of our sides—the distance between those sides is from here to Paris."

Smuckers stood straight, as if he were on the verge of giving a salute. He said, "Whatever is to come of all this, Miss Violet, rest assured that Tiberius Smuckers stands with the house. Were I to go down in a blaze of glory, I shall stand with the house. Nobody, not even the son of an Earl, shall turn me away from my duty."

Violet, quite adoring of Smuckers' various warlike speeches, said, "I have never expected anything less of you, Smuckers. You are the general to our army of sisters."

Smuckers, his feelings having been relieved upon expressing his stalwart loyalty to the family, left the library feeling rather sanguine about the fate of Lord Smythesdon. Let the lord look after Donneville, Smuckers' domain was Chemsworth Hall. He would do what he was able to forward Lady Mulholland's plans, but if he must choose sides between Donneville and Chemsworth, his attitudes were known. At least, they were known to Miss Violet. He would not go so far as to alert Lady Mulholland to this throwing down of the gauntlet.

Violet spent a pleasant hour reading, watching the rain and envisioning Lady Mulholland's vexation when she discovered she had been out-maneuvered by her eldest daughter. She had expected a soft knock on the door when the lord arrived for his tour, and so had not been prepared for the crashing in of Marigold, barely containing her disgust at being sent on such an errand. Marigold was dressed in her riding habit, as was beginning to be usual, and Violet wondered if her sister would have the temerity to ride out in such weather.

"Here it is, my lord," Marigold said, "The library, sitting here as it always does, dull as dirt. And there is my sister, Violet, sitting amidst the dullness, as *she* always does."

Lord Smythesdon stepped into the room and Violet was surprised to note that he appeared to have recovered his spirits overnight. She had put him down severely the day before, but it seemed that while one might put him down, he was not inclined to stay down. It was a very inconvenient quality.

He bowed and said, "Miss Granger, I trust you are well this morning?"

"Extremely well, indeed," Violet answered, unwilling to allow the lord to claim more wellness than herself.

"You may explore as you like," Violet said, "while I attend to my studies. I will be happy to answer any questions or direct you to anything in particular that you seek." She picked up Adam Smith's *Theory of Moral Sentiments* and looked pointedly at its pages.

Marigold threw herself into a chair and said, "I am to hang about as some sort of duenna, so mama says. I told her I ought to be out exercising Mercury or he will be wild on the morrow, but she used the excuse of a few raindrops to forbid me. A groom is to exercise him and Mercury shan't like it one bit."

Lord Smythesdon walked along the shelves, occasionally pulling out a tome and examining it before placing it back on the shelf. Violet surreptitiously watched him.

"I am a prisoner in my own house," Marigold said.

"Do something with yourself," Violet said to her sister. "Choose a book or ring for tea."

"I shall ring for tea," Marigold said. "And I shall request some of Mr. Moreau's shortbread biscuits. I require sustenance if I am not to become comatose in this room of sleeping draughts encased in leather and binding."

Marigold only needed to ring the bell once, as Smuckers had been lurking just outside of the door. Marigold and Smuckers had a long tête à tête on the likelihood of any shortbread biscuits being in the larder and the insanity that Mr. Moreau might be expected to spiral down into if he were expected to make them on such short notice and what other likely substitutes might be more easily had.

Smythesdon had finally settled on a book. Violet could see, as she peeked toward him while pretending to concentrate on the book in her hand, he had chosen the first volume of Euclid's *Elements*.

She suppressed a smile. Naturally, he would have sought out a subject that he would not dream she knew anything about. Geometry and other mathematics would only be the purview of clever young men from Oxford.

"Goodness," he said, settling himself into a chair, "there is really nobody like Euclid."

Violet let that statement hang in the air for a moment, then said, "Actually, there were quite a few people like Euclid, whether come before or after. And, as Euclid was Hellenistic, I rather think Archimedes would challenge you on that idea. Not to mention Eratosthenes, Heron, Menelaus and Diophantus."

Lord Smythesdon slowly set the book on his lap. "Are you implying, Miss Granger, that you are familiar with the work of Euclid?"

"Rather than imply a thing, Lord Smythesdon, I hope I can be counted upon to outright state it. I am certainly not a scholar of *all* of Euclid's postulations," Violet said casually. "After all, there are more than four hundred proofs and theorems."

"Four hundred sixty-four," Lord Smythesdon said.

"Four hundred sixty-five, actually."

Lord Smythesdon was silent and Violet wondered if he would have the bravery to voice his real opinions on the subject of her knowing anything whatsoever about Euclid.

"I wonder, though," he said, "what use could this knowledge be? In what household duty would it serve a purpose?"

"None at all," Marigold said. "But then, who cares for household duties anyway? The problem with household duties is that they are all in the house and not a one of them can be done on a horse."

Violet ignored Marigold. "There are any number of tasks where a calculation might come in useful," she said. "Should Mrs. Featherstone wish to know the volume of a half barrel of wheat flour, it may be easily done. But that, sir, is not at all the point. The point is simply to know it. Knowledge does not need to have a use, nor does it need to enhance a woman's household duties. A lady may have many interests beyond the usual household duties."

"Though it seems to me," Lord Smythesdon went doggedly on, "that too many interests outside the household must materially affect the workings of that household. The feminine arts are vast and, to accomplish them well, must take up a majority of a lady's time."

"The feminine arts," Violet said, "such as sewing, painting, drawing, ordering the dinner, supervising maids, visiting the neighbors, managing the household budget, taking up subscriptions and the like, are hardly activities that require the sharp intellect of any reasonable person. Most can be done while half-asleep. The curious mind must seek to expand beyond the traditional areas of interest."

"But there," Lord Smythesdon said, his voice full of agitation, "you have just said it! *Traditional* areas of interest. Tradition must always spring from history and good sense."

"Indeed?" Violet said. "I suppose the practice of burning witches was, at one time, good sense. Though we find it less so presently. The nature of man is that we are always discovering that we have made a mistake. We become enlightened only by time, generation to generation. Every generation believes they have reached the pinnacle of enlightenment, and it is never true."

"Well, that may be," Lord Smythesdon said grudgingly. "But physiology cannot change so very much and everybody knows the female mind should not be burdened with vast amounts of science or mathematics."

"Does everybody know that?" Violet asked.

"I should think so," Lord Smythesdon said. "It's bound to lead to nervousness."

"Do I appear nervous? Or do I, in fact, seemed perfectly able to sit here composedly, despite the vast amounts of knowledge stored in my mind? My lord, the very idea that there is any fundamental difference between the workings of your mind and mine is absurd. The idea that two human beings, composed of the same stuff, should be so vastly different in capability is ridiculous. Perhaps you would do well to recall Euclid's first axiom—things which are equal to the same thing are equal to each other."

"Oh bother!" Marigold said, completely uninterested in this philosophical debate. "Where are my biscuits? I must have tea and biscuits if I am to listen to this drivel. Mercury never bores me so."

Violet and Lord Smythesdon, both having been accused of drivel and being more boring than a horse, looked determinedly down at their volumes.

Smuckers entered with the tea and blessed biscuits. It appeared that shortbread was not to be had, but the more usual almond biscuits with the Viscount's coat of arms stamped on each were provided in abundance.

Marigold said, "Smuckers, I do wish you would stay. I cannot bear this room."

Smuckers smiled indulgently at the fourth eldest Granger girl. "You know that I cannot, though should you require my services I shall be just outside the door."

"It is insufferable," Marigold said, and neither Violet nor Lord Smythesdon knew if she condemned the weather, or the room, or themselves.

"The only idea that even keeps me alive is the hunt on the morrow," Marigold said. "Shall you serve brandy on the drive, Smuckers?"

"I shall, indeed, miss," Smuckers said. "Though you are well aware that Lady Mulholland shall not allow you to have it."

"Silly mama," Marigold said. "When I am eighteen, you shall see what I am like. I shall never change from my habit, I shall ride Mercury all over creation, and I shall drink brandy on the drive. I shall be a regular heathen and like it very much."

Lord Smythesdon eyed Marigold and then looked toward Violet, as if to say that this was the result of ignoring traditional feminine interests.

"Very good, madam," Smuckers said, gracing Marigold with a very formal bow. "Until the much-anticipated heathen invasion, I shall return to my post."

The next hour was long and felt so by everybody who occupied the room. Violet turned pages ever few minutes so she might appear to be deeply engrossed in her book. Smythesdon did the same, and occasionally stared off into the distance as if he were contemplating some complicated formula. Marigold paced and ate biscuits and cursed the weather.

Violet did not have the first idea how long she was to carry on with this charade. It appeared, though, that Marigold did. The clock struck eleven and she cried, "Hallelujah! We are free!"

Lord Smythesdon had practically run from the library. Marigold actually had run. Though she was forbidden to ride out in such awful weather, nobody had told Marigold that she might not attend Mercury in the stables and Violet saw her running through the rain and across the drive toward the outbuildings mere moments after she had exited the room.

Violet thought to go on with her studies now that she was to be left in peace, but she found herself too aggravated. The idea that Lord Smythesdon thought a woman's mind to be so different from a man's. The idea that, should she learn too much, she would become nervous. It was outrageous! Where had he learned such things? From his own family, of course. It was not often that Violet Granger stumbled upon a circumstance that enabled her to view her own parents from afar. This was one such circumstance. She could see, by comparison to Lord Smythesdon's views, that she had been very lucky to have a mother and father who looked upon her as just as capable as Henry. In truth, when it came to studies, she was acknowledged to be more capable.

Violet gave up attempting to learn anything new, closed her book and took herself up the stairs to seek out Rose and Daisy. She found them in Daisy's room, sorting through a pile of tangled ribbons.

"Oh, you shall never guess," Daisy said, before Violet even had time to close the door behind her. "Mama is in a right state and it is none of us that provokes her."

"Then it is Henry," Violet said. "What has he done, other than bring the awful Smythesdon to our attention."

"It is nobody in this house," Rose said. "It is Mrs. Ravencraft."

"Mrs. Ravencraft?" Violet said with some surprise. "The TFD does not give a toss for Mrs. Ravencraft."

The Ravencrafts were one of Chemsworth Hall's nearest neighbors. Mrs. Marjorie Ravencraft was a stout lady who was fond of eating, gossiping, and admiring her only daughter, in that order. Her gossip never seemed to run out, or as Marigold described it, 'She's got enough room in that belly for all the news that has occurred since the beginning of the century.'

Lady Mulholland, while civil to the family, had no use for the lady whatsoever. Mrs. Ravencraft had, early in the Viscount's marriage, been the source of some unsavory talk when she had first spotted Lady Mulholland riding astride. She had pronounced it 'mannish.' When Lady Mulholland had heard of it, she had called upon Mrs. Ravencraft, but refused to dismount her horse. Mrs. Ravencraft had been forced to come out and attend her visitor on the drive. Lady Mulholland, it was reported far and wide, had sat astride her mare and said, "Did you have a question for me pertaining to my mode of riding?"

Mrs. Ravencraft had blushed and hemmed and blurted out, "No!"

Lady Mulholland had replied, "I thought not," turned her horse and galloped off the property.

Since then, their relations were coolly polite. On occasion, because Mrs. Ravencraft really could not control her tongue, some report would meander its way back to Chemsworth Hall. The lady seemed to be obsessed with the number of daughters that continued to arrive at the house and had even remarked that there was something unnatural in it. The birth of the twins had only served to confirm this opinion.

"Mrs. Ravencraft writes to say that she will visit," Daisy said in a fit of giggles.

"Can you imagine such a thing?" Rose said. "Of course, we all know why she comes. She is intent on thrusting that daughter of hers in front of our guest. She hopes to gain a match and, if she cannot get that, wishes to at least leave with enough gossip to last a month. She frets when she is not the fountain of all falsehoods and innuendos."

"And only think, Violet," Daisy said breathlessly, "if *Miss* Ravencraft should walk off with mama's Lord Smythesdon. I cannot imagine what would come of it."

"She would be entirely thwarted," Rose said. "We can only guess how she should hold up against it. She would be insulted down to her toes."

"I do not care if Miss Ravencraft walks off with everybody in the neighborhood. I only fear what mama should be like if Mrs. Ravencraft were to come out victorious in any matter. I do not suppose the ODM can bar the door against her," Violet said.

"She attempted it," Daisy said. "That is how we know all about it. Mama and papa were talking of it in the hall. She said she would write that tactless ogress back and tell her not to come. Papa said she could not because we share a fence with Mr. Ravencraft and papa gets on perfectly fine with the man."

"And so they come this afternoon," Rose said. "The lady must be desperate beyond measure to have her carriage pulled through the mud on such a day."

"She is bold," Violet said. "I shall give her that. Imagine, visiting a house where not a single inhabitant wishes to see you."

"Oh, she is not so bad, really," Daisy said. "Only very talkative. And Miss Ravencraft can be pleasant—I saw her in town some months ago and we had a jolly conversation about bonnets."

Rose stared at Daisy as if she had just pronounced the devil himself pleasant. "They are enemies of the family," she said, as if there were a list of traitors somewhere that everybody was well aware of.

"And perhaps there is another inhabitant of the house who shall not be opposed to seeing the Ravencrafts," Daisy continued. "I do not believe Henry has ever developed the strong feelings that you have. I think he rather admires Miss Ravencraft."

"And I suppose our visiting lord shall like her, too," Rose said. "She is just the type of simpering female that men do like. Pale and appearing as if she were a young willow in a strong wind."

Violet, though she could not have said precisely why, was very much against young willows blowing about in the wind.

"But enough about the Ravencrafts," Daisy said. "Violet, how did you get on in the library?"

"I got on quite well, thank you, though I cannot say the same for either Marigold or Lord Smythesdon. Marigold pined for her horse and appeared to view books as a thing that might mortally injure her, were she to be exposed too long. The lord thought to show me my ignorance by pretending to read Euclid. As I was already well familiar with that author's *Elements*, he was sadly disappointed. I believe I then lectured him unmercifully."

"Dear me," Daisy said, "It is like the Napoleonic Wars have taken up residence within our very walls."

"I suppose he did not once throw his book down and pronounce you a horrible girl?" Rose asked.

"He did not," Violet said, "though I believe he would have very much liked to."

"And so much more the pity," Rose said. "He wanted to do it, but he could not find the courage."

"Perhaps, though, dear Violet," Daisy said, "it is not so entirely necessary to trounce the man's pride from here to London?"

Violet bristled at the hint. Daisy could not know under what duress she had been placed. This situation had nothing at all to do with her past habit of being contrary. This was Violet Granger defending her right to have a thinking mind. She would trounce Lord Smythesdon all the way to Rome if it were required.

Chapter Eight

Smuckers had been nearly dumbstruck at the news. The Ravencrafts would visit Chemsworth Hall. He did not recall them having visited in many, many years. There had been some early attempts made by Mrs. Ravencraft, but Smuckers guessed the lady had found her reception too frosty to persevere with it. In truth, there were not many in the neighborhood who dared visit the Grangers often. There was Mrs. Dallway, a great friend of Lady Mulholland's. But then, that lady was of fierce temperament and would likely stare down a dragon and tell it to move out of the way should she encounter one upon the road. The rest of the neighborhood was at once respectful of the Viscount and his family, but hesitant to be trapped overlong in a room with them. Too many tales had been told of Lady Mulholland dropping a growling Pomeranian onto somebody's unsuspecting lap or terrifying somebody's daughter who had reached for a second biscuit and been told it might lead to lumpiness, or somebody nearly freezing to death in front of a frugal fire, coming down with a cold and certain that it was purposefully done.

Were the Viscount to make an appearance in the drawing room, things might become even more alarming. There had been one hapless neighbor who had mentioned her cousin from Yorkshire and been soundly lectured on the general untrustworthiness of foreigners.

Still, if the Ravencrafts would have the temerity to step through the doors, Smuckers would meet the challenge with his usual dignified grace. Lady Mulholland had given him his direction and he would execute her wishes with all the skill he could bring to bear.

He looked over his staff and said, "We have had news. The Ravencrafts will come to call this day."

He paused to allow this unusual idea to settle into the servant's minds. Then he said, "Mr. Moreau, please be prepared to present a tea that will awe those people. We shouldn't like them to leave the house without the proper sense of awe. They are to visit the house of a Viscount and I would have them know it."

Mr. Moreau peered down his pointy nose and said, "Ravencraft cook is English," as if that was sufficient explanation as to why it would be mere child's play to awe them.

"Maids is English, too," Fleur said. Mr. Moreau nodded approvingly at his countryman. There seemed to be, amongst the French servants of the house, some secret agreement on the idea that they had emigrated to a land peopled with unsophisticated rubes and so they could, therefore, consider themselves superior.

"I suppose they will thrust their daughter upon the lord like a sacrifice to a pagan god," Peggy said.

Mr. Moreau whipped his dish towel across the back of her head, but Peggy having been hit with a dish towel for some years, did not flinch.

"Nobody is to be thrust upon anybody in this house," Smuckers said gravely. "Thrusting does not occur at Chemsworth Hall."

One of the footmen snickered and Smuckers got the idea that he'd somehow said something untoward, though he could not fathom what.

"Best tell Mrs. Ravencraft that, then," Peggy said, snorting at her own wit and bracing for a second smack with the dish towel.

Mrs. Featherstone said nothing, but merely shook her head as if it would not surprise her if the Ravencrafts were to arrive with a trebuchet to siege the place.

Smuckers said, "I hardly need tell you that our standards must rise yet again. We find ourselves serving the next Earl of Ainsworth, *and* we must ensure that all in the neighborhood are informed, through the very busy tongue of Mrs. Ravencraft, of the magnificence of this estate. We shall not make the smallest misstep and the Ravencrafts shall depart feeling decidedly small. Go forward, now, for the glory of the house!"

The drawing room was once again lit brightly. As it was warmer than usual, Violet suspected that her mother had ordered the candles set alight very early and that what burned now were a second set. The fire fairly roared and every chair had on it a fur throw, casually draped over the arm. Whatever Lady Mulholland could devise to avoid freezing the inhabitants of the house, she had done.

"This is especially...cheerful," Violet said, taking a seat next to Lady Mulholland. She scooped Dandy from her mother's lap and the Pomeranian graciously allowed himself to be petted.

"Yes, well," Lady Mulholland said grimly, "it seems we are to have more company than we expected."

"Are we?" Violet said in mock surprise, just as Rose and Daisy came into the room. "Whoever would call in this sort of weather? Certainly Mrs. Dallway does not do it. I understood her to be away in town and, were she here, she is far too practical for such a silly venture."

Daisy turned so her mother would not note her laughter. Rose picked up her sewing and stared at it.

"The Ravencrafts are coming," Lady Mulholland said, in a tone that sounded very like she had said 'the pestilence is coming.'

"Good heavens," Daisy said. "Why should the Ravencrafts come?"

The three eldest Granger daughters were certain they knew why Mrs. Ravencraft would turn up so unexpectedly, but were anxious to discover what sort of face their mother would put on it.

"I suppose," Lady Mulholland said, "since Mrs. Ravencraft is so fond of gossip, she wishes to be the first to examine our guest so that she can describe him far and wide."

Violet, highly amused with the conversation, said, "And will Miss Ravencraft accompany her mother?"

"I believe so," Lady Mulholland said, nearly choking on the words.

Violet was certain that if Lady Mulholland could discover some way to tie Miss Maribelle Ravencraft to her own bedpost to prevent her from coming, that young lady would currently be struggling against knotted ropes.

"I have not seen Miss Ravencraft in months," Rose said. "I wonder if we should find her as pasty as always. She is rarely seen in the sun and when she does venture out she is hidden under that hideous green parasol. She always does look as if she has had all the blood drained from her."

Lady Mulholland took Dandy back from Violet's lap and playfully shook his little paws. "Does she?" she said softly. Her feelings on the Ravencrafts seemed very much relieved upon hearing of Miss Ravencraft described as little better than a walking corpse.

"Violet," Lady Mulholland said, "how did you get on in the library this morning?"

Violet had been ready for the question and had decided to launch one of Lady Mulholland's own strategies against her—dodge into another subject.

"Very well, mama," Violet said, "though I cannot say the same for Marigold. She pined over Mercury, as usual. I wonder if she does not spend too much time in the stables. It must interfere with her sewing or French or whatever it is she should be doing. And this new eccentricity of wishing to wear her habit everywhere is odd, indeed. I really think something should be done about it, else she turns herself into Harriet Dunphy."

Lady Mulholland began to answer, most likely to stage a vigorous defense of her coarse cousin Harriet, but she paused and narrowed her eyes. "Leave Marigold to me. How did you get on with Lord Smythesdon?"

Violet cursed her mother's cleverness. She had seen right through the ruse to turn the conversation to Marigold. "Well enough," she said. "But perhaps our guest was surprised to find me not wholly unacquainted with Euclid."

"Euclid," Lady Mulholland said, as if Euclid were the name of a sigh that escaped oneself upon total exasperation with an eldest daughter.

"Indeed," Violet said. "The lord could not understand how knowing such formulas could benefit the female mind. Which, he notes, is prone to nervousness."

Violet watched her mother take in the information. She could well guess at the ODM's thoughts. Lady Mulholland would find it deeply offensive for anyone to imply that she or anybody connected to her was nervous. She had an abiding dislike of nervous women. It was one of the reasons she despised London so very much—the town appeared to be full of fainting females. Lady Mulholland chose to think of herself as both charming and formidable and there was no room for nervousness in those two qualities. The Viscount himself could not abide a nervous woman and was happy enough not to have one of those individuals living in his house. He did, perhaps, sometimes look askance at Lily, whose retiring ways came the closest to that unwanted state. But as Lily had not yet taken up fainting, he assured himself that she would embolden herself over time.

On the other hand, Lady Mulholland had devised the scheme to throw Violet and Lord Smythesdon together and did not like to be thwarted in anything. To be thwarted would be to admit defeat or mistake, and she was not in the habit of it.

"I suspect," Lady Mulholland said finally, "that poor Lord Smythesdon has spent too much time in town. Every swooning female from Cornwall to Northumberland has made her mincing way to that metropolis. I do not see why they should not all be kept back to periodically fall to the ground in the comfort of their own homes, but they are not. Lord Smythesdon has not been exposed to the society of sensible women until now. I suppose we must give him time to adjust to the idea."

"Mama," Violet scolded, "you cannot believe what you say. Lord Smythesdon certainly learned these attitudes from his own family."

"Nonsense," Lady Mulholland said. "Harriet tells me that she likes the family very much. Or, as Harriet would say it, Lady Ainsworth is a brick and her daughter a right jolly girl."

Violet paused. She had not for a moment believed that Harriet Dunphy had described Lord Ainsworth as an exquisite host. But a brick and a right jolly girl *did* sound like their cousin.

But what matter? They could be bricks and right jolly all they liked. That did not change the lord's ridiculous opinions.

Marigold entered and searched despairingly for the tea tray. The hem of her habit was muddy, her curls were tousled and she had Mercury's hair decorating her bodice. She had clearly come straight from the stables.

"Marigold, dear," Lady Mulholland said, eying her daughter up and down, "do go and change. You are not presentable for the drawing room."

Marigold stood her ground, as she often did. "I wished to have tea before those awful
Ravencrafts come. I was on my way to get out of these wet clothes when I heard the news from Smuckers. I am determined to elude them."

Lady Mulholland bit her lip to stop herself from laughing. "You are not to speak of our neighbors in such a tone. You are far too young to be so jaded."

"Oh, mama," Marigold said, "Am I really too young to notice how awful they are? Mrs. Ravencraft is a tattler—am I to care who said what about somebody else's dress? And that silly Miss Ravencraft is so thin she might crack into a thousand pieces if she were to fall over."

"Go and change and then return to us," Lady Mulholland directed. "And not into another habit, if you please. Bring Lilly with you, I will presume she is in her room, reading some awful novel she has borrowed from Daisy."

Marigold stomped from the room, her heavy footfalls meant to convey her general displeasure at how her afternoon was unfolding.

After she closed the door, Daisy said, "Do not blame Lily for reading novels, mama. She has my romantic heart. She cannot help but dream of brave knights who would risk everything to gain her favor."

"Let us hope the knight does not run his horse right off the Dover cliffs in the middle of a poem," Rose said.

"Why should anybody be riding round the Dover cliffs?" Lady Mulholland asked.

Before Daisy could tell her mother of the mythical gentleman who stood upon the cliffs in the rain, writing poetry about her, Lord Smythesdon and Henry entered the room.

"Good afternoon my lord," Lady Mulholland said. "Henry, tea shall be up in a moment. Until then, gentlemen, warm yourself by the fire. I understand you have been out to the stables to choose a horse for the hunt?"

"We have, Lady Mulholland," Lord Smythesdon said. "Miss Marigold Granger was gracious enough to give me a thorough background on each animal, including what they might be expected to do if faced with a high fence or wide stream and a discourse on their hardiness and how they respond to a rider's touch. I've never spoken to a Stablemaster who knew more about his horses."

"Smythesdon has chosen The Turk," Henry said proudly.

"Goodness," Lady Mulholland said. "He is a lovely specimen, but he is a bit of a handful, my lord."

Violet thought that was the largest understatement she had ever heard. The only two people who could stay on the back of The Turk were her father and Marigold. The horse was a Desert Norman, a mix of Arabian and Percheron. He stood nearly eighteen hands and while he had the brute strength of a draft horse, he had the quick mind and agile footing of a hot blood. His personality was mercurial—one moment he was happy to take an apple from one's hand and the next he attempted to eat the hand itself. He had been known to kick down his stable door when he had a mind to visit a field. The grooms, though they would not

91

admit to it, were terrified of the beast. Lord Smythesdon must consider himself quite the horseman to have chosen such a one.

"I trust my long years in the saddle on some of my father's finest horses will have prepared me for The Turk. Though I did tell Granger that I should refuse to accept the honor if the Viscount would prefer to ride him."

"Oh no," Lady Mulholland said, "my husband always takes Genesis on a foxhunt. A bit smaller, but the Viscount feels that he turns sharper."

"Is that not what I said, Smythesdon?" Henry said, looking very pleased with himself.

Violet could not make her brother out. It seemed to her that putting anybody on The Turk was risky in the extreme. If her brother had the least amount of sense, regardless of what a fine horseman Smythesdon was, he would have counseled against it. Marigold should have counseled against it.

"Smythesdon and I have talked many times of going out to the countryside together on horseback," Henry said, "but his horse was lame and then mine was here getting shod. Now we shall finally be able to do it."

"You have never even ridden out together?" Violet asked her brother.

"Violet," Henry said in a condescending tone, "we are Oxford men. We have much to accomplish while we are there. It is not a holiday where we can do as we please—it is real work."

Violet stared at her brother. Henry did not even know if his friend could, as Marigold would describe it, ride creditably and not hang on like a fool.

Before she could respond to Henry's lecturing, the Ravencrafts were announced.

Smuckers, relishing his duty to announce these upstarts and enemies of the house with all the dignified flourish that he could muster, intoned, "*Lady* Mulholland, *Mrs.* Ravencraft, accompanied by Miss Ravencraft."

Violet bit her lip. She knew perfectly well that Smuckers put the emphasis on Lady and Mrs. to point out to these invaders that they intruded upon a titled lady, while they remained, sadly, without title.

Mrs. Ravencraft was a heavyset woman decorated in all manner of frippery, as if she could not decide upon a ribbon and so had determined she had better wear them all. Her expression was one that was at once hesitant and bold. Violet was certain the woman trembled at the idea of the reception she might receive from Lady Mulholland upon this unusual visit, but trembling had not been enough to put her off.

Mrs. Ravencraft's daughter was, as Marigold had so helpfully pointed out, a thin and delicate-looking sort of person. Her manner of dress was far simpler than her mother's, being a pale-yellow silk with only small embroidered flowers of the same color around the bodice and sleeves. Though her skin was pale, there was a high flush upon her cheeks and Violet could not guess if it were on account of the cold or the shamelessness of her mother.

The Ravencrafts curtsied and Lady Mulholland rose to meet them. She glided to her guests with all the majesty that she was known to display when she meant to cow a person into submission. "Mrs. Ravencraft, Miss Ravencraft," she said.

"Lady Mulholland," they both murmured together.

"You know, of course, my daughters, Miss Granger, Miss Rose Granger and Miss Daisy Granger, and my son, Mr. Granger. This is Mr. Granger's friend, Lord Smythesdon."

The drawing room was filled with bows and curtsies and Violet could hardly keep herself from laughing.

Smuckers re-entered the room, this time leading all four footmen carrying large trays. Violet looked upon this train of food marching in with some astonishment. Lady Mulholland said, "Ah, here is tea."

Tea, indeed. They had never seen such a tea in that drawing room. Violet thought that her mother, having been denied the satisfaction of telling them not to come, had decided to paint a very elegant picture for the Ravencrafts. Lady Mulholland, by this extravagant display, said, "We do know how to entertain a lord, do we not? Naturally, I do not know how you do your own tea, though it is unlikely to matter as you will never have a lord through your own door."

The tea service was set in front of Lady Mulholland's place and she set about preparing the cups. On each tray of food currently making its way around the room, small plates were set to one side. With all the pomp and circumstance that Smuckers had infused in them, Jimmy, Johnny, Charlie and Oscar walked round to the various inhabitants and used tongs to delicately set their selections on a plate and set a small fork alongside before handing it to them. The footman then smartly snapped open a cloth napkin with the Viscount's crest and handed it down. Violet gazed upon an assortment of cheeses, lemon tarts, apple tarts, currant cakes, sponges, orange fairy cakes, seed cakes and, as always, the almond biscuits with the crest stamped upon them. Mr. Moreau had been directed to impress and Mr. Moreau had taken up the challenge with gusto.

Smythesdon, his plate piled high with currant cakes, said to the Ravencrafts, "I understand you are neighbors? That is jolly."

Both ladies nodded their heads but did not give a reply, no doubt wondering how to explain how jolly it was to live so nearby the Grangers.

Henry, nearly stammering, said, "We are to hunt on the morrow."

"I wish you good fortune," Miss Ravencraft said so softly that the gentlemen had to lean forward to hear it. "I shall try not to think of it though, because it frightens me terribly. I do not like to think of anybody having an accident."

This mild speech seemed to meet with great approbation from both Smythesdon and Henry, as they both nodded vigorously.

"I am to ride The Turk," Smythesdon said proudly. "He is a beast of a horse."

Miss Ravencraft shuddered at the mention of a beastly horse and the gentleman was much gratified by it.

"Beastly," the lord repeated, as if he would convince Miss Ravencraft to shudder again.

"My poor daughter," Mrs. Ravencraft said, "suffers from the most delicate feelings."

Lady Mulholland stared at Mrs. Ravencraft as if that lady implied that her own daughters did not suffer from delicate feelings, which no doubt the lady did mean to imply.

"There can be no shame in delicate feelings," Smythesdon said. "I rather think they must be commended."

Miss Ravencraft blushed deeply. Mrs. Ravencraft nodded vigorously. Lady Mulholland looked as if there were a gathering storm in the environs of her face. Though Violet worked to keep her expression neutral, she was as annoyed as her mother. Here they were, Lord Smythesdon and her brother, hanging on every simpering word from the girl. Miss Ravencraft was frightened of a hunt she was not even riding to? Whoever heard of such a ridiculous notion? Violet glanced at Rose, who had narrowed her eyes at Miss Ravencraft, and Daisy, who held her handkerchief over her mouth to cover her laughter.

"I will assume, then, Miss Ravencraft," Smythesdon said, "that you, yourself, do not ride to the hunt?"

Miss Ravencraft looked as if she had been asked if she were in the habit of wearing pants and swearing. "Ride to the hunt? Certainly not, Lord Smythesdon. I leave that to my father and brother, while I do the woman's work of offering prayer that they return home safely."

Lord Smythesdon nodded, in full agreement with the idea that at least one lady in the neighborhood would be safely at home, offering prayer for the men.

Just then, Marigold strode in. She looked round at the wandering footmen and their overburdened trays and said, "Is this to strengthen us for the hunt on the morrow? I shall be ready to ride all day after this."

Lady Mulholland pressed her lips together.

The Ravencrafts and Lord Smythesdon had risen at her approach. Marigold looked over Miss Ravencraft and delivered a curtsy so half-hearted as to verge on rude.

Miss Ravencraft, for her part, appeared to have understood Marigold would ride out with the men on the hunt, which she pretended shocked her greatly. Violet presumed this was for Lord Smythesdon's benefit, since the lady would well know of the practice.

Marigold filled her plate with all manner of cakes and biscuits and sat next to Violet. As she attacked those victuals with a vigor perhaps best left to a starving soldier, Lord Smythesdon and Henry plied Miss Ravencraft with questions which she very prettily answered.

Violet leaned over and whispered to Marigold, "Why have you allowed Lord Smythesdon to select The Turk? Nobody is even certain of his horsemanship."

Through a mouthful of cake, Marigold said, "I have not allowed anything. I told him to stay off The Turk. But then, he and Henry began bragging to each other about their superior skill. I could not turn them away from it. He had better have been truthful or he will regret his boastfulness by way of a broken neck. It is a long way down from eighteen hands."

Violet glanced over to Lord Smythesdon. He was just now calling over a footman to entice Miss Ravencraft to try a currant cake, while she was demurring as if to eat cake was somehow shameful and bold. It would serve him right if he did break his neck.

Violet paused. That thought was a bit too contrary to be right. It harkened back to her old bad habit. She would not really wish for him to break his neck, simply because he had some wrongheaded ideas about females. She supposed if every gentleman filled with wrongheaded ideas were to have his neck broken, the countryside should be so strewn with their lifeless bodies that one could hardly get a carriage past them.

And, even were she to wish for his broken neck, the consequences of a serious accident would be severe upon the family. Why had they allowed him on such a beast, people would wonder. A strange horse, a Desert Norman at that, on a muddy day in a previously unknown countryside? It had been madness. That is what would be said and it would be right. No, somehow, he must be dissuaded from such a rash course. He might think he understood a horse like The Turk, but he could not. He must not be allowed to have his own stupidity lead them all to disaster.

"He's all in for book smarts," Marigold said, "but he does not show a lick of commonsense. I wonder why men do that—egg each other on in such a ridiculous manner and get themselves into a situation that lacks even a hint of rationality. I have seen the grooms do it often enough."

Violet nodded, determined that she would drill some rationality into Lord Smythesdon before the evening was through. He would be better served on a horse like Merlin—strong and steady and sure-footed in mud.

Miss Ravencraft had whipped out her fan and covered her laughter at something Lord Smythesdon had said. Who on earth carried a fan in such weather? These feminine arts the lady brought to display were confounding. Violet, herself, used a fan to cool herself when she was hot, which at Chemsworth Hall did not account for more than a week's time in any given year. This waving it about as some sort of accessory to modesty was mystifying. And highly irritating, despite how charmed the gentlemen appeared to be by it.

Henry leaned in and said something else to the girl, which provoked further laughter. Lady Mulholland was not laughing. She was staring with determination at the clock on the mantel, occasionally turning to Mrs. Ravencraft and smiling, and then going back to stare at the clock.

The usual time for a call had come and gone. Violet began to wonder if the Ravencrafts had some hope of being asked to dine. If they did, that hope was sadly misplaced. Lady Mulholland would sooner eat in the stables than have Mrs. Ravencraft at her table. That lady would shortly find herself traipsing right back into the mud she came through, whether she wished it or not.

Finally, Mrs. Ravencraft could no longer avoid Lady Mulholland's broad hints on the time. The ladies rose and took their leave, amidst many compliments from the gentlemen and much assurances on Miss Ravencraft's part that she would pray for their safety on the morrow.

As far as Violet Granger was concerned, it had been a perfectly hideous tea.

Chapter Nine

Smuckers had given his congratulations on the tea to Mr. Moreau in front of all of the staff. He knew that sort of acknowledgement went a good way toward greasing the wheels of the chef's temperamental carriage. It was an old butler's trick, taught him by the butler before—rule with an iron hand, but judiciously throw bouquets of compliments to be caught by those proved worthy. The staff were to know that Mr. Moreau had been requested to awe the visitors and Mr. Moreau *had* awed them.

Mr. Moreau, for his own part, had taken these compliments in stride and merely said softly, "Ravencraft cook is English."

Now, Smuckers sat in his butler's closet with Mrs. Featherstone, drinking tea during the lull before it was time to set up for dinner.

"What news from above stairs?" Mrs. Featherstone said, drinking her tea with relish.

Smuckers set his cup down and said, "Lady Mulholland conducted herself as fine as any queen and the Ravencrafts were to understand what was what by it. Our footmen went about their duties flawlessly, if I do compliment myself on how well I have trained them. The tea service was one for the ages."

Mrs. Featherstone had begun to squirm uncomfortably in her chair at this glowing report, the housekeeper generally not in favor of such entirely happy news. There was nothing to sink her teeth into if all was to go on smoothly.

"As much as I would wish to report that nothing could have marred such a promising circumstance," Smuckers continued.

Mrs. Featherstone stopped her squirming and sat up straighter.

"I am afraid that the attentions paid to Miss Ravencraft by the gentlemen were what Lady Mulholland would consider excessive."

Mrs. Featherstone appeared as overjoyed at this news as a sailor drowning in the sea who is suddenly swept up into a rescue boat. "Ah," she said. "I might have known it. Miss Ravencraft comes in a-simpering and the gentlemen go wild for it."

Smuckers frowned, as he did not like to think of anybody going wild in the drawing room.

"Now, don't get your back up, Mr. Smuckers," Mrs. Featherstone said soothingly. "I only mean to say that Miss Ravencraft is one of those delicate types as look to faint over Shakespeare. Our Miss Grangers are of a rather more...sturdy mind. Excepting Miss Lily, of course, who seems to have been dropped in by faeries."

Smuckers did not wish to admit the truth of Mrs. Featherstone's assessment, though he could not outright deny it. There was a significant difference between Miss Ravencraft and the Miss Grangers. He had thought the difference weighed in the Miss Grangers' favor until he had seen them all together in one room. The gentlemen had been entranced by this slip of a girl. Was that usual outside of their own neighborhood? He had been used to considering the Miss Grangers as superior to all other females, but what if the rest of the world preferred the likes of Miss Ravencraft? Lord Smythesdon seemed to, and that did not bode well for Lady Mulholland's plan.

"And I suppose that little Miss Ravencraft does not hunt," Mrs. Featherstone said. "She'll be the type to swoon at the thought of it."

"You are correct," Smuckers said. "And, if I am to look upon the morrow's outing with a practical eye, I would have to admit that I am worried. Lord Smythesdon has chosen to ride The Turk."

"What?" Mrs. Featherstone said, clearly delighted with the idea. "That beast is a bad 'un."

"It is not so much that he is bad, Mrs. Featherstone," Smuckers said, unwilling to allow even a horse belonging to the family to be pronounced bad. "It is more that he is temperamental. And powerful. The Viscount once told me that it was best to ride The Turk when one had no particular destination in mind, as if that horse did not agree with a proposed direction he would simply go in another and there was little a rider could do about it."

Mrs. Featherstone heaved a contented sigh. "I see disaster runnin' round the corner, Mr. Smuckers. Runnin' round hard and fast."

The first gong had sounded and Violet had gone up. Victorine had fussed over her hair and insisted she wear her dark blue silk as it complimented her eyes. Violet had sworn she did not need her eyes complimented for anybody's pleasure, but Victorine had only laughed and told Violet that she should be ashamed of herself if she were a Parisian. Despite Violet's vehemence against the dark blue silk, she soon found herself dressed in it. Victorine, when she had a strong opinion, was very like an army of soldiers invading a peaceful market town. There was not much to do but comply with her orders.

Now, they had moved on to Rose's room and Violet said, "What do you make of Lord Smythesdon planning to ride The Turk?"

"I think he shall not ride him for long," Rose said. "Perhaps he will not get off the drive."

"That is precisely what I think. Marigold tried to talk him out of it, but she said the lord and Henry had lapsed into some sort of manly one-upmanship and he could not be persuaded. I think we ought to try though. If he breaks his neck we shall be blamed for putting him on such a horse."

"I suppose we had better be direct," Rose said. "I shall tell him he is horrible for thinking of it and you shall tell him he is stupid to even try it. Between us, we shall shame him into some sort of sense."

Violet nodded. Rose was right, there was no other way to accomplish it. They must be forceful and direct.

Victorine erupted in peals of laughter.

"What is so funny, Victorine," Violet asked.

"You no get mens to do like that! Mon Dieu! You must saves the pride."

"Save his pride? I haven't the faintest idea how we might tell him he is an idiot while saving his pride," Violet said.

"No," Victorine said pertly. "The English never does."

"Well?" Rose said. "How is this French trickery done?"

Victorine, looking pleased to be in possession of French feminine knowledge that was wholly unknown to English ladies, said, "You tells him Turk is second dangerous. No first. You see?"

"Not really," Rose said doubtfully.

Violet, though, thought she did see. Marigold had said the two men had bragged to each other on their superior horsemanship. That was what had led Lord Smythesdon to choose The Turk. He had been determined to show off on the most challenging horse. If he were to come under the impression that another horse was, in fact, the most challenging, might he not switch his choice?

"So the trick will be," Violet said, "to convince the lord that Merlin is a more frightening beast than The Turk."

Victorine began to pull the curl papers from Rose's hair. "Just so," she said.

Violet's mind raced along, examining different ideas on how it might be done. She reasoned that it was no different than understanding one of Euclid's formulas. One must only come upon the most direct and elegant solution.

She began to see how she might go about it. Before Violet could explain her idea, Daisy burst into the room.

"Oh my goodness, Victorine," she said, breathless from running down the long corridor. "You shall never guess what has happened."

Victorine shaped one of Rose's newly made curls with pomade and said, "I no guess? Gowns everywhere is guess."

"Well, yes, gowns are everywhere, I am sure I do not know how it happens," Daisy said. "But that is not the worst news. My yellow silk somehow got too close to the fire and now it has a hole burned right through it at the hem. You shall have a time of it with the repair, though I beg you do not mention it to Lady Mulholland. She always scolds me for my carelessness and this shall be one more example. More vexing, I had thought to wear the yellow this evening, now I am at sixes and sevens wondering if I should choose the pale blue? Or perhaps the lavender? Or the peach?"

"Pale blue," Violet and Rose said together.

Daisy nodded. "That *was* my first thought."

Victorine heaved a long sigh. It was the sigh that told the world that it was a heavy burden to care for these three sisters and she should get a medal for it.

Daisy kissed her cheek and said, "I know I am horrid. To make it up to you, take any ribbon you can lay your hands on that takes your fancy. Take two, if you like. Only, do not tell Lady Mulholland about this little accident."

Victorine sniffed, appeased for the moment.

Violet had left Rose and Daisy in Daisy's bedchamber, looking over the carnage. She had come down to the drawing room in good time, determined to find her chance to speak to Lord Smythesdon. Lady Mulholland, no doubt taking her daughter's early arrival as a sign of eagerness, stood Dandy on his hind legs and covered his annoyed little face with kisses in high good humor.

The Viscount sat in the chair across from his lady and looked on the scene with a satisfied expression. That gentleman was not in the habit of liking overt demonstrations of affection, except when it came to dogs and horses. Those noble creatures might be fawned over however one liked. Even though he could not look upon Dandy with the same respect he had for his hounds, and there was nothing noble about the Pomeranian except his attitude, he was a dog. Even if just barely a dog, in the Viscount's opinion.

Marigold sat on the windowsill, staring out at the darkened view. Violet might have assumed she was pining for Mercury, if she had not known perfectly well that Marigold was pining for dinner. The girl took so much exercise that she was generally ravenous at all times and would run down the stairs and take her meals in the kitchen if she could.

Violet sat next to her and said, "We must convince Lord Smythesdon to change to Merlin."

Marigold fiddled with the ribbon on her dress, no doubt irritated that she could not be in her riding habit and ready to fly off for the doctor should anybody be suddenly stricken ill.

"Merlin would be a sensible choice," she said. "He has a steady temperament and is surefooted in mud. But Violet, from what I have seen of him, the lord is not inclined to do anything sensible."

"That is true," Violet said. "However, Victorine has told me of how it might be done."

As Violet laid out her plan, Marigold at first stared in wonderment, then she laughed. "If men are to be as easily managed as that," she said, "I wonder how they came to rule the world. A horse would have a better understanding."

"Perhaps," Violet said. "But Victorine was rather certain of it and we have no other idea."

"I suppose we must try," Marigold said. "I have begun to worry that if the stupid gentleman breaks his neck, his family might demand satisfaction against The Turk. They might demand he be destroyed. I would not stand for it, mind you. If papa were to agree to it, I would have no choice but to ride him into the forest and live as a gypsy somewhere. I won't have a fine horse destroyed."

If the situation were not so dire, Violet might have been amused that a gentleman's broken neck must take second place in her sister's consideration. The horse must be saved and the man be damned.

Rose and Daisy entered, Daisy having been finally dressed. She was not in the pale blue as planned, but rather a seafoam green and so Violet assumed there had been much debate and confusion in getting her into anything at all. Poor Victorine would be just now examining the burns on the pale yellow and cursing her careless mistress in a French fury, before sorting through Daisy's ribbons and choosing a few for herself.

Henry led in Lord Smythesdon. Violet glanced at Marigold. It was time for her younger sister to play her part. Then Violet would make her move. She planned to make quick work of it.

Violet and Marigold left the window seat and joined the group. Violet stood next to Lord Smythesdon and smiled pleasantly.

"Henry," Marigold said. "Come with me, I have an idea about which covert we ought to try first. I have heard some news of it from Farmer Hellsbrink."

Henry nodded and allowed himself to be led away to a corner of the drawing room.

Violet said, "Well, my lord, you shall see how we go about it at Chemsworth Hall on the morrow. One can never be certain if it is Marigold or the master of the hunt leading us all."

"Your sister is quite the horsewoman," Lord Smythesdon said, appearing relieved that whatever had occurred between them in the library was to be forgotten.

"Indeed, she is extraordinary," Violet said. "One assumes, having another year or two's experience, she might even have the skill to attempt Merlin."

Violet then moved away, hopeful that the lord would follow her and demand to know more about Merlin. She wished to lead him away from the group so she was not overheard. It would not do for the Viscount to chime in on the steadiness of Merlin.

Lord Smythesdon had paused for a moment, but could not resist finding out more. He followed her to the window.

"Merlin?" Lord Smythesdon asked in some surprise. "But I was given to understand that your sister was skilled enough, even now, to ride The Turk."

"Oh, yes, she is," Violet said. "But The Turk is one thing and Merlin is quite another."

Lord Smythesdon was silent for a moment. Then he said, "I had been under the impression that The Turk was the most challenging horse in the stable."

"Ah," Violet said. "I suppose we do not wish you to break your neck. Very few can hang on to Merlin. His speed is unlike anything I have ever seen. I would not dare to mount him, it would be rather like being shot across the countryside like an arrow."

"I should like to try him," Lord Smythesdon said valiantly.

"Oh, I would counsel against it," Violet said. "There cannot be more than a handful of riders in England who could creditably mount him."

Lord Smythesdon, evidently feeling he must be included in the handful, said, "I must demand my chance. I shall speak to Granger about it before the night is through."

Violet had been prepared for this circumstance and determined that the lord should say nothing of switching horses. "If you are set to risk trying Merlin," she said, "I would not mention it to Henry. He would only spend the entire evening attempting to dissuade you from it. After all, I will wager he did not even mention Merlin when you visited the stables."

"Indeed, he did not," Lord Smythesdon said thoughtfully.

"If you are determined, best to just go to the stable early on the morrow and direct a groom to saddle him."

"Yes, of course," Lord Smythesdon said. "Then it will be too late to do anything about it."

"And saying nothing this evening will give you the further opportunity to consider your decision," Violet said. "There would be no shame in reversing yourself and sticking with The Turk."

"Reverse myself?" the lord said, as if any sort of reversal of thought was akin to the most vile cowardice. "I shall not reverse myself, Miss Granger. I must have my chance on Merlin and I will not be turned from it."

Violet nodded. Victorine had been all too correct in her understanding of a man's pride.

"I must thank you, Miss Granger," the lord said in real earnest. "If we had not had this conversation, I should never have even known of this wondrous Merlin."

Dinner was pleasant to most at the table, but Violet could not enjoy it. Every moment was consumed with the idea that somebody might make mention of horses, or worse, mention the ever-steady Merlin. This was only compounded by the fact that Marigold could not stop herself from talking about the hunt, all previous hunts, the weather associated with those hunts, and how they should revel in the mud on the morrow. They should come back from it all, according to Marigold, tired, cold and wet and thoroughly happy about it.

This diatribe was only occasionally interrupted by somebody else gamely trying to change the topic.

"Miss Ravencraft looked well," Henry said.

"She looked well indeed," Lord Smythesdon said. Then, seeming to realize that he had never seen her before and could not know how her looks compared to some earlier moment in time, mumbled, "At least, I assume so."

"Did she look well?" the Viscount said. "Put some weight on, has she?"

"No papa," Rose said. "She is as fragile and pale as ever."

"Some ladies carry that look very well," Henry said, a note of defensiveness in his tone. "I would not call it so much pale as I would porcelain."

"Porcelain, is it?" the Viscount said. "I suppose she is very like a little porcelain doll."

Lady Mulholland, not liking the conversation to be circling round the porcelain charms of Miss Ravenscraft, said, "Mrs. Ravenscraft came dressed. I wonder if there is a single ribbon left in town for purchase."

The Viscount, well aware of his lady's antipathy for Mrs. Ravencraft, said, "Ravencraft is a sensible neighbor, but one cannot always be rewarded with a wife as elegant as Lady Mulholland. It is not the usual thing, eh? I knew it the first time I saw her. I thought, I should not like that lady to go off and marry somebody else, so I had best make my intentions known as quick as you like."

Lady Mulholland was soothed in her feelings by her husband's declaration of her superiority to Mrs. Ravencraft and went back to contentedly dropping scraps on the floor for Dandy.

"I like Miss Ravencraft," Lily said.

Her sisters all turned to stare at Lily, as they could not remember when last she had spoken so directly, and in front of a stranger no less.

Marigold said, "Do not be silly, Lily. Miss Ravenscraft cannot even sit a horse."

"Maybe that's why I like her," Lily said, jutting out her chin.

"Now," the Viscount said to Lily, "you're not to think you are forever to sit in a carriage. Every young lady must learn to ride a horse sooner or later."

Seeing Lily's eyes well up, he said more kindly, "There now. I shall buy you the smallest pony in the world. It shall be no bigger than Dandy. And I shall walk it with you. It shall be so small that were you to fall off, it would be no worse than falling from a chair."

Lily peeked down at her own chair to measure the distance to the ground. Seeing it was not so very far, she heaved a relieved sigh.

Violet, wishing to shift the conversation away from any more talk of horses, said, "I do hope we should see an end to this rain."

"I quite agree," Lady Mulholland said. "Lord Smythesdon, it is our tradition to have a luncheon on Lookout Hill. It sits just at the west edge of the property and affords sweeping views. I fear if we find ourselves in the same deluge as we have today, it will not be suitable."

Lord Smythesdon nodded. "That can only be the case, my lady. Even if *we* were to be agreeable to standing about in the rain, it would hardly be fair to the servants. I imagine they must get there quite ahead of us and would be wretched by the time we arrived."

Violet turned toward the lord. That sentiment was the first he had expressed since he had arrived that she could unreservedly approve. She was rather surprised by the opinion—he had struck her as a gentleman who would no more concern himself over those working in a house as he would the fairies in the forest.

Smuckers, she noticed, could not help himself from nodding. As a rule, Smuckers never let on that he had overheard any conversation at dinner. He was to be the holder of all of their secrets and as silent as a grave about it. To catch him nodding in approbation of a statement was a rare thing.

"In any case," Lady Mulholland said, "we shan't be defeated by it. If the weather goes against us, we shall simply hold the picnic here. There is the armory at the back of the house that might be very suitable for such a thing, assuming we can heat it up sufficiently. It is the sort of room where one should not mind muddy boots."

"Though the point is, mama, that we shall ride," Marigold said. "We should not fret over a picnic when we shall ride."

"Yes," Lord Smythesdon said softly. "We shall ride."

Chapter Ten

"I think we have done it," Violet said to Rose and Daisy. They were now all comfortably in their robes, nibbling from a tea tray stacked with almond biscuits that Peggy had carried up the back stairs to Violet's bedchamber. There had been no need for the charade of 'Heavens, I *am* tired' on this night. A night before a hunt necessitated an early turn in and they had left Lord Smythesdon and Henry alone downstairs in the drawing room. No doubt they would pour themselves large glasses of the Viscount's port before going up.

"I only hope Lord Smythesdon is as good as his word and does not broach the subject of switching horses to Henry."

"Can he really be convinced that Merlin is so very dangerous as to make him preferred to The Turk?" Rose asked.

Violet set down her cup of tea and said, "I believe the way I described it was that riding Merlin was to find oneself shot across the countryside like an arrow."

"And he seemed terribly keen to be shot like an arrow?" Daisy asked.

"He did appear so," Violet said.

"That does mark him as a rather brave sort," Daisy said. "He could not be safer than to be upon Merlin, but he does not know that. He is ready to be launched from a bow. It cannot meet my own standards for bravery of course. My gentleman would duel Napoleon himself in pursuit of me, but it is worthy all the same."

"It seems a lot of nonsense to me," Rose said. "Why was he not railing against Henry for hiding the most dangerous horse? Was that courage? He should have told Henry he was horrible to do it."

"Now Rose," Daisy said, playfully pulling at one of her curls until it hung limp, "not everybody likes to make enemies of all the world. And anyway, I found Lord Smythesdon's care of our servants very touching. He would not wish for them to stand out in the rain and I do not wish it either."

"In truth," Violet said, "I was surprised by his attitude on that subject. It seemed to have too much sense in it for him."

"Never mind," Daisy said, rising and stretching, "all is well. Lord Smythesdon shall plod along on Merlin and think himself the finest horseman in England for having done it. My closest sisters will be up with the sunrise and braving the cold and mud while I lay gloriously abed. Lily will come to me and we will snuggle under the blankets and talk of brave knights and their princesses who are just now locked in a tower. She shall fret over the poor fox you chase, but I shall assure her that Mr. and Mrs. Fox hide their laughter behind their paws and refuse to be caught."

Though Violet would be up at dawn and on her horse, she rather wished she could be snug and warm under the covers with Daisy and Lily. Even if they did insist on talking about knights and princesses.

A bottle of sherry sat on the table between Smuckers and Mrs. Featherstone, while a merry fire warmed their feet.

"I have the honor of informing you, Mrs. Featherstone, that if the rain persists on the morrow, the picnic at Lookout Hill is entirely off." Smuckers made this announcement as if he were reading the verdict on an important court case.

Mrs. Featherstone drained her glass. "That smacks of commonsense," she said with a satisfied air. "I'll venture it was Lady Mulholland's idea."

Smuckers sat back and folded his hands over his round stomach. "It was, indeed, thought of by our mistress." He dramatically paused, and then said, "However, it was *seconded* by Lord Smythesdon."

He waited for the effect of that statement upon Mrs. Featherstone, but not noting any astonishment on her features, he said, "That esteemed gentleman noted that the servants would need to arrive well ahead of time and would be wretched in the rain. *Wretched*, is what he said."

"Wretched," Mrs. Featherstone said softly. In general, she was not opposed to wretchedness, as that state led to many interesting conversations in the butler's closet. However, she was somewhat less sanguine about any wretchedness that was to affect her own person and so was gratified to hear the lord also found himself against it.

"It is only too true, Mrs. Featherstone. That great personage has had thoughts about us."

"Thoughts," Mrs. Featherstone murmured.

"It is extraordinary, I know," Smuckers said, wishing to bring Mrs. Featherstone through the shock of the idea. "To even imagine that, amongst all the illustrious thoughts that must swirl through the mind of a future Earl, there have been thoughts about *us* cohabitating. Only think, there may have been a thought about dying for king and country *and* a thought about us, standing side by side in the regions of his mind."

"It is gratifying, to be sure," Mrs. Featherstone said, appearing genuinely touched by the lord's thoughts.

"It is the mark of true nobility," Smuckers said.

"I suppose it is only a shame," Mrs. Featherstone said, not entirely willing to forgo any ideas about disasters racing around the corner, "that he is to be on The Turk and likely to break his neck. I should hate to see a gentleman with such noble thoughts break his neck."

All of the contentment of Mr. Smuckers recollection of the pivotal moment when Lord Smythesdon spoke of the wretchedness of the servants was washed away in a moment. Mrs. Featherstone spoke the truth—the noble lord would be on The Turk and he could not see what would be the end of it.

Though Smythesdon had been determined to say nothing to Granger about switching horses, and had even reveled in imagining the look of surprise on his friend's face when he mounted the mighty Merlin, once he found himself two glasses of port in, he could not hold his tongue.

They sat together in the dim drawing room, the candles having been snuffed and the only light from the fire. He stared at Granger in the shadows across from him and said, "It's all up, my good fellow. I know about Merlin and am determined to ride him."

Henry Granger seemed oddly relieved at hearing this news. "I cannot fault you for the switch," he said. "Merlin is steady and surefooted—nobody shall blame you for foregoing The Turk."

"Why should anybody blame me for giving up The Turk when Merlin is twice the beast he is? Come now, Granger, I know all about the speed of the animal."

"The speed of Merlin?" Henry asked.

"I am to be shot across the countryside like an arrow," Lord Smythesdon said.

"On Merlin?"

"Of course, on Merlin. Oh, I know, there was some concern about me breaking my neck and so you did not even mention the horse to me. But I have discovered all and must have my chance. You can say nothing to dissuade me."

"I would not dissuade you from Merlin. He is a very steady horse. I do not know what you mean by speed, though."

Lord Smythesdon waved his hand dismissively. "Miss Violet Granger let it slip. Merlin has speed unlike any other."

Henry Granger was silent for a moment, and then he began to laugh. Had he been more sober than he actually was, he might not have informed his friend of the information he was just now getting ready to relay. "Violet," he said, "is having a laugh at your expense, I am afraid. Merlin is so steady that Lily could ride him.

He is a sixteen hand Belgian Draft. He is a fine horse, but the one thing he does not have is excessive speed."

Lord Smythesdon was silent in the face of such news. Merlin was a slow draft horse? The entire conversation in the drawing room, all of Merlin's qualities and how he might go about riding him, were only a ruse? A joke to play upon him? How dare Miss Granger think to ridicule him in such a manner. If it would not be absolutely prohibited, and likely to end in some sort of duel to defend family honor, he would tell Granger exactly what he thought of his sister. And his thoughts, at this very moment, were dark indeed.

"Perhaps, though," Henry said, sobering a bit upon viewing his friend's expression, "she only meant to get you off The Turk for your own safety. I have, myself, wrestled with the question." Henry paused, and then said, "We could always say The Turk is lame and put you on Mephistopheles. He is a thoroughbred and nearly as big as The Turk, but easier to control. You saw him yourself when we visited the stables. He is a very fine horse."

Lord Smythesdon set his empty glass on a table and said, "Granger, despite your sister's joke, I shall not be turned from The Turk." He rose and walked unsteadily out of the room.

Henry thought to pour himself one more glass of port to assist him in thinking through this latest contretemps with Violet. He meant to, but as he could generally not be counted upon to hold up after two glasses of port, he fell asleep in his chair instead. He never heard his friend leave the house, nor come back in again a half hour later.

Though it was dawn, it was not so apparent that the sun had begun its rise. The heavy clouds, misting rain and the fog that had settled into the valleys gave the effect of a twilight upon the landscape. The master of the hunt was already on his mount, having ridden over from his cottage. Marigold stood by him, no doubt discussing likely coverts with him. The dogs milled around the drive, sniffing and nipping one another and occasionally giving out a good bark to let the foxes know they would come. The whippers-in kept the hounds in reasonable order and appeared bright and eager to be off.

Violet was one of the first on the drive, just after the master and Marigold. Her father would likely be the last to arrive, she knew, as Lady Mulholland generally fussed over her husband when he was to venture out on a hunt. He would not be free to leave his dressing room until the lady had assured herself that he had drunk two cups of the tea that she'd had specially sent up, that beverage thought by her to have restorative qualities.

The grooms were bringing the horses out and, just as she suspected, Apollo appeared thoroughly disgusted. Marigold's horse, Mercury, was his polar opposite—sidestepping and yanking his head up and down in sheer joy.

Violet watched the line of horses come around the corner of the house. Then she looked at Marigold. Her sister was staring in some amazement as The Turk was led onto the drive.

Violet hurried over. "I believe you have made a mistake," she said to Tim, the groom holding The Turk's reins. "Lord Smythesdon meant to change to Merlin. He has no doubt not had the time to tell you. Please change horses immediately."

The groom smirked, as Violet noted he was in the unpleasant habit of doing, and said, "That gentleman paid us a visit late last night, pr'haps a bit worse for the drink, and said 'I shan't be turned from The Turk. Nobody ain't gonna turn me from 'im.'"

Though Violet was not convinced that Lord Smythesdon had said 'ain't gonna,' she was convinced of the groom's truthfulness in the tale. Tim was cheeky, but he would not dare invent such a story. Why had it happened? Lord Smythesdon had appeared so set on Merlin. He had appeared so entirely taken in by the idea of being shot like an arrow. All she had needed to do was get him on and going and then it would be too late to change once he discovered that Merlin was not a particularly fast horse. He might have been annoyed by the discovery, his pride might have been injured, but his person would have remained intact.

"I suppose men are not as stupid as we thought," Marigold said next to her.

"No, Marigold," Violet said. "Somehow, they are even more stupid than we thought. We have tried to save the lord from his own idiocy and we have failed."

"Miss Granger."

Violet heard herself being addressed, and she knew perfectly well who it was. She slowly turned and said, "Lord Smythesdon."

Marigold backed away, seeming to have no interest in being incriminated with her sister. Smythesdon, Violet thought, looked as if he had been up half the night carousing with her brother. He was in no shape to ride any horse, much less The Turk.

"I have uncovered your effort to make a mockery of me," the lord said curtly. "As you can see," he said waving at The Turk, "I will not be riding out on a Belgian draft horse."

"My lord, I only meant to make some effort in averting you from disaster," Violet said.

"Your efforts are not required, even if I believed in them. You have done nothing, up to this point, to welcome me as a guest, and so I should not believe you had suddenly been inspired to begin."

The lord's words stung sharply. Though her motives had been innocent in this particular matter, she could not defend against the charge that she had not treated him with all the deference due a guest. Before Violet could muster some sort of defense, and she planned to do so vigorously once she had invented it, Henry joined them. Henry looked as poorly as his friend and if they had any sense at all they would both sit out.

"You should not have done it, Violet," her brother said.

"Of course, I should have done it," Violet said vehemently. "I was forced to do it because *you* put us all into this ridiculous situation. You know perfectly well he will not stay on The Turk!"

Henry reddened and Violet knew that he understood the truth of her words. That he would not take her part was some sort of ludicrous loyalty to Lord Smythesdon's pride, though it might cost his friend dearly.

The footmen came round with trays laden with glasses of champagne and brandy. Marigold, having been absolutely forbidden to have brandy, grabbed a glass of champagne and gulped it down before anybody could protest against it.

Both Smythesdon and Henry took glasses of brandy, though Violet was of the opinion that it was the very last libation they should have drunk.

Rose skipped down the stairs to the drive, looking glorious in her dark green habit. "Good lord," she said. "Why is The Turk out?"

Henry snatched another cup of brandy from Jimmy's tray, held it up and said, "Because my friend, Lord Bertram Smythesdon is an excellent horseman and chooses to ride him."

Lord Smythesdon, following his friend's lead and taking a second cup of brandy, bowed to Rose.

The Viscount came out of the house, followed by his lady. Everybody knew that once he had made his appearance, departure was at hand. Even the hounds seemed to know it and there were various hi-pitched yelps. Daisy and Lily waved handkerchiefs out of Daisy's bedchamber window. Even Poppy and Pansy, still relegated to the nursery on the other side of the house, had managed to escape Miss Millthorpe to wave from a window.

Violet was helped on to Apollo. She had been so occupied with the problem of The Turk that she had entirely forgotten that Lord Smythesdon would be, as yet, unacquainted with the fact that the Granger ladies rode astride. It occurred to her now, as she watched his horrified face as she let down either side of her skirt. Apparently, he had not noticed that of all the horses led out, not one had worn a sidesaddle.

He recovered himself quickly and marched, with some swagger, over to The Turk. He was the last to mount and viewed by the various members of the hunt with some trepidation. Violet, Rose, Marigold and Henry surreptitiously watched the maneuver.

A groom gave him a hoist up and he was in the saddle. The Turk, as was his habit upon finding a rider on his back, widened his eyes and snorted. Violet thought the horse always had a look of madness at such a time—his eyes rolling around in his head and showing their whites, his mouth in a grimace to reveal his teeth. Still, Smythesdon was on him and had not yet been thrown off.

Henry seemed relieved to see that his friend was to last at least a minute upon the horse's back. Smythesdon wore rather a smug look.

The master said, "We shall ride west until we near the border to Sunnydale Farm, there is a likely covert there." He blew his horn in one short burst to signal that the hunt had commenced.

The master set off in a canter and the rest of the riders made room for the Viscount and Marigold to pass. Marigold, though she did not take precedence, was always behind the Viscount, being generally acknowledged to be highly skilled. Violet kept herself at the back with Rose. Henry had followed Smythesdon, who was behind Marigold.

The Turk did not appear to have any regard for precedence. Though Violet could see Lord Smythesdon's arm muscles straining on the reins through his coat, the animal paid no more attention than if a fly attempted to slow him down.

They had gone through a wooded trail with The Turk nudging Mercury from behind. Marigold had turned twice to note that fact to Lord Smythesdon, but he seemed able to do little about it. Now the wood came to an abrupt end, leading into open fields segmented with wood fences.

The Turk, seeming to approve of this wide-open vista, and appearing to have little care for where the hunt was going, took off at a gallop. The horse passed Marigold and brushed against the Viscount's horse, nearly unseating him.

"Slow down, man," the Viscount called.

Violet watched in horror as The Turk, not bothering to wait for his rider's signals, chose to give himself his head. He galloped across a field as if he really had been shot from a bow. Violet had never seen him rebel in such a manner when the Viscount or Marigold had been on him. He was in general a difficult horse to control, but at the moment he was an impossible horse to control.

Lord Smythesdon appeared to be hanging on rather than riding. Violet saw one foot come loose from its stirrup. Horse and rider were barreling toward a high fence.

"Jump!" Henry called. "Jump off!"

It was too late. The Turk sailed through the air and Lord Smythesdon was unseated. He hit the ground and then Violet cried out when she saw that his opposite foot was caught in its stirrup. The Turk dragged his rider behind him before finally slowing to a stop and bending his neck down to eat grass, satisfied that he had unburdened himself. His rider lay motionless on the ground.

Violet spurred Apollo. Marigold was already half way down the field.

Lord Smythesdon lay still, his leg bent back in an unnatural position. That it was broken could not be doubted. Violet only feared what else might be broken.

Violet sailed over the field fence, Apollo taking her up and over as if he were always meant to fly. Marigold was already dismounted ahead of her.

Marigold had gently removed the lord's foot from the caught stirrup. The Turk glanced at the carnage he had created and then casually walked off toward the stables.

The lord groaned and his eyes fluttered. Violet leapt down from Apollo. "My lord," she said quietly. "You have been severely injured. Do not attempt to move."

Lord Smythesdon did not answer, but just let out a further groan. By this time, Henry had reached them. "Is he alive," her brother asked.

"Yes, and no thanks to you," Violet said spitefully. Recalling herself, she said, "Marigold, fetch the doctor. You are the swiftest and can reach him quickly."

Marigold nodded and said, "I know a shortcut. I've practiced it many times for just such an emergency. I can take

Megthorn back with me on my horse instead of waiting for his slow riding. I shall return in under an hour if he is at home, longer if he is out." Then she turned and glared at Henry. "This is not The Turk's fault. I won't have him harmed." She leapt on Mercury and galloped in the direction of Doctor Megthorn's house.

Violet said, "Henry, go get a litter. There is one in the stables. Bring grooms back with you to carry him upon it. And bring brandy. A lot of it."

Henry Granger, appearing to now recognize the folly he had engineered and the damage that it had caused, was motionless. Shock had appeared to overtake him.

"Go Henry!" Violet scolded. "Go now."

Henry seemed to wake up to her voice. He turned his horse and galloped away, his face as white as flour.

"Merlin. You tried," the lord said in a whisper.

"Never mind that now," Violet said.

The Viscount, the master and Rose had finally reached them. "Whoever put him on such a horse?" the master asked.

The Viscount shrugged. "He was certain of his skill, and he is a guest after all. Though had I known it was only to be youthful boastfulness I should not have allowed it."

The lord's cheeks, though his face had been deadly white, bloomed red at this speech.

"Papa, let us not enter into recriminations against the injured party," Rose said. "Henry has been perfectly horrible and I shall let him know it. For now, we must plan how to get Lord Smythesdon on the litter."

"Henry is bringing brandy," Violet said. "A lot of it."

"That's the thing," the Viscount said. He paused and said softly, "Lady Mulholland shall not like this at all."

"Perhaps, father," Violet said, "you might return to the house and prepare our mother. I am certain she will wish to have the fire built up in the lord's bedchamber. She will also wish to gather the supplies that Doctor Megthorn will require—clean bandages, hot water, she will know what to do. Henry is bringing the grooms and a litter and we should be at the house in not too long a time."

The Viscount nodded. "I had better go up and smooth the way." He bent down over Lord Smythesdon and said, "Not to worry, my lord, we shall have you fixed up in no time at all." He tipped his hat, turned his horse and cantered toward the house.

Violet thought, as her mind raced through everything that must be done, that at least the accident had happened close to the house. The grooms, once they began to carry, would not take ten minutes to get the lord inside. She must only get him very drunk to get him on the litter to begin.

While she waited for the grooms to return, Lord Smythesdon mumbled various phrases between groans of pain. He cursed The Turk, he cursed Henry, he cursed himself.

"I suppose it is well," Rose said, "that he took two glasses of brandy before he ever even got on that blasted horse."

"Blasted horse," Lord Smythesdon murmured.

"We did our very best to get him onto Merlin," Violet said. "I do not know what else we could have done."

"Very best," Lord Smythesdon whispered.

Violet and Rose lapsed into silence. Violet's thoughts began to calm after the initial rush of the emergency. With that calmness came the knowledge of everything she knew about broken bones. It might be set, or the doctor might determine that the bone was shattered and it would be...taken off. The lord might think he was in pain now, but it was nothing compared to what was to come. Even a setting would be excruciating. Were chance to work in the lord's favor and the leg set, danger still remained. Gangrene could set in. If he were to come through all of that, he might walk with a limp or need a cane. Somebody would have to inform the Earl of Ainsworth that his one and only son had been gravely injured.

Violet gazed down at his pale face. Without the accompaniment of ridiculous speeches, the lord was more handsome than ever. His hair fell over his forehead and his dark lashes fluttered against closed eyes.

"He is not so horrible when he is not talking," Rose observed.

"Not so horrible," the lord repeated, seeming to drift in and out of consciousness.

Violet saw Henry and the grooms hurrying out of the wood, carrying a litter between them. A bottle of brandy bounced along atop the sturdy cloth stretched between two long poles.

Now came the difficult part. Lord Smythesdon must be transferred to the litter. Violet knew what was to come upon moving him—she had seen what it had been when a tenant's farmhand had fallen from a roof and broken a leg. His screams when he had been lifted onto a waiting cart had been the stuff of nightmares.

Lord Smythesdon's senses need be dulled by brandy if he was to stand the pain of it, something that poor farmhand had not had the benefit of. She must see that he became drunk enough to not feel the full force of the shock, but it must be done soon as continuing to lie on cold, wet grass could only cause further harm. He was hardly conscious, but she knew the move would slap him awake.

The grooms followed Henry, all appearing pale as if they would pay the price for the lord being mounted upon The Turk. Violet had a very great wish to inform them that it was only Henry that was to blame, but held her tongue. There was no time for it.

"Lay the litter right beside him and give me the brandy. You," she said, pointing at Tim, "Come round behind his head and gently raise it so he can drink."

The groom had lost the smirk he had sported on the drive earlier in the morning and hurried over, handing Violet the brandy.

"My lord," Violet said in a loud voice. "My lord, Tim will lift you up and you must drink as much brandy as you can."

The lord's eyes fluttered and he said, "No thank you."

"It was not a question," Violet said. "Believe me, you must. Drink as much as you can."

As Tim lifted his head, Lord Smythesdon seemed to regain his senses and realize what Violet was trying to tell him. He gulped down the brandy.

"Give it a minute to take effect," Violet said to the grooms. "When we are ready, we shall not lift him up off the ground, but rather we shall carefully roll him on his uninjured side and slide the litter underneath him before gently setting him back down. Then we shall carefully move the leg that is injured, fully supporting it in the position it is now, onto the litter."

The grooms nodded, white-faced.

"When it is time to carry, you must all move as one, no jostling of any sort. I shall give you direction. Just follow my commands. Henry shall be at the front and guide you through the wood.

Henry nodded, now entirely incapable of speech.

"Goodness, you are rather wonderful, Violet," Rose said.

"Ravver wonferal," the lord slurred.

Violet looked down at the lord, encouraged by his slurred speech. "My lord," she said, "do you begin to feel the effects of the brandy?"

"Ravver wonferal," he said, his voice fading into hardly a whisper.

Violet knew this comfortable state would not last long. The pain of being moved would wake him from his brandy stupor. However, she did not suppose she could get him more drunk than he was at present.

"We begin," she said quietly.

Chapter Eleven

The procedure of getting Lord Smythesdon onto the litter and through the wood, into the house and up the stairs to his bedchamber was not one that Violet would soon forget. The initial move to the litter had been the worst of it—it had been the farmhand's screams in her ears all over again. The lord had bitten his tongue and a stream of blood had run down his chin. His skin had become ghostly and took on a bluish hue. Henry had nearly fainted. Violet had pinched her brother to bring him back to the task at hand and he and the grooms had carried him to the house as carefully as they could manage. Despite their slow and careful progression, the path through the wood was uneven and littered with rocks and tree roots. Every jostle had been accompanied by shouts and oaths.

Lady Mulholland stood on the drive to meet them. It had been well to direct the Viscount to prepare her for the sight. She had composed herself and was prepared to manage the incoming disaster. Smuckers, on the other hand, appeared as pale as the lord upon seeing their houseguest laid out on the litter.

Lady Mulholland said, "Take him up directly. I sent my husband to saw off the bedposts at the foot of the bed—Dr. Megthorn will need room to work."

Violet shivered at her mother's words.

Lady Mulholland followed Henry and the grooms up the stairs. Lord Smythesdon, the effects of the brandy having been driven away by pain and now finding himself bounced up the stairs, shouted oaths all the way up.

Rose said, "Well Smuckers, the Grangers have made a fine mess this morning. When you can, and not above anything our mother asks to be done, I think we might have tea. It seems to me that when one cannot be certain what to do in a situation, one had better start with tea."

Smuckers nodded and Rose ran up the stairs and into the house.

Violet stood motionless in the drive. She had been all action, but now that she had delivered the patient to the house, she felt her energy draining from her. "What if he dies, Smuckers?" she said softly.

"Now, miss," the butler said unsteadily, "you are not to think like that."

"How am I not to think like that?" Violet said. "His leg is surely broken. He is an only son! Think how our father would take it if something were to happen to Henry."

Smuckers could find no answer to that, as he knew very well that while the Viscount was a gruff old eccentric, he would be destroyed over it.

"And I!" Violet said. "I, Smuckers. I have been so...I have been contrary. That is what I have been."

"No miss," Smuckers said with some vehemence. "You were not responsible for putting him on that horse."

"That is the only thing I did *not* do," Violet said. "Think of all the smartly delivered insults I hurled. All the teasing. All the provoking to prove that I knew more than he. What was it all for? If he is to die, or lose his leg, what matter that he carried with him some incorrect assumptions that were never in danger of having any material effect upon me? It was all so petty!"

Smuckers was silent and Violet knew that he could not refute what she said. He had watched her grow up and knew her almost as well as she knew herself. It had always been Smuckers that had helped her extricate herself from problems of her own making—if she were to declare that she was not so certain she liked trifle and then go without, he would find a way to deliver it to her later. He knew, just as she knew, of this unfortunate habit of hers.

"Try as I might," she continued, "though I do remind myself often, I cannot seem to grasp that my life is not at all hard. I am continually swept up into piques and fits. Am I a soldier risking my life? Am I a beggar on the streets, wondering about my next meal? No! I am petted and pampered and yet, I always seem to grab hold of some silly notion and it becomes my raison d'être. A gentleman comes to stay, and he and I do not agree on a particular subject. That really should have been the end of it. But no, that could not be the end of it. Rather, I must turn myself into Margaret of Anjou and destroy my enemies to protect my pride. I am shallow, Smuckers. You must be embarrassed to know me."

This was going entirely too far for Smuckers. "Miss Violet Granger is to be compared to Margaret of Anjou? An ill-advised and vindictive Frenchwoman? No, I will not agree to that," he said, sticking his chest out. "Not even were I to be ordered to agree to it. There is not one family member in this household that I am not honored to know. In truth, I will go even further and say that if I were pressed to declare a favorite, and only if I were pressed to reveal it, it must be the eldest Miss Granger."

Mr. Smuckers dabbed at his eyes, nearly overcome by his own sentiment.

"Dear Smuckers," Violet said, brushing at her own eyes. "You always do lift me up when I have fallen particularly hard. I am afraid you are biased, though, on account of your loyalty to the house."

"Everything for the house, miss."

"Yet here we are, and the days when my problems were only a matter of missing dessert have long fled."

"Perhaps," Smuckers said. "Though you were just as sorry then as you are now. Trifle, at the age of ten, is a matter of vital importance."

Violet laughed, as Smuckers knew she would. He took great pride in his ability to cheer up all the Granger children, except perhaps Marigold when she was kept from her horse. That circumstance could not be viewed with any levity whatsoever.

And so they went into the house, both wiping their eyes.

Violet and Smuckers had only just got inside the door and closed it when the clatter of hooves sounded on the drive.

127

"Doctor Megthorn so soon?" Violet said. "How could Marigold fetch him that quickly?"

Smuckers swung the door open. Marigold reined in Mercury, the horse looking wild with excitement. Doctor Megthorn, mounted behind Marigold, appeared less excited. His expression leaned more toward terror.

"Let me off this beast this instant," he shouted.

There were no grooms to assist, they all being up the stairs with the litter. The footmen had disappeared somewhere, no doubt on errands for Lady Mulholland. Violet ran down the steps as Marigold said, "Well, doctor? You are behind so I cannot dismount until you do."

Violet took the doctor's bag from him and set it on the drive. She steadied him as he slid off the horse. "Great Scot!" the doctor cried. "I have never been carried in such a deranged manner in all my life. It was as if the hounds of hell were on our heels. How we are both still alive, I hardly know."

"You are both still alive because Marigold is an expert horsewoman and you are very good at hanging on," Violet said soothingly. "Time is of the essence so I am sorry she frightened you, but very glad she returned with you in such haste."

"I told you it was only a matter of time before I must go racing off to the doctor, Violet," Marigold said. "Now you see how fast I can do it."

The doctor, gruff as he appeared, was not generally in ill humour. "Very well, I am here in one piece and so we will forget it. I understand you suspect a broken leg?"

"Yes," Violet said, as Marigold turned her horse and rode in victory toward the stables. "I am certain of it. Lord Bertram Smythesdon, the next Earl of Ainsworth, has been carried upstairs."

"An Earl, eh?" the doctor said. "I suppose he'll want some fancy physician from London down to consult. Then I'll have to deliver the bad news that I do not consult with fancy physicians."

"Never mind such thoughts," Violet said. "You are the only doctor here and we have full confidence in you."

Doctor Megthorn was mollified by this tribute to his skill.

"My father has sawed off the bedposts so that you will have room to work."

"Sawed off the bedposts, has he?" The doctor said, picking up his bag. "I'll give this house one thing anyway—there's plenty of commonsense lurking about. I suppose you've plied the fellow with brandy?"

"Quite a lot," Violet said.

"Very good. I've laudanum in my bag, we will see what can be done."

Violet had shown the doctor up the stairs. She had thought to go in and assist her mother as best she could, but as they appeared to be cutting off the lord's clothing, Lady Mulholland had pushed her out the door. Now, she sat in Daisy's room, that room being the closest to the other wing of the house and Lord Smythesdon's bedchamber. Rose had the tea things brought up by Peggy and now they sat around morosely, listening for any sound they might hear in the hall and waiting for news.

"I suppose we shall know it if the Doctor takes his leg," Rose said. "Even the neighbors will know it. There is not enough laudanum for that, I do not think."

"Oh Rose, do stop!" Daisy cried. "I cannot bear to think of it. Our poor Lord Smythesdon. And only think of what Henry is feeling just now."

"Henry?" Violet asked. "Why are we to feel sorry for Henry? He is the idiot that caused this."

"Of course, he is," Daisy said. "He must know it. It must tear him to pieces."

Rose sighed. "It had been better that Henry tore himself to pieces *before* he allowed his friend on The Turk."

From somewhere beneath the gowns strewn across Daisy's bed came a soft little cry. The gowns shifted of their own accord. Violet stared at the moving mound of silk.

Daisy saw her look and said, "It is only Lily under my dresses. She is too terrified to come out—precisely what she feared about horses has come to pass. Before you came in, I heard her whisper, 'I knew it, I just knew it.'"

"I did know it," Lily said, her voice muffled by fabric.

Before Violet could rescue Lily from underneath the silks, her attention was caught by the sound of the door opening. It swung open slowly and one small face, then two, peered in. Two faces identical, but for the small moles on their upper cheeks. Poppy's mole was on her right cheek and Pansy's on the left. The twins were not side by side identical as was usual, they were mirror images.

Somehow, they had made an escape from Miss Millthorpe. The girls raced into the room and threw themselves on Violet. "Is it true?" Poppy whispered in her ear. "Shall the doctor cut off the lord's leg?"

Pansy pushed in front of her sister. "I told Poppy that good old doctor Megthorn would not dare do it," she said. "A lord needs two legs and everybody knows it." Then her voice dropped to a whisper. "But if the doctor does saw it off, what shall we do with it? With the leg, I mean? Shall we bury it in the garden? Would we put a headstone there? What if Dandy dug it up? What then?"

Poppy, evidently struck by her sister's considerations, said, "I should not like to think of that poor lord looking out the window from his sickroom and seeing Dandy running around with his leg." She laid her hand over her heart and, her voice full of feeling, said, "I should just cry at the sight of it."

"I suppose you would not cry more than Lord Smythesdon would," Rose said.

Violet gave Poppy and Pansy both a squeeze and said, "You are very morbid children. We should not talk of what may or may not happen as we have no news whatsoever. Further, do not inform anybody else of your speculations on headstones or what Dandy might do in the garden."

"How in the world did you escape the ever-vigilant Miss Millthorpe?" Rose asked.

Poppy and Pansy, at an age when they could still be easily distracted, forgot all about Dandy running around the garden with the lord's poor leg as they launched into a tale of intrigue and daring suitable for any self-respecting British spy. They had happened to be in the third-floor hall when the commotion struck up and they had raced to the nearest window. Neither of them had expected to see anything very interesting so they were transfixed by the gruesome scene of the lord on the litter. Miss Millthorpe had most unfairly made them come away and then, when they could not settle to their studies, had insisted they take a nap. They had been up since four in the morning to be certain they would be awake to wave off the hunters and Miss Millthorpe was certain their inability to concentrate was due to not getting enough sleep. This, Pansy noted, had been the height of good luck. As far as Miss Millthorpe was concerned, they were even now napping peacefully in their beds. The governess, as was her habit, had fallen into a doze in the outer room of the nursery. They had crept with all stealth right past her, biting their tongues so they would not laugh and be caught out. They could only speculate on when that lady might discover that the lumps under the coverlets were, in fact, piles of clothes.

"You've been very naughty and I quite adore it," Daisy said.

"They *have* been very naughty," Violet said. "And they shall go right back up to the nursery and do their best to get back into their beds before Miss Millthorpe wakes."

Seeing her sisters' crestfallen faces, Violet relented and said, "And they may fill their pockets with biscuits before they go."

Biscuits being one of the temptations, along with fairy cakes, that the twins could not hold out against, they scooped handfuls from the tea tray before dashing out the door. Violet heard them giggling and whispering as they made their way up the stairs to the nursery and did not hold out much hope that they should get back into it unobserved by Miss Millthorpe. They would probably be punished with no dinner, so it was just as well they took the biscuits.

After the twins left, the sisters sat in silence, only broken occasionally by a sad little sigh from beneath Daisy's gowns.

Just as Violet thought she might go in search of news, a cry rang through the halls. A cry such as Violet had never heard, a cry as terrifying as the first time she had heard a fox scream. It seemed to come from the very walls of the house.

Violet, Rose and Daisy stared at each other. Rose said, "Whatever was to be done, it has been done."

As soon as The Turk had taken off with him, Smythesdon had known he had made a grave mistake. The animal was unlike any in his father's stable. Even the largest horse owned by the Earl could be convinced to do as he was asked with a skilled horseman in his saddle. This beast seemed to have no more care that there was anybody on his back than a dog must care for a flea.

He'd known he was in trouble as soon as they had started off. The Turk had not liked being confined in a line while going through the wood. He had pushed against the horse in front of him, trying to hurry him forward. Once the trail broke to open countryside, all was bedlam.

The race across the field had felt as if it had gone on for an hour. He'd heard Granger shout that he ought to jump. He ought to have, but he had clung to a shred of hope that he might bring the horse under control. It had not been possible.

The sound of the sickening snap when he hit the ground still rang in his ears. It had been pain such as he had never felt and he had been awake, then not awake, then awake again.

The whole thing had been so pointless! What had he tried to prove? Of course, he knew what he tried to prove. He had happily joined in with Granger on a contest of one-upmanship. Miss Violet Granger had done her best to show herself superior and he had intended to do *his* best to show her she was not. She could not ride The Turk, and so he must show that he could. Then, of course, he became even more determined when he discovered Miss Granger had attempted to put him on a draft horse. Add that ridiculous reasoning to the pleasant imaginings he'd had of all of Oxford hearing that he had subdued The Turk, and the tantalizing idea that Miss Ravencraft would hear of it and be frightened—it could only have ended as badly as it, in fact, did.

He had paid for his pride and stupidity with a nightmarish trip back to the house. Miss Granger had poured brandy down his throat, but it had been as water for all the good it did him. Now, however, the kind fellow that had taken charge of him had given him something for the pain. He was told it was laudanum. He had never taken it before and was fairly amazed at the way it seemed to glide like silk down every limb, soothing as it went. Under the influence of this delightful substance, he had begun to feel a bit more sanguine about the mishap. As if, suddenly, things did not seem as grim as they had. All these nice people, the doctor somebody, Lord and Lady Mulholland, the two tall footmen, were rushing around and consulting with each other regarding his comfort.

Just now, all these nice people surrounded him and bent over his leg. He vaguely heard the man with the wonderful laudanum say, "When I say pull, pull hard."

A streak of searing agony shot through him and he screamed himself into oblivion.

Mrs. Featherstone pretended to sip her tea, but in truth the lady was far too excited to hear news of the calamity that had befallen the house to attend to it. There was not in her memory a more dire event that had occurred at Chemsworth Hall and she meant to savor every detail.

"We can be grateful, Mrs. Featherstone," Smuckers said, "that the leg has been set. Doctor Megthorn was pleased with the result, he says the legs have come perfectly even. He believes it was a clean break and should heal with time."

Mrs. Featherstone, unwilling to allow such a disaster to be so easily resolved, said, "That is a blessing, to be sure. We must only pray he does not succumb to the gangrene."

"This is Chemsworth Hall," Smuckers said sternly. "The gangrene would not dare enter this house, Mrs. Featherstone."

Mrs. Featherstone, seeing she was to be thwarted in her hopes for the gangrene, said, "When you say it will heal in time, Mr. Smuckers, exactly how long will the lord be a-staying with us?"

"I believe he will be here for some time, though only the doctor can say for certain," Smuckers said. "Lady Mulholland has written the Earl with the distressing news and advised that it would be far too dangerous to move him. She invites the Earl and his lady to come here, so they may assure themselves of their son's safety. The lord's valet has taken the letter to deliver personally, as it was thought to be too much of a shock to have delivered by post, with nobody at hand to answer the Earl's questions."

"The Earl and his Countess are to come here?" Mrs. Featherstone asked. "I suppose we shall all be in a lather then!"

Smuckers, not liking to imagine any of his staff in a lather, said, "We shall do as we always have done, Mrs. Featherstone. We shall work for the glory of the house. That we must raise our already high standards once again goes without saying."

"Them standards must be nearing the moon by now," Mrs. Featherstone muttered.

After the haunting cry that had shaken them, Violet, Rose and Daisy had sat silent for some time. Violet wished to go for news, but was terrified to do so. She did not know what she would discover and perhaps it was better, for now, to know nothing at all.

They heard various closings of doors and whispers in the hall. They heard their father and mother discussing something too softly to be understood. They heard Jimmy talking to Doctor Megthorn about which bedchamber he would occupy. Of course, Violet thought, her mother would not allow the doctor to leave. He would be kept here, under Lady Mulholland's dictatorship, for as long as it was determined that he was needed. It had been so those many years ago when the house had been taken with fever—the doctor had become such a regular inmate that the kitchens had given up complaining about his odd meal times or his penchant for dark toast. He had only been released when Mrs. Megthorn arrived and demanded him back.

Peggy tiptoed in to collect the tea things and Violet found she could not stand not knowing the worst any longer. "Peggy," she said. "What have you heard?"

Chapter Twelve

Peggy, relishing the unusual circumstance of somebody wanting to hear something from the kitchen maid, said to Violet, "Well, miss, as I heard it, the doctor and Jimmy and Charlie grabbed hold of that mangled leg and, on the count of three, they heaved on it like they was pulling a wagon out of deep mud. Jimmy says they heard the bone snap back into place and it was jarrin' to his feelings to hear it. The doctor rigged the leg up into some kind of contraption his assistant brought, so it don't move around and undo their handiwork. The lord, for all his going to be a high and mighty Earl, went dead faint over it."

"The leg is set, then?" Violet asked. "It was not taken off?"

"No miss, it warn't taken. It's as attached to him as a bee to a rose," Peggy answered. "I can't say that Charlie ain't the littlest bit disappointed as he'd been wonderin' what the sawing off should be like."

Peggy paused, seeming to reflect upon Charlie's dashed hopes. Then she said, "Though I suppose, all things considered, that it's better for the lord that Charlie be disappointed."

"I should say so," Rose said.

"'Course, I don't like to speak on things I ain't been asked," Peggy said, winking at Violet.

"But we did ask you, Peggy," Violet said. "I asked you what you had heard."

"Ah! So you did, miss," Peggy said, a note of triumph in her voice. "I done forgot you worded the thing so broadly. Pr'haps that gives me leave to mention another bit of news."

Violet waited expectantly, but Peggy did not seem to be able to go on without encouragement. "The other bit of news, Peggy? What is it?"

Peggy, seeming to forget she was not in the kitchens, set down the tray and plunked herself down into a chair. She leaned forward and, in a confidential tone, she said, "It appears that Lady Mulholland thinks to bring the Earl and Countess to Chemsworth. The injured party being their son, you see. We're to have an Earl and a Countess in the house, unless they don't like him much and don't care to visit. Though I bet they do visit and I bet Mr. Smuckers comes upon the idea that our standards got to be raised again, though where we will go with them now, I cannot say. Seems to me we been raising them every half hour."

"Thank you, Peggy," Rose said, eyeing her sitting in the chair.

Peggy, noticing that she had sat herself down as cool as ice, leapt up. "God in heaven," she said, "how did I ever come to be sittin' down?"

As none of the sisters could have explained how Peggy had sat herself down like a duchess, none of them answered. She quickly gathered the tea things and headed for the door amidst Daisy's muffled laughter.

Violet considered Peggy's news. The leg had been set. All danger was not past, but the first and most immediate danger was. There was a chance, at least, of a full recovery. She did not quite know what to make of the second piece of news. Of course, it would be far too dangerous to move the lord and of course his mother and father should wish to see him. It was the most natural thing in the world that Lady Mulholland should invite them here. Still, it would be strange to have Lord Smythesdon's parents in the house.

"Heavens," Daisy said, giggling, "what shall papa make of an Earl from the foreign environs of Hampshire?"

The next days at Chemsworth Hall were a very slow dawn. The first day after the accident had verged on black, the only person in the household who remained unaffected by the general malaise being Marigold. That young lady was far more interested in discussing precisely how fast she had been able to retrieve the doctor. The only matter that could have disturbed Marigold's mind at all was the fate of The Turk, but her father privately told her that if the Earl insisted the horse be destroyed they would just move him to a tenant's farm with nobody the wiser. Marigold and the Viscount were in firm agreement that a fine animal should not pay for the folly of a young gentleman. No man nor horse, the Viscount sagely noted, should pay for the folly of a young gentleman, as young gentlemen were always carried this way and that by folly.

The rest of the Grangers milled around aimlessly and drank their tea distractedly. Every open and close of the door above stairs seemed momentous. Doctor Megthorn could not even be pressed with questions as he had so far been rarely away from his patient and had taken his meals in his room.

By the third day the sky had begun to lighten. There remained no sign of infection. The lord was able to take some soup. Having heard he was given white soup, as that was the lord's favorite, Daisy had even jokingly whispered to Violet, "I suppose you will not argue the dates of white soup *now*."

Though Daisy had joked, Violet had been stung by the remark. The mere mention of white soup brought all of her remorse back to her again. White soup! She blushed to think of how she had gloried in pointing out the mistake of the dates. Who on earth cared when white soup had been invented? The argument would have been too silly for even Poppy and Pansy.

She resolved that while she could not undo the past, she could avoid falling into any similar traps in future. Once and for all, she must give up contrariness. She must not react to every slight with a full-blown attack. She must not pull up the drawbridge and shoot flaming arrows each time she heard an opinion that offended her sensibilities. She would simply allow it to be nonsense and say nothing of it.

Smuckers had been a deal of help in that regard. He had noted her wandering forlorn in the library, unable to attend to her studies, and had said, "Only the most intelligent of us are prone to self-reflection. Be cheered that you are one of them." Then, as he was in the habit of doing, he waxed on about the glory of the house and made her laugh.

By the time a week had passed with no setbacks in the sickroom, the sun had begun to shine on Chemsworth Hall. Doctor Megthorn was convinced that the danger of infection had come and gone and Lady Mulholland even allowed the doctor to go home and sleep in his own bed. The doctor was relieved by this, though he found he could not complain overmuch about his treatment at the hands of Lady Mulholland. He was sent home in the Viscount's carriage, a hefty fee in his pocket and surrounded by boxes and packages for his wife. There were bolts of fine cloth, a set of dishes, preserves, cakes, a basket of apples, a delicate bonnet decorated by Lily, an apron stitched upon by Poppy and Pansy under the watchful eye of Miss Millthorpe, six silver teaspoons, six china cups and a newly made goose down comforter. Doctor Megthorn felt that going home in state and bearing gifts was a vast improvement over his arrival, hanging on for his life on the back of Miss Marigold Granger's horse. Mrs. Megthorn, upon viewing the treasure sent her, commented that they should be very comfortable indeed if some nob would be kind enough to break his leg in the neighborhood once a year.

The tempo of the house had quickened. Much would happen before the sun had set—Doctor Megthorn had arrived the day previous and performed a new treatment on Lord Smythesdon's leg. He released it from the box that had held it motionless and splinted it, then wrapped the splint in bandages soaked with starch and plaster of Paris. It was a new and daring treatment, and Smuckers frowned upon it as it had come from the

French, but it would allow the lord to be out of bed and into a specially modified chair. This, the doctor said, was vitally important. Bed rest was all well and good for a time, but too much could congeal the blood, unbalance the body's humours, and depress the patient's spirits. The new treatment was given overnight to dry and then Lord Smythesdon would be carried downstairs to rejoin the living. His outings were to be cautious and brief, but it was a sign that all the house took to mean that any real danger was truly at an end.

Also on this day, the Earl of Ainsworth and his lady were set to arrive. This, it seemed to Violet, would be the more complicated operation. The Countess had sent word that they would bring a valet, a lady's maid, two grooms and the coachman. All of them, and their horses, would need to be housed. Lady Mulholland had had a long conference with Smuckers, Mrs. Featherstone and Mr. Moreau to ensure that every detail had been thought of. Rooms were to be aired, the finest bedding installed, curtains changed from brocade to velvet, bell ropes tested, fireplaces scrubbed and elaborate meals planned. Mrs. Featherstone had emerged from the meeting appearing harried, Mr. Moreau had looked slightly offended as was his habit, but Smuckers had strode out triumphant. Violet knew that having an Earl and Countess in the house would only serve to animate his every step and begin the imaginings of a Marquess, Duke or even the King, himself, strolling in next.

Violet had not seen Lord Smythesdon since he had been carried up the stairs on the day of the accident. She had offered her assistance, but while her mother was satisfied to throw her into the library with the lord, she could not see her way clear to allow any of her daughters into his bedchamber. Rose had noted that if anybody posed less danger than a man with his leg strapped into a box, she did not know him. Lady Mulholland had frowned—the expression that was understood by the family to mean that her iron fist was poised in the air and debate was at an end.

Various reports had described Lord Smythesdon as pale, but alert. His temper might not have been admirable over the past few days, as the doctor had weaned him from the laudanum. Gone was the comfortable drifting and painless hours and back was the harsh light of day. Lady Mulholland said he had arrived at that delicate moment in a sickroom where the patient began to feel confined but was not yet ready to be free. The patient was not in agony, but remained in discomfort. She had thought to soothe the lord with the Viscount's good port and by all accounts the strategy proved successful.

Each time Violet walked from her bedchamber to the top of the staircase, she could not help but stare down the hall of the other wing and wonder what occurred there. This morning, she spied some unusual activity—the small figures of Poppy and Pansy raced down the corridor towards her, covering their mouths in laughter.

Violet stood in their way, and they screeched to a halt.

"Well?" she said. "Why are you racing about like that in a wing you have no business to be in? Where is Miss Millthorpe?"

The twins threw themselves on their sister's mercy. They clutched the skirts of her morning dress and said, "Pray, do not give us away, Violet. We have only been spying on the lord to see how he gets on."

"We wanted to be sure he still had his leg on," Poppy whispered. "We were terribly worried over it. Miss Millthorpe told us he did, but might she not claim it true so that we would not have nightmares?"

"She is not to be trusted when it comes to nightmares," Pansy said. "She gets very out of sorts when she has to get up in the middle of the night because Poppy dreamed of monsters who have stormed the house and are even now creeping up the stairs."

"Or when Pansy has dreamed of terrible sea creatures who capture her ship," Poppy said, "dragging it down to the bottom of the sea while she screams from her cabin."

The twins shivered in the face of such horrors. Violet was unmoved.

"Spying on the lord?" Violet asked, ignoring the specters of monsters and sea creatures. Her mind raced along furiously, trying to work out how the girls could possibly have observed Lord Smythesdon in his own room.

She took them by the arms and marched them to her bedchamber. "Now," she said, "sit down and tell me precisely what you have been doing."

Poppy and Pansy pointed at each other, as if the other one should be the first to confess the misdeed. Then Poppy said, "Well, it just so happens, Violet, that we have made a thorough study of the house. We had to do it, you see, in case of invaders. Remember, we are the reigning queens of the Inviolate Kingdom and we watch for knights and dragons from the third-floor balcony."

"Of course," Pansy said, "it is usually only Cassie coming with cheese. But we would not be put off and we began to wonder, what should we do if a dragon gets inside the house?"

Pansy made this pronouncement as if dragons were indeed in the habit of crashing through the doors of the various estates of England.

"We decided we must acquaint ourselves with every hidey-hole, obviously," Poppy said. "It would be the only way to survive a dragon attack."

Violet had yet to see how any of their imaginative story-telling had to do with spying on Lord Smythesdon. "And?" she said.

"It occurred to us," Pansy said, "that if we did need to hide from a dragon, the lord and his poor old leg would have a time of it. How was he to run? Even if he still had it on, and we were not certain he did, he could not use it yet."

"And it occurred to us," Poppy said, "that we had better determine how we might be able to rescue him."

"One cannot rescue a person," Pansy said, with all the authority of an individual who was long in the habit of conducting such operations, "unless one knows the particulars of the situation. A captain does not try to rescue his men without first understanding the lay of the land. Did the lord have his leg on, or did the lord have his leg off?"

"Then it occurred to us," Poppy said, "that we had discovered a hole in the wall of the empty bedchamber next door some time ago."

"And so we have been going nearly every day," Pansy said proudly. "You cannot even guess how many dinners we have missed over it—Miss Millthorpe is cross as anything that we keep running off."

"She is convinced we have set up another Inviolate Kingdom somewhere," Poppy said. "She is entirely vexed that she cannot find it."

"But she would not dare to search the east wing," Pansy said, laughing.

Though Violet thought her youngest sisters were the naughtiest two children to have ever arrived in Chemsworth Hall, she could not quite overcome her curiosity as to what they might have seen.

"You had better tell me everything you saw," Violet said. "Then I will be in an informed position to tell you what you must forget forever."

Both Poppy and Pansy seemed to believe this was a remarkably sensible suggestion and, in any case, were fairly bursting to tell somebody of their exploits.

"First we confirmed that he had his leg on. We could not actually see it, but Doctor Megthorn talked about it a lot," Pansy said. "We were vastly relieved over it."

"The poor old lord was very happy for a while," Poppy said. "Even with his leg strapped into a box. Doctor Megthorn would come and give him something to drink, then he would joke and laugh and then fall asleep in mid-sentence. But three days ago, Doctor Megthorn said he was not to have any more of the drink and the lord grew very out of sorts."

"*Very* out of sorts. He was like we are when we are overtired," Pansy said, to better paint a picture of the lord's frame of mind. "You know, when Miss Millthorpe call us Huns. Mama brought him some port to cheer him up."

"He was better today, I thought," Poppy said.

"He was," Pansy concurred. "But, shall we tell Violet the funniest thing?"

"Oh, let's do," Poppy said. She leaned confidentially over to Violet. "Henry has been coming every day and they do have very silly conversations. First, they talked of how it was only a strange accident that the lord could not stay on The Turk. Perhaps the ground was slippery and the horse lost his footing, or perhaps the saddle was not properly tightened."

"They even talked of how the lord might try him again when his leg was healed," Pansy said, snorting.

"They made all sorts of plans about it," Poppy said. "It was like they forgot all about the lord being carried in with his leg bent wrong. Until yesterday…"

"Yes, yesterday," Pansy picked up for her sister, "Lord Smythesdon very suddenly said, 'Granger, we are idiots. I should have listened to Miss Granger and rode Merlin instead.'"

"You cannot imagine how many shades of red Henry turned," Poppy said with glee. "He sputtered and mumbled and said he could not quite say that they were idiots, but the lord said they most certainly were idiots and he owed Miss Granger an apology."

"Now we have been trying to find out which Miss Granger he means. Which sister does he think to throw himself before in abject sorrow and remorse? We are guessing it is Marigold."

"Of course, it must be Marigold," Poppy said. "Though she is not sentimental unless you are a horse and so I think she shall be rather unmoved. If it were me, I should cry at the sight of it."

"But I wonder," Pansy said, "might he not hurt his leg all over again if he were to throw himself down on the ground to beg forgiveness?"

"He would," Poppy said, "but if he is a real knight he will not care a thing about it. He'd rather die than care a thing about his poor old leg."

Violet ignored their chatter. The lord owed Miss Granger an apology. Of course, Violet knew it to be herself. It was she who had attempted to trick him onto Merlin. Well, she supposed she could be gratified that he had seen the error of his ways.

Violet paused. She felt in herself a little too much smugness at having been proved right. As well, being proved right in the matter of the Turk did not prove her right in everything. She must not lose sight of that fact. She had treated him abominably, with the exception of trying to keep him off The Turk.

She vowed that if the lord were to apologize, she would accept gracefully without a hint of superiority. It would dash his pride to do it, and if he did have the courage to do it, she would accept as graciously as a benevolent queen. It was to be her new outlook and she must stick to it.

She eyed her two sisters. "You must cease your spying and being naughty," she said. "Every person has the right to be in their own bedchamber without worrying that two very bad children are staring at them."

Poppy and Pansy seemed to deflate in the face of this order. "But," Poppy said softly, "we were hoping to spy on the Countess."

"Yes," Pansy said. "She is to come today and do not you wonder what a Countess does when nobody is looking?"

"I do not," Violet said firmly, though of course she did. One could not but help wonder what sort of beauty rituals a Countess might employ. "You shall not dare spy on anybody else ever again. I should not like to inform Miss Millthorpe of your crimes, you would never eat another dinner in your lives."

This idea seemed to effect Poppy and Pansy greatly. "We have missed so many dinners already," Poppy said.

"We would become martyrs, starved on the third floor," Pansy said sadly.

"But, Pans," Poppy said, a note of hope in her voice, "we might be able to become ghosts and haunt the third floor forevermore."

Pansy seemed much affected by this idea. "People might tell stories and write ballads about us."

"You shall not be starved to death, just made extremely uncomfortable if you do not pay heed. This is the end of your criminal career," Violet said. "Now, go up to the nursery and apologize profusely to Miss Millthorpe. Promise her you will never run off again, and mean it."

The twins left, swearing they would throw themselves on Miss Millthorpe's mercy and draw flowers for her and attend to their sewing and kiss her cheeks until she was happy once more. Their promise never to run off again was made somewhat less convincingly. In any case, they were happy to go up because they must watch for incoming intruders to the Inviolate Kingdom, otherwise known as Lord and Lady Ainsworth. Regardless of how aggravated she was, Miss Millthorpe would not keep them from that lofty task. The governess felt that being able to inform the family of a pending arrival was by far one of her more interesting duties.

Chapter Thirteen

Violet watched her sisters run up the stairs to the nursery and then proceeded down to the great hall. As she descended she saw Smuckers and Doctor Megthorn examining a wheeled chair that had just arrived. It was made of dark wood with a caned back and two enormous wheels on either side. The leg rests were some inches from the floor and Doctor Megthorn was adjusting one higher to hold Lord Smythesdon's casted leg straight out in front of him.

"Lady Mulholland," Smuckers said, with all the air of a general managing a campaign, "wishes it to be set in the drawing room. The lord will be carried down by our footmen and placed in the chair to receive his mother and father."

Violet examined the seat, which was of polished wood. "Perhaps we ought to put a cushion on it?" she said.

"Excellent notion, Miss Granger," the doctor said. "I think we ought to do the same on the leg rest that will hold the healing limb, perhaps some batting covered over with cloth."

"I will see that Mrs. Featherstone makes the adjustments," Smuckers said.

"You and Mrs. Featherstone are far too busy with other arrangements, Smuckers," Violet said. "I am perfectly able to find a cushion that fits and sew a padded casing for the leg rest."

"You should like to take charge of the lord's conveyance?" Smuckers asked in some surprise.

Violet felt Smuckers' curiosity on the subject and her face flushed. It had been a perfectly reasonable suggestion, and yet she was embarrassed over it. Smuckers read too much into the idea and it was mortifying. He was grinning at her as if there was hope for Lady Mulholland's scheme after all.

"It is only a bit of sewing," she said. "If one is to practice sewing since the age of six and then have no ability when it is needed, one mightn't have bothered at all."

Doctor Megthorn, approving of all things sensible, nodded. Smuckers appeared quietly satisfied.

Violet grasped the handles of the chair and pushed it into the drawing room, glad to be away from the butler's surmises. She hardly knew what she thought of it herself. Now that she had got hold of the chair, it seemed somehow very private. Too private. Lord Smythesdon would put his person in this chair that she would have fixed for his comfort.

She scolded herself that it was only a chair, after all. Everybody must put their person into a chair.

Violet scanned the drawing room. She instantly recognized that she would need a footman to rearrange some of the furniture. The wheeled chair was bulky and it must be situated near the fire and have room enough to be pushed there and then out again to the dining room. There must be a wide path from the door to the fireplace.

She rang the bell and it was, blessedly, answered by Jimmy rather than Smuckers. He followed her direction, pushing chairs and sofas this way and that, while she looked through the sewing baskets to find what she needed. She found ample batting and a dark green worsted that would do very well for the leg rest. A cushion from one of the Queen Anne chairs in the corner of the room fit the seat perfectly. That the scene on the cushion was that of a fox hunt she hoped would go unremarked.

Lady Mulholland swept in. She gazed around at the disorder of the furniture, and at Jimmy dragging the last chair across the carpet. "What in heavens," she said. "Jimmy, everything in this room has been placed with much planning and precision. Each piece in its own place. There is no regularity to this new arrangement at all."

"Mama," Violet said, "I ordered it to be done. This chair is bulky and there was not near enough room to wheel it to the fire."

"Ah," Lady Mulholland said, still looking uncomfortable in the face of this willy nilly moving of furniture in all directions. "I see." She examined Violet's hands, just now full of batting and material.

"The doctor wishes that there be a cushion on the seat and padding for the leg rest," Violet said, the defensive tone ringing loud in her ears.

"And you shall sew it?" Lady Mulholland asked, looking far more pleased at the notion than she ought.

Violet did not answer. It was becoming entirely inconvenient to have her softened attitude toward Lord Smythesdon so noticed and commented upon, if not directly pointed out. She knew what her mother was thinking and it vexed her to have her own improved temperament held against her.

Lady Mulholland came and inspected the seat cushion. "That," she said, pointing to the fox hunting scene, "is very unfortunate. I shall have Fleur bring down a cushion from my dressing room. It is a garden scene that will offend nobody."

Violet nodded.

"Though very good of you, darling, to see to the chair."

"There is nothing so very good about it," Violet said. As soon as she said it, she wished she had not said it. It was the trifle all over again. Why must she leap to the opposing view so unnecessarily?

Lady Mulholland, being an expert on her daughter's contrariness, merely smiled.

Just as they had for Lord Smythesdon, the family and servants were lined on the drive to welcome the Earl and Countess of Ainsworth. Violet could almost feel the nerves emanating from Smuckers as he examined his footmen and continually told them to stand straighter. As much as he tried though, Smuckers could not make Oscar grow any taller than he was. Even Fleur, the perennially bored Parisian, seemed on the alert. It occurred to Violet that Fleur was girding herself to encounter a lady's maid that served a higher ranked mistress and was determined not to be bested.

Lady Mulholland was speaking quietly to the Viscount about how they could not hold arriving from Hampshire against the Earl as it had been Chemsworth Hall that had so unfortunately allowed their son on The Turk to such disastrous results. The Viscount pondered this idea and only replied that if the Earl and his lady demanded The Turk be destroyed, he should not do it.

At his mother's words, Henry flushed, which was not surprising since he was in a near constant state of mortification at having been implicated in the disastrous result. Marigold nodded approvingly at her father's good sense. She wore her habit and Violet presumed she would be ready to ride The Turk to safety in a moment's notice.

Two carriages rumbled toward the house, both capable of carrying four passengers and both sporting the Earl's crest. Violet presumed they should find the Earl and his lady in one and the servants in the other. They rolled to a stop and Chemsworth Hall's grooms and footmen sprang into action, determined to make Mr. Smuckers proud.

The Earl of Ainsworth was very like his son—he was tall and dark-haired, with Lord Smythesdon's deep blue eyes. Lady Ainsworth appeared petite next to her husband and had a mass of blond curls very like Daisy's.

The Earl and the Viscount greeted one another and Lady Mulholland, as was her habit, smoothed the introduction with charming compliments and encouragements. The Earl and his lady were assured of their son's continuing recovery and the delight with which they were received to the house. They were quickly introduced to the rest of the family.

Poor Henry kept a good face on it, though Violet thought he looked as if he feared that any moment the Earl would accuse him of nearly killing his only son. The Earl, however, did not seem to be in possession of precisely how the accident had occurred. Violet knew this would be thanks to Lady Mulholland and only hoped the hazy account she had written in a letter would hold.

The Earl appeared most happy to be introduced to Violet, Rose and Daisy, and repeated, "Excellent, yes, indeed," to all three in their turn.

"My lord," Lady Mulholland said, "we shall not keep you on the drive another moment as I know you are anxious to be reunited with your son. He has been brought down to the drawing room to receive you."

With that, the party made their way into the house and, from what Violet could gather, Smuckers viewed this first hurdle of creditably entertaining an Earl and his Countess as a great success.

Violet was acutely aware that this would be the first time she would see Lord Smythesdon since the day of the accident. There was no reason on earth that she should find herself embarrassed over it, and yet she was. She wished she had not caught Poppy and Pansy spying and that she would not know what the lord had said of her. She felt as if she were perennially rehearsing in her thoughts what she would say to the great apology.

The drawing room was the scene of an affectionate reunion of father, mother and son. Lord Smythesdon, to his credit, did all he could to make light of the injury and made no mention of he and Henry having been idiots to have even considered The Turk. The horse's name was not even spoken.

Tea was served, and not the ridiculous tea that had been rolled out for the Ravencrafts. This tea was all the refinement and elegance that Smuckers could inspire in Mr. Moreau. The chef had sent up a tea service that might have graced the rooms of Marie Antoinette. The trays were filled in the center with petite savarins, delicate rosewater macarons and citron tartes, a second ring housed Mr. Moreau's famous mince pastries and all were surrounded by the crested almond biscuits. Lady Ainsworth was enchanted and she and Lady Mulholland leaned their heads together to converse on the benefits and pitfalls of keeping a

French cook. According to Lady Mulholland, the benefit was the food and the pitfall was the ferocious temper the cook might find himself in if he were crossed too often in the span of a single day. The remedy to this was simple—inform the staff of your wishes well ahead of time and never change one's mind. Lady Mulholland was of the opinion that the French, in general, did not take well to surprises and one had best avoid them where possible.

Violet had so far evaded Lord Smythesdon's eye and so could not say where his attention was focused. Much to her surprise, Lord Ainsworth said, "Dear Miss Granger, I wonder if you would be so kind to arrange the fire screen for my son? I find I am no good at the operation and I wish to speak to the Viscount about his ideas on crop rotation."

Violet was momentarily frozen as she considered how much had been accomplished in those two sentences. She was to be thrown into Lord Smythesdon's notice and her father was to be pleased beyond measure. Certainly, Lord Smythesdon must have written the Earl and alerted him to where the Viscount's interests lay. In one fell swoop, she was to have her first conversation with the lord and her father was to throw off any reservations, on account of crop rotation, that he may have harbored upon receiving guests from another county.

She nodded and set her plate down. Violet assumed it was the last she would see of the plate, as Marigold had already relieved her of the citron tarte that had been on it.

She knew she was blushing. It was so entirely stupid to blush like a schoolgirl. She would not be blushing at all if she had not seen Rose and Daisy smiling at her and her mother surreptitiously peeking at her. Even Smuckers appeared to be consumed with curiosity, no matter how he attempted to appear oblivious to what occurred around him. It was not that she was embarrassed to adjust the pole screen in front of the wheeled chair, it was that so many people in the room found it so interesting. Why should they not attend to themselves? Why should they be so intrigued by her every movement?

Violet walked as regally and calmly as she could to the pole screen. She would have it fixed in a moment. Nobody who resided in Chemsworth Hall could survive long without becoming expert at fire screens and all other methods to direct whatever paltry heat the fireplaces could be convinced to give up. She nodded to Lord Smythesdon by way of greeting and raised the screen so that his face was shielded.

Feeling the intense awkwardness of the silence, she said, "I trust your recovery proceeds satisfactorily."

What was wrong with her? I trust your recovery proceeds satisfactorily? She sounded as if she were addressing Parliament! Her face grew even hotter and she hoped the heat of the fire could account for it.

Lord Smythesdon smiled. "Well enough," he said. "Though I would not just now be engaged in a recovery if I had been guided by your advice. I must apologize for my rudeness upon discovering you had very sensibly attempted to put me on Merlin to stop me from killing myself."

"It was not entirely your error," Violet said, gratified by his speech. "Henry and Marigold should not have even mentioned The Turk,"

The lord appeared rueful as he said, "Your brother and I have agreed that we were idiots to even think of it. At least, I have made an attempt at convincing Granger of that fact. I cannot find fault with your sister, though. She, herself, is capable of controlling the beast and so could not take blame for others who claimed the same skill."

Violet was surprised by his tone. Of course, based on reports from Poppy and Pansy, she had expected an apology, but she had not foreseen such a dramatic change in attitude.

"I wonder, Miss Granger," the lord went on, "if there are not other things I have been mistaken about."

Violet could not be certain if he spoke of his attitude toward learned women. If that was what he alluded to, she could not be certain if he meant it, or if he were just saying what he thought she would like to hear.

"After all," he said, "As Euclid noted in his axioms, things that coincide with one another are equal to one another. Many of my attitudes and opinions have coincided these past weeks, with a rather unpleasant outcome."

Lady Ainsworth had approached and fussed with the blanket covering Lord Smythesdon's propped up leg. "Euclid, my dear?" she said. "Heavens, I doubt Miss Granger will be interested in Euclid of all things, we do not all attend Oxford, you know. Miss Granger, do sit down and have Bertram tell you of the gardens at Donneville."

Violet sat down but did not know in which direction to look. Just when Lord Smythesdon had introduced the subject of Euclid and they might have engaged in a conversation about the meaning of the axiom, his mother had dismissed her as only being worthy to discuss flowers.

Of course, this was where Lord Smythesdon would have got his erroneous opinions to begin. Euclid was not to be a part of polite conversation with a lady.

Lord Smythesdon reddened at the rebuke as his mother moved back to her place beside Lady Mulholland. Lord Ainsworth and the Viscount were by the window, animatedly discussing all the business of their respective estates. Violet assumed her father was becoming acquainted with the idea that farming in Hampshire was not as wildly different as he would have thought. Rose and Daisy talked desultorily. Daisy winked at her when she caught Violet's eye. Marigold was engrossed in relieving Mr. Moreau's tray of its savarins.

"I do not know much about Donneville's gardens," Lord Smythesdon said, "other than they are pleasant to walk through. I have dabbled a bit in studying the efficacy of plants in medical treatments, but cannot consider myself an expert."

Waxing on about the beauty of flowers was quite beyond Violet Granger. Medical treatments, however, were a subject she found intensely interesting. She had been treating people in the village since she was twelve. "I find Culpeper's Herbal indispensable," Violet said. "There are no end of remedies in the average English garden. Though I find I cannot agree with his use of astrology in describing the efficacy of a plant."

"Precisely," Lord Smythesdon said. "Why should picking Celandine when the sun is in Leo and the moon in Aries be necessary? Celandine is right to pick in August and be done with it."

"My thoughts exactly," Violet said, entirely forgetting her embarrassment. "The properties of flora cannot be affected by a precise position of the moon. It is only the growth period, and therefore the season, that can make any material difference. Seasons do vary in sun and rain and therefore no heavenly body can predict when something ought to be picked."

"I wonder at such a learned man giving way to such superstitions," Lord Smythesdon said.

"Well, the dear, old man did not invent such nonsense, it was quite the tradition for centuries."

"One can only speculate on what people a hundred years from now will pronounce nonsense though it seems so very sensible to us."

"Each generation believes they have discovered everything, and they are never right."

"Yes, I believe you said something similar in the library."

"Oh, let us not speak of the library."

And so they circled back to where Culpeper had gone wrong for the next half hour. Violet was entirely startled to hear the first gong. A footman arrived and wheeled Lord Smythesdon to the stairs, where the others waited to carry him to his bedchamber. She found herself sorry that the conversation had ended so suddenly.

Victorine was in high spirits as she buttoned up the back of Violet's rose silk.

"I suppose it is very lively below stairs," Violet said. "To have new faces in the servant's hall."

"We is supérieur," Victorine said pertly.

"I am sure Mr. Smuckers would be pleased to hear that his staff is superior," Violet said.

"No him," Victorine said, laughing. "Me and Fleur. We is supérieur of Martha. *Martha*," she said, laughing over the name. "She don't know nothing."

"Well I hope you did not say so to her," Violet said.

Victorine shrugged. "Nous avons besoin de ne rien dire."

They had not seen the need to say anything at all. Violet took this to mean that Victorine and Fleur had donned their most superior French faces for poor Martha. She could only hope the visiting lady's maid could hold up against it. Especially against Fleur, who could make a Marquess feel small if she were so inclined.

Violet followed Victorine to Rose's bedchamber, and then on to Daisy's room. Daisy, as always, was torn between multiple dresses and Violet and Rose made the error of not agreeing on the same dress. Violet thought she said green first and Rose thought it was cream. This had led to a lengthy debate held by Daisy with herself until Victorine had taken over, chosen a peach silk and wrestled her into it. They had been late coming down.

Smuckers waited at his post in the hall, appearing grieved.

"We know we are late," Violet said.

"It is entirely my fault," Daisy admitted. "Violet and Rose did not agree on my first instinct and it threw me topsy-turvy. My first instinct is invariably right, but it seems to have fled me this evening."

"You know how Daisy goes on," Rose said. "She is as straightforward as her curls. If there is a way to go round in circles she will find it."

"Straightforward as my curls?" Daisy said. "Rose, I am very much surprised. That sounds almost poetic."

Smuckers was desperately looking toward the drawing room door as if he could not stand another moment of their lateness.

"Never mind, Smuckers," Violet said. "The lord and lady are not Poppy and Pansy's dragons and cannot eat us up. In any case, if there is ever to be a dispute of any sort, big or small, we know you stand with the house."

With this reminder of his stalwart heart, Smuckers stood straighter and his brow cleared. Whatever problems he encountered, whatever decisions he must make, whatever action must be taken, there was one constant in his life—he would stand with the house.

"You are such a darling, Smuckers," Daisy said. "When we are all married we shall spend all of our time trying to steal you away for our own."

"That is very true," Violet said. "I must have a butler-general for my own children." She paused, then said, "Though that circumstance is not in the near future."

"For myself," Rose said, "I must have Smuckers because I insist my children be bold and scheme like demons to get sweets run up the backstairs. Our Smuckers is already thoroughly acquainted with the operation."

The idea of being sought after by any number of great houses was extremely gratifying to Smuckers. He had not ever imagined such a circumstance. There was no question but he would stick with Chemsworth Hall, he would never let down the Viscount and his lady. Still, it cheered him to think of the daughters of the hall fretting over how they might secure him. He nodded gravely at the honor as they passed into the drawing room.

Chapter Fourteen

The drawing room was as lit up as it had been on the day of the lord's arrival. The Viscount and the Earl were settled comfortably in front of the fire, the Viscount seeming to have got over any reluctance to associate with a foreigner. Henry sat nearby, listening with deference to what the two elder men discussed.

Lily played on the pianoforte while Marigold turned the pages for her. Turning pages, Violet presumed, was as far as Marigold had ever got in her musical career. One could not play the pianoforte upon a horse and so it would have gone the way of so many other things Marigold should have learnt.

Lord Smythesdon was nowhere to be seen. Violet felt a small disappointment upon noting it. She had thought of a few more points on Culpeper that she would have liked to discuss. It was not so much that she wished to see Lord Smythesdon, but that it had been very pleasant to disparage certain of Culpeper's ideas. It was not often that she could have such a conversation and express conclusions she had come to while studying alone in the library. She reasoned with herself that simply because such a conversation were attached to the person of Lord Smythesdon did not signify. It was the conversation that was so interesting, not the person.

Lady Mulholland and Lady Ainsworth had their heads together talking confidentially and Violet became mortified when they looked up. Both of their gazes had settled upon her. And remained settled upon her. Whatever they had spoken of, she very much felt she had been a subject of the conversation.

Certainly, her mother would not have had the temerity to discuss her ridiculous plans with Lady Ainsworth! The house had just recently come close to killing her only son! Lady Mulholland could not think it the right time...no time would be the right time. Not even The Friendly Dragon would dare.

"Violet, dear," Lady Mulholland said, in the smooth tone that generally signaled her iron fist poised overhead, "come and join us."

Violet had no choice but to do as she was asked. She went forward, hearing Rose's snort and Daisy's soft laughter behind her. She sat down and found herself stared at by the two women. Were they to say something? Or would they just continue to peer at her in such a way?

"Violet," Lady Mulholland said, "I was just telling Lady Ainsworth of your various interests."

Violet glanced at Lady Mulholland. Had her mother invented interests that she did not, in fact, have? It seemed too unlikely that the TFD had spoken of her real interests.

"I am so ashamed," Lady Ainsworth said. "You must have thought I was quite condescending to advise my son to cease speaking of Euclid. I, myself, do not know a thing about it, but I should not have presumed that you did not."

Violet was wholly taken aback.

"I suppose," Lady Ainsworth said, "that I have become too accustomed to London girls. One never expects them to know more than what is in front of them. Each one is more silly than the next."

Lady Mulholland nodded approvingly at this sentiment. "Fanning and fainting at the slightest provocation," she said. "One wonders why their fathers do not keep them at home to swoon in the comfort of their own drawing rooms."

Both Lady Mulholland and Lady Ainsworth found this idea highly amusing. Lady Ainsworth said, "I recently hosted a girl, and I shan't tell you the name, who positively shrank from the very idea of reading novels. She claimed to only read Fordyce's Sermons. I did not believe a word of it, of course. But there she was, attempting to paint herself as some drooping flower not even hardy enough to stand up to prose."

"I should be mortified if one of my girls claimed she could not hold up against a novel," Lady Mulholland said.

"My son," Lady Ainsworth said, "has a great desire to become a leading intellect. My lord does not think much of the idea, though I see no harm in it. One must have interests, after all. I only fear…"

Lady Mulholland laid her hand on Lady Ainsworth's arm. "What do you fear, Lady Ainsworth?"

The lady looked away as if she could hardly bear to speak of it. Softly, she said, "I only fear that if my son were to marry such a one as the young Fordyce's Sermons girl, he should not be happy."

"Of course, he would not," Lady Mulholland said. "He must choose a lady who can participate in his interests. A lady who can hold up her end of a conversation."

"I quite agree with you," Lady Ainsworth said.

Violet looked back and forth between her mother and Lady Ainsworth. It was a regular stage play. That they had been conspiring together, she no longer doubted. They had positively rehearsed. What surprised her more was that they should acknowledge her scholarship and yet think she was such a simpleton as to be taken in by this farce.

"It is the greatest gamble in life," Lady Mulholland said, "to attach oneself forevermore to a husband. One had best be certain that the temperaments are suited."

Lady Ainsworth nodded solemnly and Violet was vastly relieved when the gong sounded. Not even these two ladies, enacting their stage play, would dare delay Mr. Moreau.

The seating at dinner was more formal than usual, due to the arrival of Lord and Lady Ainsworth. Lady Ainsworth was seated to the right of the Viscount, while Violet sat on his left. Lord Ainsworth was to Lady Mulholland's right, and Henry to her left.

Marigold was seated to the Lord's right and Violet dearly hoped she could hold her tongue on the specifics of the accident.

The poor Viscount, generally preferring to talk of estate management, seemed at a loss as to what might be discussed with Lady Ainsworth. The lady, however, was well-used to carrying on a dinner conversation.

"You have very fine daughters, Lord Mulholland," Lady Ainsworth said.

"I do, indeed," the Viscount said. "and no shortage of them either. I believe there are two more of them lurking about somewhere."

"Poppy and Pansy, papa," Violet said. "They are still in the nursery."

"That's right, Poppy and Pansy. That's the last of them, eh?"

Violet nodded and the Viscount went on. "I count myself lucky in daughters, Lady Ainsworth. One never knows what to do with too many sons. I understand your Lord Smythesdon is an only son."

"He is, my lord."

"Very sensible," the Viscount replied.

Lady Ainsworth, not to be put off by the Viscount's unique views, carried on. "How wonderful that Miss Violet Granger has educated herself so well," she said.

"Has she?" the Viscount said. "I suppose she has. One wonders where she might be found if we did not have a library."

"Of course," Lady Ainsworth said, "one can only pray she marries a gentleman of equal intellect."

Violet knew she was blushing furiously. Lady Ainsworth was as bold and determined as her own mother.

"Should she, though?" the Viscount asked. "I am not so certain but that my Violet might prefer being the superior mind of a match. Eh, dear? Run rings around the poor fellow?"

Violet's mortification felt to be increasing by leaps and bounds. The only thing she could take some small comfort in was the realization that her father did not have the first clue what Lady

Ainsworth hinted at. The TFD had enacted her plan with no help from the Viscount.

Violet prayed the conversation would come to an end. Before she could think of a suitable way to guide it in another direction, she heard Lord Ainsworth say, "What's this about The Turk?"

She shuddered as she turned her head. Marigold said, "I only say, my lord, that a fine horse should not be harmed on account of a gentleman's stupidity."

Lord Ainsworth was silent for a moment, then he said, "And you are implying that my son is stupid?"

"No," Marigold said. "I am saying that he *acted* stupidly. Though you may comfort yourself to know that he was not alone. My brother acted equally stupidly."

Lord Ainsworth's face was grave. Henry appeared frozen in time, as if he were a Greek statue forever immortalized in marble. Lady Mulholland was clearly alarmed, which was highly unusual. Lady Mulholland was never alarmed.

"Anyway," Marigold went on, oblivious to the faces around her, "I shan't allow good old Turk to be harmed. He's a first-rate specimen and I should rather take him into the forest and live like a gypsy."

Lord Ainsworth suddenly roared with laughter. "Great heavens," he said to Marigold, "what I wouldn't give to have my own stablemaster gripped with such a passion for horses."

Marigold beamed at the lord, his character gone up significantly in her estimation.

"You may consider The Turk safe. I'll not fault anybody, or any horse, for a decision my son chose to make," Lord Ainsworth said. "If a young gentleman did not commit egregious errors in judgment, one would wonder if he did anything at all. In any case, I have only two requirements from him—that he recover sufficiently and that he marry before I die. As I am in the habit of drinking vast amounts of port, I would prefer he get on with it."

It seemed that wherever Violet turned, there must be talk of marriage. The Viscount, for his part, seemed most interested in the

165

idea that Lord Ainsworth was fond of port. He was an aficionado himself and that commonality could only further bridge the divide between Oxfordshire and the foreign county of Hampshire.

Marigold only said, "Whoever he marries, my lord, let us hope she can ride creditably and is not just hanging on like a fool."

After they had retired to the drawing room, Violet played the pianoforte to avoid any further conversation with Lady Ainsworth and her mother. The Viscount, the Earl and Henry had stayed long over their port and she assumed her father and Lord Ainsworth were engaged in the copious amounts of port that the Earl had so fondly mentioned. When they rejoined the party, a card table was set up and the Viscount and his lady were joined by the Earl and his wife at whist. The rest of the evening passed quietly.

Now, Violet, Rose and Daisy lounged comfortably around Violet's fireplace, discussing the dinner.

"I tried to kick Marigold to stop her from talking, but I could not reach her under the table," Rose said.

"The only saving grace to it," Violet said, "was that it put an end to Lady Ainsworth's broad hints. She is as bold as the ODM."

"It seems everybody works against you, Violet. I do not see how you shall stand up to it," Daisy said.

"If you require reinforcements, I could pronounce them all horrible at dinner on the morrow," Rose said. "I would have to go and live with Marigold and The Turk in the forest, but I would do it."

"*You* do not work against me, Daisy," Violet said. "What if she were to foist upon you some gentleman who was not at all romantic? Not standing upon the Dover cliffs? What then? Rose does not work against me. She is fully prepared to throw down her napkin at dinner and cause a scene. What if mama should present her with a milksop who couldn't insult a chicken? What then?"

"I should dig my heels in," Daisy said. "I must have my poet."

"I should make very short work of a milksop, if he dared speak to me at all," Rose said.

"But, Violet," Daisy said. "Is this not different? You wish to marry an intellect and Lord Smythesdon plans to become a *leading* intellect. How many of them could there be? Surely, you might change your mind now that we have nearly crippled him and he's ever so much nicer."

"If that's what it took to make the man nice," Rose said, "we should have put him on The Turk the first day he arrived."

"You would not have believed how they conspired together," Violet said. "I do not know what the TFD and Lady Ainsworth spoke of, but they are in league. In *league*."

"We ought to think up a name for Lady Ainsworth," Daisy said. "How about the SIW, for Smythesdon's Indomitable Warrior?"

"Or," Rose said, "how about the DCC for the Dragon's Co-Conspirator?"

"I do not care what you call her, I would just like to know how long they plan to stay," Violet said. "I cannot imagine having too many more encounters such as I had this evening."

"Perhaps Lord Smythesdon can be moved now that he's got that great bandage pasted on his leg," Rose said. "Perhaps they will tell us on the morrow that they are moving him back to Hampshire or to their house in town."

Though Violet had so recently stated that she would wish to know when the lord and lady would depart, she had not thought of the possibility that they might take their son with them. She felt a surprising pang at this suggestion, but quickly attributed it to her wish to continue disparaging Culpeper's love of astrology.

The madeira had come out in the butler's closet and Mrs. Featherstone waited to hear what was the cause. The madeira was only for momentous occasions and Christmas Day.

Smuckers had poured two glasses and he now stared contentedly into the fire. He knew, of course, that Mrs. Featherstone would be on the edge of her seat to know his news. The madeira was a subtle hint that this day had not been as other days. He stayed quiet, relishing the high drama of the silence.

"Out with it, Mr. Smuckers," Mrs. Featherstone said. "You don't fool me one bit. I have a glass of madeira in front of me and I would know the meaning of it."

Smuckers had dwelled on the act of imparting this news all evening. He had even made the smallest misstep in serving the soup as it had wholly consumed his thoughts. With great relish, he said, "One goes on, year after year, Mrs. Featherstone, striving to do one's best. It is the English way. One such as myself strives to honor the house at all personal costs. One does not dare, however, hope that such striving has been noticed."

A long silence filled the butler's closet. Finally, Mrs. Featherstone said, "And has your strivin' been noted?"

"It has," Smuckers said proudly. "It has been noticed and remarked upon."

Mrs. Featherstone let out a quiet sigh. The sort of sigh she made when a traveling tinker had knocked on the kitchen door and then waxed on too long about his wondrous wares. She would get to the heart of the matter at once.

"And what were the remarks, Mr. Smuckers?" she asked.

Smuckers now prepared to impart the most glorious sentiment ever relayed to his ears. "It appears, Mrs. Featherstone, that when the Miss Grangers are married, they will scheme to secure my services. It shall be for naught, of course. I am as much a part of Chemsworth Hall as the stones in the walls. Nonetheless, it is a pleasant prospect to consider. It is the sort of sentiment that one will cherish in one's old age. The knowledge that strivings have been noticed."

Mrs. Featherstone did not appear as overcome by the happy imaginings of Mr. Smucker's old age as he would have thought.

"Well," she said, "'tis always handy to have options. Now, tell of the great lord and lady as has come to us."

Smuckers was forced to come to the realization that nobody, not even Mrs. Featherstone, could fully comprehend the honor that had been bestowed upon him by the Miss Grangers. It must be enough that *he* knew it.

"I believe the cause of the accident has been got over," he said. "Miss Marigold charged Lord Smythesdon and master Henry as acting stupid and the lord was very amused by it."

"So the lord ain't ragin' at the house and demandin' the beast be destroyed?"

"Not in the slightest," Smuckers said.

"And there ain't to be any dire consequences over it?"

"It appears not."

Mrs. Featherstone gulped down her madeira. It had been a most unsatisfactory interview in the butler's closet. Absolutely nothing had gone wrong.

Lord Smythesdon lay back on the pillows and sipped his port. He'd had a tray brought up to him for dinner and, as always, that wonderful cook of theirs had sent up an array of desserts. It had been severely tiring to be carried downstairs and sat up for a full hour and he was glad of the soothing quality of a well-made savarin and good quality port. Still, it had been quite wonderful to see another view than could be had from his own room. He had begun to feel like an elegantly housed prisoner.

He had been very much relieved that he had got over the apology to Miss Granger. The knowledge that it must be done had weighed heavily upon him. And, he knew, it must be done. His sense of honor required it. The conversation had turned out more pleasant than he would have anticipated. She had not greeted his regret with smugness, as he had been very much afraid she would.

Then, it had been so very interesting to discuss Culpeper. Her eyes had been so bright and her manner so engaging. But perhaps the most interesting circumstance was the mention of the library. There had not been anything explicit said about their previous unfortunate encounter there, but it seemed to him that when Miss Granger said, 'Let us not speak of the library,' it must indicate some sort of regret.

He did not suppose she meant to regret that she was learned. He had quite got over that idea. It was unusual, there was no getting around it. That the ladies of the house hunted, and rode astride, was also unusual. But just because a thing was unusual, did that make it wrong? That was the question he had been asking himself. Before The Turk, he had not been in the habit of questioning his own opinions. They had felt, he realized now, not just as opinions but facts. Now, however, he felt as if he must review every preconceived idea and deem it suspect until proven otherwise. He should not wish, for the whole of the rest of his life, to make such a stupid mistake again.

He was cheerful, in spite of his injury. The only circumstance that marred this general sense of well-being was his mother and father's arrival. He had been happy to see them. But then his father had come to him and given him the same old lecture about being on the edge of his grave, ready to fall into it at any moment. His mother had come in and waxed on, all too obviously, about Miss Granger. They were plotters, the both of them.

Perhaps they thought they could overcome him in his weakened state. Perhaps they thought it was very convenient for him to have a reason to make an extended stay in the house. He did not like to disappoint them, but for now he would carry on just as he always had.

It was a shame, though, that he was not quite ready to marry. Miss Granger did have the most remarkable looks and, when she was inclined to be friendly, their conversation was a delight. Her manners and background were everything suitable.

The air she had about her, as if she were a sister to the king—regal and composed—he could not help but admire.

Smythesdon sighed. He must only hope that when he *was* ready to settle, another similar lady should come into his view.

172

Chapter Fifteen

Henry Granger paced his room, just as he had paced ever since Smythesdon had fallen. It seemed laughable now that he had worried so much over his mother's schemes. That was nothing compared to what had actually happened. The man could have died!

Worse, Marigold was right and his poor judgment had been there for all to see. Even Smythesdon knew it. He had hoped they could laugh off the accident and blame it on the saddle or some such mistake. That they might go on speaking as if riding The Turk was still a possibility. But Smythesdon had pronounced them both idiots.

What would Oxford say? He was very much afraid that they would not both be pronounced idiots. It would be Henry Granger, and Granger alone, who would be found to be the idiot. He had been so caught up in showing Smythesdon the impressive horseflesh to be found in Chemsworth's stables that by the time he realized where the situation was going it had been too late to stop it.

He supposed the only bright spot was that Lord Ainsworth did not seem to think that a pair of young gentlemen conducting themselves as idiots was anything out of the ordinary. He would be tempted to blame his mother for all of it when he went back to Oxford, except he could imagine the ridicule of a gentleman blaming his mother for anything. And the ire of Lady Mulholland should she hear of it.

He supposed it was a shame, after all, that his mother's plan had not worked. If Smythesdon *had* wished to marry Violet, he could not very well go round blaming Henry for his broken leg. Romance and blame, he was sure, could not coexist together.

The only circumstance that kept him from falling into despair was that the Ravencrafts, after years of not calling, had suddenly decided to call on Lady Mulholland. Miss Ravencraft was everything wonderful. She was pretty in that delicate way he found so lovely. Her manner was refined. Smythesdon had clearly approved of the lady. He could not understand what his sisters held against Miss Ravencraft. Her mother, to be sure, was a frightful gossip. But was that to doom Miss Ravencraft in anybody's estimation? He could not think that fair.

Henry walked to the window and stared out into the night. He imagined Miss Ravencraft sitting in front of the fire at Holby House, working on her sewing. He had no direct knowledge of how she spent her time, but he always did imagine it was filled with the feminine arts and bashful conversations. It was very pleasant to think of.

Violet had tossed and turned through the night, robbed of her usual sound sleep. She had risen and dressed early and descended the stairs.

The evening before, she had not dared to enquire why Lord Smythesdon had not been to dinner. She did not know if it were some previously designed plan or whether he had become overtired at his first outing from his bedchamber. She did not dare ask about it as she knew that any small inquiry from her would be pounced upon by Lady Mulholland. And, apparently, Lady Ainsworth too.

Her wondering was soon at an end, though. Doctor Megthorn was just coming down the stairs from seeing his patient and they met in the hall.

"Ah, Miss Granger," Doctor Megthorn said. "I did not see Lady Mulholland upon my arrival and I must be off—Farmer

Kendrick's rheumatism is flaring and he writes that if he does not see me today he shall set his dogs after me."

"Goodness," Violet said, "he sounds an irascible patient."

Doctor Megthorn shrugged. "The rheumatism will make anybody irascible. I wonder if you might inform Lady Mulholland that our plan appears to be working nicely. There was no harm done in the excursion to the drawing room yesterday and so we might continue to lengthen the trips downstairs. Having a care, naturally, that Lord Smythesdon does not become overtired. We should not like to have a setback."

Violet nodded. "And so you think he might dine downstairs this evening?"

"No, no," Doctor Megthorn said. "That would be entirely too much too soon. He was down for one hour yesterday, he may be down one hour and a half today and so on."

Violet had taken the message to her mother, and somehow felt embarrassed at it. The way her mother looked at her, it was as if Violet had been staking out the hall to get news of Lord Smythesdon from the doctor, when she had done no such thing.

She had closeted herself in the library for the rest of the day, though she could not claim she had learned anything by it. Finally, she had given up and went to her room, determined to spend a half hour quietly before it was time to go down for tea. Lord Smythesdon would be brought to the drawing room and Lord and Lady Ainsworth would be there. She was certain she would be stared at again by her mother and Lady Ainsworth and she knew not who else. She could not understand those unfortunate individuals who took to the stage. How could those theater people bear to have so many eyes upon them night after night?

Victorine came in and fussed about in a general air of unhappiness. The lady's maid did not care for tea dresses—she found them overly plain and, in the worst possible way, fastidieux. She sighed a long and exaggerated sigh as she examined a simple white dress.

She had laid Violet's things on the bed and was ready to help her change when the door burst open.

Poppy and Pansy rushed in as if their hair was on fire. "Violet," Poppy breathed, "we do not have much time as Miss Millthorpe is looking for us even now."

"Heavens girls," Violet scolded, "You promised you would do no more running off."

"It was an emergency, Violet," Pansy said. "We take our responsibility of guarding the house very seriously and we will not give up our sentry duties."

"We will not," Poppy said, "even if it means we must starve on account of it. You will be very happy that we did not on this day because who do you suppose is on their way to our door?"

"A dragon?" Pansy asked, snorting.

"Almost," Poppy said, erupting in peals of laughter. "It is Mrs. Ravencraft!"

"Mrs. Ravencraft," Poppy and Pansy shouted, jumping up and down with the delightful mirth of it.

"Mrs. Ravencraft?" Violet said in disbelief.

"Truly," Poppy said. "We know her carriage, she has that silly yellow flag atop it. You know, the flag she won at the flower show for her dear roses? We watched until she had positively turned onto our land."

"She will be here in a quarter of an hour," Pansy said.

Violet frowned, her suspicion writ on her expression. "I see," she said. "I do wonder though, how your eyes have sharpened to that of a hawk's to be able to see clearly the details of a carriage at the turn off, yellow flag or no. It is a mile away."

Poppy looked at Pansy, Pansy shrugged. "If you must know, Violet, and you must keep this to yourself, Henry gave us a spyglass when he came home," Poppy said. "It is one of the treasures of the Inviolate Kingdom."

"*Henry* understands the vital importance of guarding the house," Pansy said, as if no other inhabitant of it could be trusted to understand it.

Miss Millthorpe appeared in the doorway. She was a thin and pinched-looking lady and had a harried look about her. Violet did not wonder why. Chasing Poppy and Pansy day after day must exhaust anybody. It had occurred to her that caring for twins was not just caring for two, it was as if the sum were greater than its parts and poor Miss Millthorpe was charged with keeping a battalion in order.

"Miss Millthorpe," Violet said, "here are your two very naughty children."

Glancing at Poppy and Pansy, and seeing their defeated gazes, Violet softened her tone. "Of course," she said, "they have just brought me news of a visitor and I am certain Lady Mulholland will be gratified to have warning of it so I do not suppose they should go without dinner."

Miss Millthorpe, not finding herself able to hold up against the idea of Lady Mulholland being gratified, relaxed her features. "Very well," she said. She leaned down over Poppy and Pansy and said, "Ladies? We return to the nursery. Now, march."

The girls dutifully filed out of Violet's room, unwilling captives of Miss Millthorpe once more.

"Help me dress quickly, Victorine," Violet said. "I believe my mother would wish to know that the Huns are nearly at our door."

"Elle est une upstart," Victorine said dismissively.

Lady Mulholland's sitting room was a study in cream and white silks and brocades. Velvet curtains in the darkest blue contrasted with the light décor. Dandy lay on a sofa, nearly camouflaged as his fur and the white velvet were indistinguishable—only two black eyes with little red rims gave him away.

Lady Mulholland was at her desk writing letters. She kept up a constant correspondence with ladies all across England. This had the happy result of allowing her to know what went on everywhere, despite never choosing to go anywhere. Violet presumed this was how her mother knew that young ladies from all over the countryside were just now fainting in London.

She scattered sand across the fresh ink and turned as Violet burst in.

Without ado, Violet said, "Poppy and Pansy have spotted the Ravencrafts. They have turned upon our land."

Lady Mulholland appeared a queen having just been informed that an enemy army had crossed a border and invaded her country. "They cannot dare to call upon us again," she said. "Not under the present circumstances."

"I rather think they do dare," Violet said.

"She is as bold as a magpie," Lady Mulholland said softly, "and collects just as much gossip into her nest. She would knock down our doors to get a look at Lord and Lady Ainsworth and thrust her daughter in front of them."

Violet was rather amused by this dignified diatribe. "You could always direct Smuckers to say that you are not at home."

Lady Mulholland considered this strategy for a moment. Then she said, "Unfortunately I cannot. Your father absolutely forbids it. He puts his foot down on so few matters that I do not like to cross him on it. If he suddenly feels as if he has got to fight for every point, I shall find him looking into how much I spend on furnishings or how many dresses you girls own. Best not to rock the boat lest you sink it. The real question in this particular matter is not whether they are allowed in, but what they are served once in."

"What can you mean?" Violet asked. "Surely Mr. Moreau can accommodate two more persons. It is only tea."

"It is not the quantity," Lady Mulholland said. "It is the type."

"Oh," Violet said, remembering the ridiculous display that had been put out for the Ravencraft's last visit. Mrs. Ravencraft's eyes missed nothing and she would surely wonder, aloud and loudly, why the tea had been reduced to normal proportions when there was an Earl and Countess in the house.

"Why do not you carry on with the usual tea," Violet said. "I am sure Mr. Moreau will send up savarins. Then, all you need do is comment upon how much your visitors prefer savarins above anything else. That would account for the change."

"Indeed," Lady Mulholland said, appearing pleased. "Very clever, Violet. You shall make a fine lady of the house someday."

Violet narrowed her eyes at her mother. "Someday," she answered back.

Fleur had come in. She smiled at her lady and pretended she did not even see Violet. As far as Fleur was concerned, only three things existed in the world—herself, Lady Mulholland and France.

"Fleur," Lady Mulholland said. "I will wear my best today. My finest afternoon dress and my best jewels. We have enemies approaching and I plan to defeat them with an imposing figure."

Fleur nodded and said, "Satin vert and the èmeraudes. Très imposant."

Lady Mulholland nodded. "I knew you should know what to do. Now Violet, since you are dressed, do be a dear and go down and alert Smuckers that the neighbors are determined to inconvenience us once more."

Violet found Smuckers lurking in the hall. While she had no wish to meet with the Ravencrafts so soon again, she was rather delighted at the outrage the butler displayed upon hearing the news. One would have thought, upon considering his facial expressions and exclamations of horror, that papists were rushing in to convert them all to Rome.

He had been somewhat mollified on being informed of two important points: Mr. Moreau need not change his plan for tea, and Lady Mulholland was just now donning her emeralds. He stalked off with dignity to alert the downstairs to the unwelcome visitors.

Violet thought she ought to go to the drawing room and see that the fire had been suitably built up. Nobody was expected down for another quarter hour and she knew she had left an interesting book lying on a table—she could sit and compose herself for the tedious visit to come.

Much to her surprise, she found Lord Smythesdon seated in front of the fire. The footmen had brought him down before she descended.

Lord Smythesdon seemed equally surprised to see her upon turning his head at her entrance.

She took a deep breath. "My lord," she said, "how do you do this afternoon?"

"Very well," he said. Then he looked at his leg, sticking straight out and bandaged, and laughed. "Perhaps not *very* well, but well enough."

Violet felt awkward standing there in front of Lord Smythesdon and sat herself down on the sofa across from his chair.

"I have given some thought to our conversation on Culpeper," Lord Smythesdon said.

"As have I," Violet answered.

"I wonder if the fellow even believed what he said," Lord Smythesdon said. "After all, the effect of a sugar pill on a suggestable individual is well known. Any number of people suffering from vague complaints that reside solely in their mind have been relieved by such."

"And the person dosing must display all confidence in the remedy for it to have a chance at being effective."

"Yes, and so perhaps Culpeper added these allusions to astrology to imbue the treating individual with the confidence that the medicine would be effective."

"Thereby, imbuing the patient with the same idea," Violet said.

"He may very well have thought, this is utter nonsense, but as they believe it, I will pretend that I do too."

"And belief is no small thing," Violet said. "What else could account for a spontaneous healing of a condition thought to be fatal? We have all witnessed such miracles."

"Ah, the vicar will claim it is God's work, but the vicar cannot explain how God chose to save the petulant old woman and take the innocent babe."

"I have long held that our God is a God of systems within nature, not perching upon a cloud and capriciously selecting individuals for good fortune or ruin," Violet said, scarcely believing she dared voice an opinion she had long ago settled upon, but which was perhaps best left unspoken in society.

"Naturally," Lord Smythesdon said. "I cannot believe in a wrathful God, and what else is a God who takes a beloved child from loving parents? In any case, capriciousness is the purview of man, not God, and so therefore there must be systems and logic. That the clergy do not yet understand these systems does not make them invalid."

They were interrupted in this lively discussion by Smuckers announcing Mrs. Ravencraft and Miss Ravencraft.

Violet sighed and rose. "Mrs. Ravencraft, Miss Ravencraft," she said, with a slight dip into a curtsy. "How good of you to call. My mother and sisters have not yet come down, but please do make yourself at home. Tea will be in shortly."

Mrs. Ravencraft was all bustle, "My lord," she exclaimed. "What in heavens name happened to you?"

Lord Smythesdon seemed amused by this inquiry and said, "What sort of neighborhood is this! All news is not known by everybody in a moment? In my own neighborhood, if a goose lays an egg we will all know it before the goose knows it."

Miss Ravencraft blushed. Violet thought she blushed so often that her cheeks would have an easier time of it if they just stayed blushed instead of having to go back and forth so frequently. "We did hear there had been some sort of riding accident," she said as softly as ever.

"Exactly so," Lord Smythesdon said. "It was a riding accident and I suppose no more need be said about it."

Violet approved of Lord Smythesdon's unwillingness to repeat the details of the accident. She guessed that many young gentlemen would be pleased to recount every last horrid detail and showcase their bravery throughout the ordeal. She only wished Marigold had the good fortune to witness his response to Mrs. Ravencraft's attempt at gathering gossip.

"As we did hear that you were indisposed, my lord," Miss Ravencraft said, "I took the liberty of bringing you a book that might idle away some hours."

"Did you?" Lord Smythesdon said. "Very thoughtful indeed."

Violet found herself very much against Miss Ravencraft's thoughtfulness. Perhaps she was most annoyed that she had a whole library of books and had not thought of it herself.

"Ah, I see," Lord Smythesdon said, taking the book. As he opened its pages, Miss Ravencraft sat beside him to show him various interesting points. Violet could not overhear much of what they said, as Mrs. Ravencraft appeared determined to keep her attention. The lady had leaned over confidentially and said, "Of course, we *did* hear bits and pieces. It is said that the poor lord was put on that awful Turk."

Violet did not answer, unwilling to give Mrs. Ravencraft any information she might trot around the neighborhood.

"It is said that the leg was badly broken, but that Doctor Megthorn thinks it shall be a full recovery."

"Doctor Megthorn must know best," Violet said.

"It is further said that the Earl and his Countess have come to assure themselves of his health. Of course, that is very good of them, but only to be expected from such as Lord and Lady Ainsworth."

Violet eyed Mrs. Ravencraft coolly. It irked her no end that this woman would be so free with whatever she had heard and determined to wring even more from her. As her mother had noted, she was a magpie collecting gossip. "You appear familiar with Lord and Lady Ainsworth," she said. "Are you, indeed, acquainted?"

Violet watched with interest to see how Mrs. Ravencraft would respond to that particular inquiry.

Mrs. Ravencraft blanched. "I have not had the honor," she said.

Lady Mulholland glided into the room, trailed by Rose, Daisy and Marigold. Her mother had indeed gone to great lengths to ensure she was an imposing figure. In the firelight of the waning afternoon, the green satin dress shimmered and the emeralds sparkled. She was all elegance to Mrs. Ravencraft's busy assortment of ribbons and bits and bobs.

Rose stared at Miss Ravencraft as if she was on the verge of pronouncing her horrible for stepping through their doors. Daisy was, as always, vastly amused at the absurdity of it all. Marigold barely acknowledge the visitors and stood staring at the door, willing the tea tray to come in.

"Mrs. Ravencraft," Lady Mulholland said smoothly, "how delightful for you to call again. So soon. It seems only yesterday when we saw you last and we have not yet had a moment to even return the call."

Mrs. Ravencraft had the good sense to blush, but Violet supposed that would not turn her away from her purpose. The lady was bound to lock herself in their drawing room for as long as necessary to be introduced to Lord and Lady Ainsworth and her mother could stare at the clock and drop hints as much as she liked to no effect.

Smuckers brought in the tea and his footmen came in behind him with trays of savarins, savory tarts and biscuits. Mrs. Ravencraft eyed the trays and Lady Mulholland said, "Dear Lord Ainsworth cannot abide anything but savarins at this time of day."

Mrs. Ravencraft seemed to consider this preference for savarins as a view held by the nobility that had somehow eluded her notice, but had best be imitated. She said, "Naturally. What else but savarins will do at this time in the afternoon? I know I cannot abide anything else."

Lord and Lady Ainsworth entered the drawing room. They were introduced to Mrs. Ravencraft, who curtsied so low that Violet wondered if she would touch the carpet with her forehead, and Miss Ravencraft who very prettily curtsied and blushed furiously.

Lord Ainsworth sat in front of the fire next to an empty chair that was no doubt meant for the Viscount. The two men had spent the day with Mr. Tidewater, touring the estate, and had much to discuss. Lady Ainsworth and Lady Mulholland retired to a corner of the room and spoke in soft tones. Violet could not hear what they said, but from their glances she surmised that neither were pleased that Miss Ravencraft had seated herself beside Lord Smythesdon. She presumed her mother was telling the lady all about the Ravencrafts, and none of it flattering.

Rose and Daisy looked through music at the pianoforte, while Violet found herself left next to Mrs. Ravencraft and Marigold. Marigold was attacking her heaping plate when Mrs. Ravencraft attempted to use her wiles once more.

"They are saying the lord was upon the Turk and *that* is what caused his accident," she said to Marigold.

Violet glanced toward the ceiling, fairly certain what was to come next.

Chapter Sixteen

Marigold slowly deposited a half of an uneaten tart on her plate. She stared at Mrs. Ravencraft as if that lady had grown two heads. "The Turk," she said coldly, "was not at fault in Lord Smythesdon's accident."

"Oh," Mrs. Ravencraft said, "they did say it was The Turk. I suppose they were mistaken."

"*They*," Marigold said. "I often wonder who *they* are. I also often wonder that I do not find you spying around the stables attempting to squeeze information from the grooms, as we all know perfectly well that *they* is you."

"Marigold!" Violet scolded.

Marigold shrugged. "I only speak the truth, Violet. I shall see you at dinner. I have a mind to go and check on The Turk. He is a fine specimen of a horse and has the further recommendation of being pleasant company."

Marigold stomped out of the room, carrying her plate with her. Violet peeked at her mother to see if she had noted the outburst, but Lady Mulholland was far too engrossed in watching Miss Ravencraft ply her pretty wares.

"Your dear sister is quite outspoken," Mrs. Ravencraft said, smoothing out her skirt.

"She is, indeed," Violet answered. She knew very well that she ought to apologize for Marigold, but she was too disinclined to make the attempt.

Henry came into the drawing room and scanned it like a hawk over a field. He was, perhaps, the only person present who was unequivocally delighted to see the Ravencrafts. He nodded and bowed his way over to Miss Ravencraft.

Violet watched him. She knew he did not hold the same views on Miss Ravencraft that his sisters held. However, she had never thought much about it. Now she began to wonder if his interest was not more pronounced than she had thought. Lord Smythesdon and her brother were once again vying to be the most amusing, the most cordial and the most considerate. From what she could hear from across the room, Miss Ravencraft was to be celebrated on her choice of book as if it were some very great feat. It was tedious. Entirely tedious.

"My daughter makes such a pretty picture, does she not?" Mrs. Ravencraft said.

Violet was desperate to avoid giving up such a point, but there was no suitable response but, "Yes, indeed."

"She was born to be at a gentleman's hearth, keeping his house with all good cheer. She shall be a fine wife."

Violet could not bear to play along with this insipid conversation. "Do you hint that she is engaged, Mrs. Ravencraft?"

"Dear me, no," Mrs. Ravencraft said hurriedly. Then she gazed at the two gentlemen hanging on her daughter's every utterance and said, "Though I would not be at all surprised to find my husband approached sometime soon."

Violet followed her gaze. Did she mean Henry? Did she mean Lord Smythesdon? The woman was intolerable. Either choice would be intolerable. Married to her own brother? To Henry? Or perhaps Mrs. Ravencraft took aim higher than Henry. Perhaps Lord Smythesdon would be her quarry. Both ridiculous. Both impossible.

Violet paused. Why should she care if it were Lord Smythesdon in the lady's sights? Of course, she knew that Miss Ravencraft was too silly for such a learned man, but it was no concern of her own whether the lord made a good match. Certainly, he must be the judge of that. And, if he did not make a good match, what matter to her?

"I said to Mr. Ravencraft," Mrs. Ravencraft continued on, "she's in possession of remarkable looks and they cannot long go unnoticed. Her temperament is the sweetest in the county. Do not feign shock if some eminently eligible gentleman comes knocking on the door."

Violet thought the said gentleman would do well to knock hard on the door to be heard over Mrs. Ravencraft's never-ending chatter. She thought she should also congratulate herself on her restraint, as she did not say so aloud.

"Miss Granger," Lord Smythesdon called. "I would show you this remarkable book if you can be tempted to leave Mrs. Ravencraft's side."

Mrs. Ravencraft pursed her lips and Violet found she could be very tempted to leave the lady behind. She rose and eagerly joined the party in front of the fire. The only blot on this happy circumstance was noting that her mother and Lady Ainsworth seemed entirely delighted with the request and watched her intently.

"Miss Ravencraft has been kind enough to give me a book and what do you suppose it is?" Lord Smythesdon said with enthusiasm. Before Violet could make a guess, he said, "It is by a local scholar and it elaborates on flora to be found in the county and their medicinal purposes."

"It has ever so many pretty drawings," Miss Ravencraft said.

"And does this local scholar make reference to astrology as Culpeper does?" Violet asked.

"He does not," Lord Smythesdon answered. "He entirely dismisses the notion in the introduction."

"Then we must admire his good sense," Violet said.

"One must always admire rationality," Lord Smythesdon agreed.

Seeing that Miss Ravencraft appeared confused, Lord Smythesdon went on to explain the various points that he and Violet Granger had settled between them as pertained to the medical use of plants, the nonsense of astrology and the efficacy of sugar pills.

Miss Ravencraft attempted to follow this rush of ideas she had never heard of. Finally, she said softly. "Oh my. I suppose I must be a simpleton for only admiring the drawings."

"Not at all," Henry said fiercely. "It takes a fine eye, a fine understanding, to appreciate the art of it."

"Indeed, Miss Ravencraft," Lord Smythesdon said. "the whole world cannot be only knowledge, there must be beauty, too."

Miss Ravencraft whipped open her fan and prettily fanned herself, as if her appreciation of the drawings had overwhelmed her.

Violet suppressed a sigh.

Lady Mulholland had risen and approached Mrs. Ravencraft. Loudly, she said, "Clouds are rolling in, Mrs. Ravencraft. We are to have an early sunset and I shouldn't like you to be caught on the roads in a dim twilight. There is icing, I hear."

Once being apprised of danger on the roads, Henry and Lord Smythesdon were in a competition to see who could most violently urge the ladies to avoid putting themselves in any danger. The Ravencrafts, facing this onslaught of concern, could have no excuse for delaying taking their leave. Violet had a great urge to throw open the front doors to hurry them on their way. But then, her mother had already done the job.

Violet had thought she might continue her conversation with Lord Smythesdon without the overly delicate interruptions of Miss Ravencraft, but Jimmy and Johnny had no sooner put the Ravencrafts in their carriage than they had come to wheel him out.

Smythesdon was placed back in bed by Jimmy and Johnny. He had not, until his unfortunate accident, had many in-depth conversations with footmen. However, these two lads had been with him from the first. They had carried him up on that terrible day, they had been in and out of his room at all hours ever since—carrying messages, bringing him anything he requested, keeping the fire up, opening and closing the curtains, and generally breaking up the silence of the sickroom. His valet had been sent to Donneville with Lady Mulholland's letter to ease the shock of the news of the accident. Upon arrival, he had been noted to have a cold and Lady Ainsworth had forbid him to return until he was clear of it. Smythesdon had remained in the care of the footmen and they had all grown very comfortable together. He was continually fascinated by their unique thoughts on a variety of subjects.

Smythesdon had discovered that footmen knew everything that went on in a house. It almost appeared as if they knew everybody's *thoughts* in the house. He had already learned a great deal of what occurred below stairs. Smuckers was their general, ready to defend the house at all costs. Fleur hated anybody who was not French with the exception of Lady Mulholland. Victorine's beauty was unparalleled but she looked down upon them as lowly creatures. Mrs. Featherstone was a depressing sort. Mr. Moreau had moods that were either high flying or low flying and Peggy was bold as anything no matter how many times she was smacked with a dishtowel. It tickled him to wonder what sort of adventures occurred in his own servant's hall. It alarmed him to think that all his dodging of his father before he had come away had been duly noted by his own footmen. Judgments and opinions had been formed. Matters had been discussed.

Johnny was adjusting his blanket and Jimmy was stirring the fire when Smythesdon said, "Miss Ravencraft looked well."

Jimmy paused, poker in hand, and said, "Well enough for her sort, anyway."

Smythesdon had no idea what her sort was, but was interested to discover what conclusion Jimmy had come to. "What sort is that, Jimmy?"

Jimmy rubbed his chin and Smythesdon was delighted to understand that he was on the verge of hearing a considered opinion. An opinion that Jimmy had given much thought to.

"It's like this, my lord," Jimmy said. "There's them, like the Miss Grangers, that appears to be born with nobility runnin' in their veins. They have a certain air about them. A confidence, like. And then there's them like Miss Ravencraft who tiptoe around, never sure if they are in the right place. Like somebody left the door open and they just wandered in. They are neither here nor there and it affects my feelins' something awful."

Smythesdon had not expected Jimmy's feelings to be involved.

Johnny tucked Smythesdon's blanket under his arms and said, "What Jimmy's tryin' to communicate, my lord, is that everybody oughta know where they fit. They aren't to go around leapin' into other places. Jimmy, there, is first footman, you see. Now how is it goin' to be if Oscar, the lowliest and shortest footman in the house, starts tellin' people he oughta be first? It don't make no sense. There ain't no logic in it."

"And you think that is what Miss Ravencraft does?" Smythesdon asked. "I had thought her rather charming."

"Oh, she's nice enough," Jimmy said. "We don't blame her one bit, it's her mama that's attemptin' all the leapin' around. But for all that, Miss Ravencraft don't got the spirit of the likes of a Miss Granger. She weren't born to it, you see. Just like Oscar weren't born to be first footman. T'would be unnatural."

"But the Miss Grangers are born to it, you think? What qualities, other than breeding, would you assign to such?" Smythesdon asked, certain he was about to hear some very original opinions.

Jimmy began to pace the room as if he were delivering a lecture at Oxford. "My lord, it ain't somethin' you can put your finger right on. It's the spirit of the thing. Now, you have a look at all the Miss Grangers, you ain't gonna find more different sisters anywhere. Miss Violet Granger is a fearful academic. Miss Rose Granger has the heart of a warrior. Miss Daisy Granger is all sunshine. Miss Marigold Granger would live in the stables if she could. Miss Lily Granger is like a fairy, flittin' around all delicate-like. Miss Pansy and Poppy Granger, well, we can't know just yet what they will be like as they're still devlopin' into their personalities. All different, but for all that, all the same. They all got that quality about them. If you was to see them on the street, you would know they belong to a house such as this without bein' told it."

"As the Miss Grangers *are* all so different," Lord Smythesdon said, delighted with Jimmy's thoughts on the matter, "which of the various personalities do you most admire?"

This set off much shuffling around the room. Jimmy mercilessly stabbed at the fire. Johnny threw open the curtains and then, realizing it was night, threw them closed again. Jimmy poured him an oversized glass of port and set it dripping on the night table. Johnny brushed his clothes with such a ferocity that Smythesdon began to fear he might put holes in the coat.

Amidst red faces, Jimmy mumbled, "We are all much admirin' of Miss Daisy Granger, my lord. We are of one mind when it comes to that."

Having revealed their preference, the footmen hurriedly left the room. Smythesdon leaned back on his pillows. It was so very highly interesting to know that the footmen, down to a man, were half in love with Daisy Granger. She was comely enough, but she was no Violet Granger. She had not the cool and sophisticated countenance of Violet Granger. Perhaps a footman could not appreciate the likes of Miss Violet Granger. It would be a simpler matter for them to admire the always laughing Miss Daisy Granger.

And then there was the matter of Miss Ravencraft. She was the sort of lady he had been used to seeing in London. He began to get an uncomfortable feeling that the reason he had found her company so pleasant was because she showed so much deference and mildness. This, somehow, made him feel more than he was. More important. More intelligent. More worldly. Where Miss Violet Granger made him feel as if he were struggling to keep his head above water and might well drown over his next sentence.

On the other hand, his conversations with Miss Granger on Culpeper had been something altogether different. He had felt they were two equal minds. Equally matched. Exchanging ideas rapid-fire, the time flying before them. It had been very like a debate in the *Queen's Lane*.

And then, there really was nobody prettier than Violet Granger. Miss Ravencraft was pretty in her own way, a delicate and small sort of person. Many would find that appealing, and yet he could not. It was Miss Granger's regal looks that were compelling.

Smythesdon suddenly propped himself up on his elbows.

Good Lord. Was he falling in love with Violet Granger?

No. It could not be. He had come to the house with the express purpose of escaping such a fate. It must only be his weakened state, the footmen's opinions and the Viscount's good port that muddled his mind.

Violet had not, as was her usual habit, invited her sisters into her room nor asked Smuckers to send tea up the back stairs. The dinner had been weary, with Lady Ainsworth quizzing her on all sorts of subjects as if she were interviewing for a position in her household. Which, Violet supposed, Lady Ainsworth assumed she was.

Violet had thought she should be grateful that Lord Smythesdon had been carried up so early in the evening. She had at least avoided all the staring from her own mother and his. Yet, she found her thoughts continually going back to the scene in the drawing room. Little Miss Ravencraft bringing him a book. Miss Ravencraft feeling sorry that she only admired the pictures and Lord Smythesdon and Henry leaping to her defense. In fact, had not Lord Smythesdon even made reference to beauty? Had he not said that knowledge was all well and good, but the world required beauty as well?

Violet sat at her dressing table, having sent Victorine on her way to Rose. A lone candle burned next to her and she examined her reflection. Was she as pretty as Miss Ravencraft? She had not the delicacy of feature. She was not dainty like Miss Ravencraft. It had not, until this moment, occurred to her to wonder what gentlemen liked. Her mother had always fussed over her looks and pronounced them wonderful, but then her mother had done the same with all of her daughters. Lady Mulholland could not judge it properly—she could not help but think highly of her own children.

No matter. It did not signify to her that Miss Ravencraft was to be admired. Lord Smythesdon might go about admiring any person he liked and she shouldn't mind it. Though she would admit that he had become ever so much more pleasant since he had nearly lost his life on The Turk.

And their conversations about Culpeper! Those had been a real pleasure. She supposed that when she did decide to marry, those conversations could be used as a measuring stick. Did the gentleman she considered engage her in such lively debates? For if he could not, she did not see how she would agree to go hand in hand forevermore with such an individual.

But as Daisy had pointed out, she sought an intellect and how many could there be?

She supposed she must give up on the idea that she would find someone as learned as Lord Smythesdon. If she did find such a person, she could not hope for his sort of looks. It would be too unusual to find both in one person. She had best resign herself to a homely sort of person, as she had so thoroughly decided that intelligence must take precedent.

Violet blew out the candle and crawled into bed. She stared at the ceiling, her face flushed with the memory of him calling her over in the drawing room. He was determined that she should see the book and comment upon it. As if her thoughts were of some importance to him. Then, there had been an ease between them, they had so easily dropped into the Culpeper discussion as if they had never left it off. She could see, in her mind's eye, his face upturned toward hers, his sly smile as he announced the dismissal of Culpeper's astrology in the introduction to the new book.

Violet suddenly sat up, propping herself on her elbows.

Good Lord. Was she falling in love with Lord Smythesdon?

No. Certainly not. And even if she were, which she was not, she would never own to it. She could not bear to cause the satisfaction of Lady Mulholland and Lady Ainsworth. She could not countenance being forced into anything. She would not be managed.

Chapter Seventeen

The butler's closet glowed a cheerful orange from the fire in the grate. "It is all a muddle, Mrs. Featherstone," Smuckers said, sipping his sherry. "Those Ravencrafts are creating quite the muddle."

Mrs. Featherstone had long ago downed her glass of sherry and looked determinedly at the bottle until Smuckers noticed and refilled her glass. Taking a satisfying gulp, she said, "What's the muddle then?"

"It had begun to appear as if there was some warming of temperatures between Miss Violet and the lord, but then Mrs. Ravencraft comes in as cool as you like with her daughter. That daughter brings the lord a book, which he appears to appreciate very much."

"And so the book is causing the muddle?" Mrs. Featherstone asked. Not being a great reader herself, the lady was uncertain as to what sort of trouble that particular article could be capable of getting up to.

"No, it is not the book on its own. It is the type of lady that Miss Ravencraft is. She is all gratifying mildness and the gentleman make so much of it. Why should they not recognize the natural superiority of Miss Granger? I cannot understand it at all."

Mrs. Featherstone, always preferring to see the other side of a question, said, "Perhaps the lord *does* see the superiority of Miss Granger but he don't like to admit it is as such."

195

Smuckers mulled over this opinion. He brightened and said, "Mrs. Featherstone, I believe you may be on to something. It would account for my inability to pinpoint where they stand on the matter. One moment they are talking so animatedly that one would think they were courting, and the next they are not."

"Well," Mrs. Featherstone said, wiggling her feet in front of the fire, "there's naught you can do about the thing."

Smuckers had set down his glass, even though he knew it would leave the contents of the glass in some danger of being confiscated by his worthy housekeeper. "Is that quite true, Mrs. Featherstone? Might I not be able to do something? All along I have looked at this matter as a general would look upon his maps to devise a winning campaign. You see, I have gone about the thing all wrong!"

"I always did say there was no use you treatin' us all like an army. We ain't never going to war with nobody, 'cept maybe the Ravencrafts."

"What I should have done," Smuckers went on, "was approached this as a diplomatic mission. I should have acted as Pope Leo I at his meeting with Attila the Hun on the shores of Lake Garda. It was that very diplomacy that saved Rome from being sacked. And, as Rome was saved, so too can Lady Mulholland's plans."

Mrs. Featherstone, not being a student of history and not particularly caring what happened to Rome today or yesterday, appeared unmoved.

"I shall begin such diplomacy on the morrow," Smuckers said.

"As long as it don't mean we're attemptin' to raise our standards again, I suppose there ain't no harm in it," Mrs. Featherstone said. "Though it strikes me that disaster is sprintin' round the corner. I can feel it in my very bones."

Smuckers heaved a sigh. He supposed he should be grateful that, while Mrs. Featherstone's disasters were always poised to run round the corner, they rarely managed to actually *get* around the corner.

Smuckers had been in the great hall earlier than was his habit. He knew Doctor Megthorn arrived before breakfast so that he might check on his patient before setting off on his rounds. The hall had been quiet and still, except for the brief explosion of Miss Marigold thundering down the stairs and out the door to leap upon Mercury and go off for her early morning gallop.

It had not been long before he heard the sound of carriage wheels on the drive. He had fully expected to see Doctor Megthorn, but instead it had been the intrepid Mrs. Dallway. The lady was a staunch friend of the house and Smuckers had a great admiration for her, though that admiration was very slightly dosed with anxiety. The lady was formidable and one could never be certain what she might say at any given moment.

He had thrown open the door and before he could say a word, the lady had descended from her carriage and was charging up the steps two at a time. She was a small and highly active woman and was currently nearly lost in a large fur coat and oversized hat.

"Well, Smuckers?" she said. "Your lady's letter finally reached me in London and I have come straight here. Is he alive?"

"Yes, Mrs. Dallway. The lord lives and is primed to make a full recovery."

"Very good. And what goes on with Lady Mulholland's plans for the gentleman? Oh, do not be shy with me, Smuckers! You are all-seeing in this house, that I know. I demand to be told where we are with the romance."

Smuckers conceded to himself that it really was impossible, even for an old hand such as himself, to keep anything from Mrs. Dallway. "I cannot be sure," he said. "In the beginning, it appeared grim, but there have been moments when it has seemed more hopeful. Strangely, the lord's accident appears to have assisted. But it is a very tenuous matter, Mrs. Dallway. I was planning to attempt some diplomatic strategy on the case."

"Ah hah! The lord falls from his horse and gets the idea that he's not as high and mighty as he thought. Is that it? Of course, it is. It always does take some sort of shock to jolt a young gentleman from callow youth to somewhat less annoying callowness, thereby setting him off on the great journey to manhood. He cannot be blamed, it is the nature of things."

Though Smuckers was certain he had never been callow in his life, he decided not to argue the point. "I was just now thinking, Mrs. Dallway," Smuckers said, "that I might suggest to Doctor Megthorn that the lord be carried down to the library for an hour each morning. It might prove efficacious to Lady Mulholland's plans."

Mrs. Dallway rubbed her hands together. "The library. Of course, the library. For where else is Violet Granger to be found at all hours of the day? You are a sly one, Smuckers."

Smuckers unconsciously clutched at his heart. "I hope I can never be described as sly, Mrs. Dallway! Sly is a pickpocket, not a butler."

Mrs. Dallway, always amused by Chemworth's butler, said, "There now, I think you know my meaning. Let's call it deep, then. You are a deep one, Smuckers. If it would not crush Lady Mulholland, I'd steal you for my own. Carry on with your plans, my good man, and we shall see where we go. Now," she said, handing over her heavy fur and her hat, "I shall show myself up. I am certain Lady Mulholland is still abed but she shan't mind. We shall have a cozy early morning tea and I shall do my best to pretend that I have not noticed that devil dog of hers is coating my dress with his shedding. I always leave this house wearing more dog fur than the actual dog."

Smuckers nodded in sympathy in regards to Dandy's white hairs, which were indeed diabolical. Mrs. Dallway sped into the house with her usual energetic dash and disappeared up the stairs.

He had a pleasant half hour awaiting Doctor Megthorn's arrival, as it gave him ample time to reflect upon the knowledge that there was yet another person who would wish to steal him away to their own household. He could see now that all his efforts over the years had not been in vain. Those efforts had been noted all along and he had been sought after. He was sought. There could be no warmer a compliment than to be sought. He wondered how many other households had, unbeknownst to him, dreams of capturing Smuckers for their own. He wondered if there had been conversations regarding his skill. One lady might say to another, "It could be accomplished, but only if you had a Smuckers." Or perhaps, "All the credit cannot go to Lady Mulholland. After all, she *does* have Smuckers." It was gratifying to think of.

Doctor Megthorn arrived and Smuckers used all his diplomacy to convince him that Lord Smythesdon must visit the library in the mornings. There were such facts laid out as it was the warmest room in the house, though it was not. That Smuckers, himself, should remain nearby to attend to the lord's every need, which was true. That the lord's absence from his bedchamber would give the maids time to wash it with the lye soap that Doctor Megthorn believed so efficacious, though Smuckers knew that to be hogwash. And finally, that the windows might be thrown open and the bedchamber aired as Doctor Megthorn advised, though Smuckers had no intention of opening a window and considered the idea akin to madness.

Doctor Megthorn was convinced the project might be attempted after broaching the idea to Lord Smythesdon and hearing his enthusiasm on the subject. This heartened Smuckers enormously, as he thought that enthusiasm was a feeling that could not be pretended at. Lord Smythesdon would know that Miss Granger would be found in the library and Lord Smythesdon was enthusiastic at the prospect.

Let the diplomacy begin.

Violet had made her way into the library, determined to accomplish something. The day before had been most unsatisfactory and she would not countenance more wasted hours. She had a mind to do further research into medical botany. She had, sometime ago, been inquiring into the properties of willow bark. A saline draught made from it was the most reliable treatment of fever, but she had noticed something else about the mixture. Those elders in the village who took it most regularly appeared to suffer less from illnesses of the heart. Was that a coincidence or was there a connection? Was the compound that reduced fevers the same that protected the heart, or was there some other ingredient at work? She wondered what Lord Smythesdon would say of it.

As she wondered what might be his opinion, she found herself vaguely uncomfortable. It felt difficult to sit still and she moved around the room, collecting every possible book that might reference saline draughts. Her thoughts of the evening before, when she was quite alone in her bedchamber, had disturbed her. Naturally, her feelings had softened toward Lord Smythesdon. His whole manner had changed and so it was only to be expected. She had briefly wondered if she was falling in love with him, and dismissed it as too ridiculous. That she should be falling in love with anybody was too ridiculous.

Yet, the remembrance of the drawing room and him calling her over as if her opinion was paramount had insisted on coming back and back and back to her like a fish swimming the banks of a pond—seeming to go forward, but always arriving at the same place.

The door was thrown open and Violet fully expected to see Smuckers poking his head in to inquire if she should like tea brought in. Instead, it was Jimmy wheeling Lord Smythesdon through the door.

"S'cuse me, Miss Granger," Jimmy said. "Doctor Megthorn ordered that the patient be brought down to the library for a time. A half hour he says."

Lord Smythesdon appeared slightly embarrassed over his abrupt arrival. "Only if it does not disturb," he said. "I do not wish to be a nuisance and could just as well be wheeled to a window somewhere to admire the view."

Smuckers stepped in and said, "I am afraid not, my lord. I have assured Doctor Megthorn that this is the warmest room and he seemed quite set on it."

Violet eyed Smuckers. Warmest room, indeed. Still, she found she could not be entirely unhappy with the arrangement.

"It is no disruption at all, Lord Smythesdon," she said. "As I was just beginning an inquiry into a particular herbal remedy, perhaps you will find you have some thoughts on the matter."

Lord Smythesdon appeared pleased, though Violet was not certain that anybody could be more pleased than Smuckers. He waved Jimmy ahead and the lord was wheeled in.

"I shall bring tea and biscuits," Smuckers said. "Such scholarly pursuits will require ample sustenance."

Violet nodded. She thought she had seen Jimmy wink at the lord as he made his exit. If she had, it was quite impertinent. But perhaps she had been mistaken, as the lord appeared to not have noticed.

"I am inquiring into willow bark, my lord," Violet said.

"Ah, a very old remedy against fever," he said.

Violet nodded. "But I have noticed, in treating local people, that there may be another effect."

Violet went on to tell Lord Smythesdon of her theory. Smuckers brought in the tea and nearly ran from the room, so anxious was he not to disturb their conference.

Lord Smythesdon said, "There is much to consider. Perhaps the improved effect on the heart is to do with the medicine, or perhaps it is to do with the people who take it."

Violet leaned forward. "How so, my lord?"

"These elderly people you describe take the medicine regularly for such things as rheumatism and old injuries. These sorts of people may not take the same exercise as others and therefore do not put the same strain on the heart. Perhaps that is where the improved result originates."

"I might admit that as a theory," Violet said. "were I unaware that gross inactivity leads to so many other health concerns. One must only note that gout is prevalent among the upper classes and not very often seen in the lower. One would therefore expect, if these individuals were indeed so very idle, that they would be struck with the gout as well. Even without the rich diet which is so often noted as the cause, they must develop it."

"Ah, I had not considered that."

"As well," Violet went on, "I know these men personally and they remain active because they must. A living must be had."

And so they went on, rolling various facts and ideas back and forth between them, until Smuckers had let a full three quarters of an hour pass and was forced to come in and wheel Lord Smythesdon away.

"I hope I may be permitted to return on the morrow," Lord Smythesdon asked. "I have many idle hours in the sickroom and will enjoy giving this matter thought. It is very pleasant to have something of import to think upon."

Violet clasped her hands, which had unaccountably begun to shake. "Of course," she said, nodding. "And you will be in the drawing room for tea?"

"Yes, tea," the lord said.

Smuckers had closed the library door behind him. Jimmy and Johnny should have been waiting to carry the lord up the stairs, but Smuckers had conveniently sent all four footmen in different directions, hoping he might find a way to converse with Lord Smythesdon in the minutes those boys were away from the hall. The war of diplomacy had commenced and he would not like to allow a single opportunity to slip though his fingers.

"Jimmy and Johnny are on their way, my lord," Smuckers said.

Lord Smythesdon nodded, but was otherwise silent. Smuckers saw at once that he would have to initiate any conversation to be had.

"It was a great honor, my lord, to see two such intellects at work in our beloved library."

Lord Smythesdon looked up. "She is a very great intellect, is she not? I would not be at all surprised if she were to make some new and important discovery in future."

"Indeed," Smuckers said. "Naturally, Miss Granger will someday be the jewel in some lucky individual's crown. To have such a one as Miss Granger presiding over a table, one might be confident in inviting the great minds of the day to dine."

"That is true," Lord Smythesdon said thoughtfully.

"One so often pities a man whose wife cannot hold up her end of the table."

"Indeed," Lord Smythesdon said.

"Naturally," Smuckers said, entirely emboldened, "Miss Granger's beauty alone guarantees her suitors. They would storm the doors if we allowed such a thing. But I suspect Miss Granger to be in possession of very high standards as it relates to who she will like and who she will not like."

"Of course," Lord Smythesdon said softly. "She is rather regal-looking."

"Entirely regal," Smuckers said. "As regal as any queen."

"And there are a lot of suitors, you say?" Lord Smythesdon asked.

Smuckers, determined in his mission and yet reluctant to tell a bold-faced lie, merely said, "It would hardly be surprising to know that every man in the neighborhood admires Miss Granger." This was perfectly true. While Miss Granger had not had any particular suitor, it would not be at all surprising to Smuckers to discover such a thing.

"Of course," Lord Smythesdon said, appearing distracted by the notion. "Nothing more natural."

Victorine had dressed Violet, and then dressed Rose, and now found herself at the ever-onerous task of dressing Daisy.

"This must stop, Daisy," Rose said, looking over her disaster of a bedchamber. "I should not like to hear that Victorine has quit because of it."

"She hears first," Victorine said, pointing at Daisy. "Then you hears it."

"Oh, my darling Victorine," Daisy said. "Do not give up on me. I shall do anything you say."

"You shall do as *I* say," Rose said forcefully. "You shall not go anywhere near your wardrobe again. You shall trust Victorine in everything. She will choose for you and blessedly release you from all of your pondering and debating."

"I should not even wonder what to wear?" Daisy asked, this appearing to be a new idea.

"Not even wonder," Rose said. "She shall choose and you will be delighted."

"That is clever, Rose," Daisy said. "It shall be a surprise every day. What do you think, Victorine? You shan't leave if I am always to be surprised?"

"Que va faire," Victorine said, marching toward Daisy with a tea dress.

"Goodness," Daisy said. "I am surprised already. I should not have chosen that one."

"Daisy," Rose said sternly.

Violet had stayed silent during the exchange. She had more weighty matters on her mind than Daisy's disorganization and Rose and Victorine's disgust over it. She had, up until this moment, condemned Lord Smythesdon to her sisters. She had begun the campaign before he had even arrived. She had only given him the slightest reprieve upon his accident. She had been willing to admit that he had grown more pleasant. Now, though, she was beginning to have rather warmer feelings. She did not particularly wish to name the feelings, she only wished that any thought of animosity between them should be put at an end. She wished to soften or smooth over some of her harshest criticisms. But where to begin?

"Lord Smythesdon came to the library this morning," she said.

"Did he?" Rose asked. "Was this some scheme of the TFD's?"

"No," Violet said. "Doctor Megthorn ordered it."

"Poor darling Violet," Daisy said. "She is not even allowed peace in her own library."

Violet colored and stammered, "It was perfectly alright. We discussed willow bark. It was quite interesting."

"Dear me," Daisy said. "You and Lord Smythesdon are the only two people in the wide world who could discuss willow bark and declare it interesting."

"Well," Violet said, "it's true that we do have a number of interests in common."

Rose peered at Violet. "Do I detect some sort of sea change?" she asked. "Is there some sort of melting of icebergs occurring?"

Violet should have seen that Rose would cut to the quick of the matter. She had better get it over with. "I only say, that since his accident, his better qualities have been allowed to surface. That is all I say. So I only look to be released from certain...former opinions."

Daisy broke free of Victorine and clasped her sister in an embrace. "Dear Violet, I change my mind, minute to minute, and nobody cares a thing about it. Why should you not change your mind on occasion?"

"Because Violet is far less mercurial than you are, Daisy," Rose said. "However, our sister has declared that she wishes to revise an opinion and we shall accept it and not say another word about it. How ever she wishes to think of our guest, that is how *we* shall think of him."

Rose and Daisy nodded together. Violet was vastly relieved. She had felt that attempting to hide her changed feelings toward the lord from her sisters was very like crossing a stream over slippery rocks—she was bound to fall in eventually. Now, there could be no cause for any remarks if she were to speak with Lord

Smythesdon at tea. At least, no further remarks from her dearest sisters. She could not hope for the same from her mother and Lady Ainsworth.

Chapter Eighteen

After his visit to the library, Jimmy and Johnny had lifted Lord Smythesdon into bed. He had lain back, finding himself not well-pleased to be locked away again in his bedchamber. His trip downstairs had been gratifying. And yet, it had also been disturbing to his peace.

"I understand," he said to the footmen, "that there are many suitors to the eldest Miss Grangers. Particularly, Miss Violet Granger."

Jimmy glanced at Johnny, then said, "If you'll pardon my opinion, my lord, Miss Granger ain't been approached by any that's worthy."

"Ah, I see. So you have high standards for such suitors?"

"It weren't my place to judge," Jimmy said, "but I go ahead and judge all the same. A fellow like me can't serve a family all loyal-like and not be led into thinkin' on it. Me and Johnny and Charlie and Oscar are of one mind when it comes to suitors. They got to be up to snuff."

Johnny nodded vigorously.

Smythesdon smiled. Whoever all these suitors were that Smuckers had spoken of, they did not pass muster with the footmen. He could not know what Jimmy would deem up to snuff, but he was cheerful in the idea that, whatever it was, those rogues had been found lacking.

"Take Miss Violet Granger, for instance," Jimmy said. "What's to say she marries some regular fellow. There ain't nothin' wrong with the man, maybe he's even a high and mighty type. A Duke, even. But in the brains department he's average. How's that gonna be?"

"I cannot say that I know," Smythesdon said. "How *would* that be?"

"A regular disaster," Johnny said.

"Or worse," Jimmy said darkly. "What's to say he don't wake up one day and have a thought? The thought might come over him that his wife has got more in the noggin than he do. How's that gonna go over? Then he gets all angry-like 'cause he can do naught about it. He can't make himself smarter and he can't make her dumber."

"T'would be a dark time," Johnny said. "And is Miss Violet Granger gonna keep her smarts all hidden away in her sewin' basket where he don't see 'em?"

"That seems doubtful," Lord Smythesdon said.

"Ain't no doubt about it. She ain't never done it and she ain't never would."

"Well," Smythesdon said, "let us hope that Miss Granger makes a suitable match. May she marry a gentleman that can appreciate her intellect, rather than be frightened of it."

Jimmy and Johnny stared down at the lord with determined expressions. Jimmy folded his arms and said, "That's what we're a-hoping for, my lord."

Violet had gone down for tea well before the gong sounded. She was embarrassed to do it, though that did not quite put her off. Lord Smythesdon had been brought down early the day before and she thought if that was the case today, they might continue their conversation on willow bark. Victorine, upon being hurried along, had the impertinence to say, "Bravo pour l'amour." Violet had scolded her right out of the room, though she did not think it had much effect upon the saucy maid.

She was mortified to note Smuckers peeking around a doorframe as she made her way down the stairs and headed for the drawing room. It would be Smuckers usual habit to leap out and discover if she wished for anything, but he had not. She guessed he did not want to delay her journey into the drawing room by even a moment. There was naught she could do about such a ridiculous scene but pretend she had not spotted him.

Violet found her heart unaccountably gaining speed as she reached the drawing room doors. She passed through and found Lord Smythesdon in front of the fire.

"My lord," she said, willing her voice steady, "I pray you have not overtired yourself."

It was a perfectly stupid thing to say, as the lord had no doubt just arrived and was sitting in a chair, not running around the room.

"I have not," he said, "and I very much look forward to the day when I might be allowed to stay down to dine. Doctor Megthorn is in league with my parents *and* yours and I am ruled by cruel despots. You are early for tea, Miss Granger."

Violet started. You are early. He noted she was early. Of course she was early, but she had not expected him to note it. What in heaven's name was she to say to that?

"Indeed, it appears that I am," she said. "I suppose my clock is not at all accurate and I had been better served to listen for the gong."

"Ah," Lord Smythesdon said, looking down at his hands. "I had hoped you were early to have further conversation, but I find I flattered myself."

Violet felt of pang of regret at making up such an excuse to account for her arrival before the gong. She said, "Well, I will admit that I did hope to speak on the matter of the willow bark."

Lord Smythesdon appeared much gratified by her statement and not at all inclined to tease her over her claim that her clock had broken. "I have brought Miss Ravencraft's book," he said, pulling it from the side of his wheeled chair.

Violet found she was entirely annoyed to see the book and would not mind pitching it into the fire if she would not appear a lunatic in doing it. "How kind Miss Ravencraft was to give it to you," she said.

"Yes," Lord Smythesdon said. "She is a most pleasant person."

Violet felt a stinging on her skin, as if Miss Ravencraft's pleasantness was some sort of rash. "She certainly is ardently admired by gentlemen," she said, with a touch of bitterness in her voice and more than a touch of bitterness in her heart. Why must they speak of Miss Ravencraft at all?

"Is she?" the lord said. "Oh, I suppose some must admire her ardently. I cannot see it, though."

"Can you not?" Violet asked, thinking of the lord's eagerness to hear any little drivel emanating from that small person.

"The way I see it," Lord Smythesdon said, "is that if I were to assign ladies a role from Henry Tudor's court, would not Miss Ravencraft be poor little Kitty Howard? Pretty enough, but all lightness and no substance?"

"Indeed, I do not know," Violet said. "I have never considered such a thing."

"I think it so, though I do not mean any disrespect to her to say it. Do you wonder what role I would assign to you in the old king's court?" the lord asked.

Violet did very much wonder, and prayed it was not Anne Boleyn. She would not like herself compared to the woman who dared too much. The woman who thought she could manage a king, until on the scaffold she knew she could not. Undone, by her own cleverness.

"I would make you Katheryn Parr," the lord continued. "She was the scholar, the only one of them who could outwit her king."

Violet knew she should be pleased to be compared to Katheryn Parr. She should be gratified to be assigned the scholar.

However, she found, just at this moment, that she would not be entirely against being cast as pretty Kitty Howard.

"For myself," Lord Smythesdon went on, "I have noticed that when I admire a Kitty Howard, and there are many such in London, it is not so much the lady that brings pleasure. It is my own sense of self-importance in remaining unchallenged in any matter. It is a fault I am determined to correct."

"Perhaps one can be both pretty and scholarly," Violet said stiffly.

"You are offended at my choice?" Lord Smythesdon asked. "I did not wish it. Katheryn Parr had that particular something, just as Anne Boleyn had that particular something. But unlike Anne, she survived. I rather account for that by her unique combination of beauty *and* intellect."

This was not at all what Violet had expected to hear. Was she to understand that the lord deemed her pretty? Was she to understand that her intellect was now to be firmly admired?

"My lord, Kitty Howard was precisely the sort of lady who would not bother with Euclid and would concern herself solely with feminine arts and wiles. You could not have changed your opinion so drastically as to prefer Katheryn Parr—a lady who fancied herself at the heart of the reformist movement while other ladies were quietly sewing."

"Could not I have?" Lord Smythesdon asked. "One of the great advantages of a sickroom is the enforced amounts of time that must be filled with thinking. Thinking, I have noticed, very readily exposes any faults in opinions that may have been masquerading as facts. Nothing can be hidden from time and thought."

"I am amazed, my lord," Violet said. "What else have you discovered from all this thought?"

Lord Smythesdon was silent for a moment. "Perhaps I know my own mind better than I did."

Violet was silent, waiting to hear what else Lord Smythesdon would reveal from his thinking in the sickroom, but it was not to be. The gong sounded and not a moment passed before Marigold came charging into the room.

"No tea yet?" she asked, looking around. Seeing that the drawing room was entirely devoid of anything consumable, Marigold heaved a long and heavy sigh. She walked over to Lord Smythesdon and Violet and said, "How does your leg come on, my lord?"

"Very nicely, Miss Granger," he answered.

"Once it is healed, I should very much like to take you out for a ride. I know all the best spots in a ten-mile radius. It is very important that you ride as soon as possible and do not avoid it because of your accident. But you must agree to go on Merlin. I'll not have you break your other leg—mama would be entirely put out about it."

"Not to mention Lord Smythesdon," Violet said.

Lord Smythesdon laughed. "Indeed, I should be very put out to find my other leg casted for it would mark me an unrepentant idiot. I graciously accept your offer to be my guide, Miss Granger. On Merlin."

Marigold peered at the lord, seeming to examine him closely. "Well," she said, "I do not know how it has happened, but it sounds like you are developing commonsense."

"Marigold!" Violet scolded.

Marigold shrugged. The lord said, "I take no offense at the truth, and I dearly hope it *is* the truth."

Lady Mulholland and Lady Ainsworth entered and behind them came everybody else. The drawing room quickly filled. Violet found Lord Ainsworth seated to her side and her father next to Lord Smythesdon. All conversation about Kitty Howard and Katheryn Parr was at an end.

Violet was both disappointed and relieved. She hardly knew what she thought about being compared to Katheryn Parr.

Lady Mulholland brought Lord Smythesdon's tea to him. She noted that she had prepared it just as he liked it—strong—as if this was something Violet should take note of. Her mother lingered for a moment, but as Violet was determined to say nothing while she hovered, the lady eventually returned to her huddle with Lady Ainsworth.

Her father and Lord Ainsworth were happily discussing some plan that had been settled upon with the assistance of Mr. Tidewater, and how likely the same thing could be done at Donneville. As far as Violet could tell, they had earlier in the day rode out to a field prone to flooding and designed a unique drainage scheme.

The Viscount paused in his discussion and said, "Violet, before I forget entirely, we encountered Will Masters on the road. He asked if he could borrow more books. I said you would not mind it." The Viscount paused, then said, "He's a funny fellow. Seems he's always arriving to borrow more books from our library. No idea where he finds the time to read them all."

Lord Smythesdon listened with interest to this news. Violet merely nodded as the Viscount returned to his discussion with Lord Ainsworth.

"This Mr. Masters is a regular visitor to the library?" Lord Smythesdon asked.

"He is," Violet said. "He is a local squire and quite well read."

"Ah," Lord Smythesdon said, "I suppose he and his wife do enjoy the proximity to a well-stocked library."

"He is unmarried, my lord," Violet said. "Though I would suspect that when he does marry, it will be to a lady that enjoys reading as he does. As it is, he manages things quite on his own and, as my father noted, I cannot imagine where he finds the time."

"Perhaps he does not," Lord Smythesdon said. "Perhaps he only enjoys visiting the library. Does this Masters fellow stay long?"

Does he stay long? What sort of question was that. Was the lord...no he could not be. The future Earl of Ainsworth could not be jealous of such a one as Will Masters.

"Not an unusual amount of time, I'm sure," Violet said.

"I suppose, now that I am thinking of it," the lord said, "I would not actually know how long a time would be usual in such an endeavor. How long does he stay?"

Violet thought back to Will Masters' visits to the library. It took some doing as she rarely thought of him at all. For all his learning, he was a milquetoast sort of man.

"It seems to me that it depends what he is seeking. Sometimes he is there and gone fairly quickly, and sometimes he lingers," Violet said.

"Lingers, does he?"

Jimmy and Johnny arrived on either side of Lord Smythesdon's chair. They would wheel him to the bottom of the stairs and carry him up to his bedchamber.

"Already?" the lord asked upon spying the footmen. "Really, I do not see why I should not stay down."

"Doctor Megthorn's strict orders, my lord," Jimmy said. "We don't dare defy him."

Violet wished he were not to go so soon. So much had been said, but so much she could not positively gauge the meaning of. Rose had mentioned that there had been a melting of icebergs. But this encounter foretold of more than that. Much more than that. She must just determine what he meant by it and what she thought of it.

But for all her wondering, Doctor Megthorn would prevail.

Lord Smythesdon had been wheeled from the drawing room against his wishes, not that anybody had consulted his wishes. He really was being managed by Tartars. It felt as if he had only been downstairs for a moment.

Jimmy and Johnny transferred him to his bed smoothly, they had become expert at avoiding knocking his leg. They propped him up with pillows and served him his dinner on a tray. The chef had grown to understand his tastes and there was an ample dish of savarins for dessert.

He said, "I am given to understand that this Will Masters fellow from the neighborhood is in the habit of visiting the library."

"Yes, my lord," Jimmy said. "He's a regular one. Seems like he turns up more and more. I just said to Johnny, not a fortnight ago, well look who it is. Weren't he just here?"

"The Viscount wondered where he found the time to read so much," Lord Smythesdon said.

"T'weren't my place to wonder on such a matter," Johnny said, building up the fire, "but I wondered on it all the same. He farms a good bit a land and he's got his dear old mother to care for and no sisters to help out. Seems like he ought to have his hands full without pilin' on the literature."

"If he were to seek my advice," Jimmy said, "which he never did and never will do, I'd tell 'im—you need a wife in that big old house of yours."

"It is a fine house, then?" the lord asked.

"Very fine," Johnny said. "It ain't no Chemsworth Hall, mind. It ain't got the history, it bein' new-like. But one of the finest round here all the same."

"Perhaps he takes your advice, Jimmy. Perhaps he *does* look for a wife," Lord Smythesdon said.

Jimmy snorted. "He'd be better off puttin' the books down and actually looking round him, then."

"Perhaps he looks for a wife in Chemsworth's library," Lord Smythesdon said.

The idea that Lord Smythesdon had been uncomfortably brewing in his thoughts penetrated both Jimmy and Johnny at the same moment.

"Miss Granger!" Johnny cried.

Jimmy shook his head sorrowfully. "My thoughts had not gone runnin' in that direction, though it would account for his regular appearances. I'd not like to see it," he said. "I'd not like to see it at all."

"Do you find him unworthy of Miss Granger?" Lord Smythesdon said, finding himself hoping that this neighborhood rogue would be found unequivocally unworthy.

"It ain't that he's unworthy exactly," Johnny said. "It's just that we don't like to see it."

Jimmy slammed a glass of port on the bedside table, the liquid splashing over the rim, and said, "It ain't our first choice."

The two footmen hurried from the room, looking as if they had somehow overstepped their bounds. Smythesdon supposed that they had—footmen were not generally consulted on the marriage of a peer's daughter. For all that, he could not fault them. After all, they would not like to see that scallywag Masters prevail.

Lord Smythesdon leaned back and sipped his port. He was perfectly well aware that he would not like to see that scallywag Masters prevail either. He had been very firm in his wish to delay marriage, but now that this Masters character had appeared on the horizon he was not so certain. The arrival of Masters had seemed to represent a ticking clock. Who knew when the man might make his move?

He found that he could not wish to see Miss Violet Granger gracing somebody else's table. What a waste it would be for her to become a squire's wife! Did she not have the bearing to be a Countess? Was she not a lady who could assist him in his pursuits? Was she not uncommonly pretty? Was she not perfect in every way?

Smythesdon paused. No, he could not claim that. He could not claim she was perfect in every way. However, it was beginning to appear that she might be perfect for him. He would not have known it when he had arrived to the house. She had seemed a bit of a harridan then, set on correcting him at every turn. But then, had he known her temperament better he might have seen that he had been continually throwing down the gauntlet. A lady like Violet Granger did not go meekly into the night. If a gauntlet was thrown in the vicinity of Miss Granger, that gauntlet should expect to be taken up.

Masters must be run off and Miss Granger must be secured. But would she view it in the same light? She had not liked him when he arrived, that much was clear. And yet, he felt that now she rather did like him. She had sought him out in the drawing room. There had been no errant clock sending her down early after all.

All he could do, he decided, downing his port, was try. His mother and father would favor it, that he knew. He suspected Lady Mulholland would look upon it as a good match too. And then there were the footmen. Jimmy and Johnny had dropped enough heavy hints—they were staunchly anti-Masters and pro-Smythesdon. Surely, that would count for something. He must only discover what Granger thought about it. Granger might know how best to proceed with his sister.

He leaned back, contemplating the savarins in front of him. How odd that he should so thoroughly change his mind on the subject of marriage. He supposed this was how it happened for everybody—one moment a person was scheming to avoid the state and the next they were plotting to get into it.

Chapter Nineteen

Violet had excused herself early after dinner, and had not announced, 'heavens, I *am* tired.' Rose and Daisy had watched her leave the room, both of them with curiosity writ large on their faces. She did not go immediately up the stairs, but rather went into the library. She lit a few candles and scanned the shelves for what she looked for, but could not find a book that might contain a portrait of Katheryn Parr. She would very much like to see what the lady looked like.

Smuckers poked his head around the doorframe. "I saw the candles, miss, and wondered if Jimmy had been so careless as to leave them burning."

"He did not," Violet said. "I lit them myself. Smuckers, do you think me a Katheryn Parr?"

Smuckers, always enjoying being asked a question, stepped into the room. "Katheryn Parr, miss?"

"One of Henry the VIII's wives."

"Oh," Smuckers said. "That Parr. The last one."

"Do you suppose I am like her?"

Smuckers considered this. He could not claim to be an expert on history that occurred so long ago. And, of what he did know, he found that particular Tudor king to be a bit...unfortunate. "I seem to recall that Queen Katheryn very narrowly escaped a warrant. She was on her way to the scaffold and was clever enough

219

to talk round her king who, if I may be so very bold to say so, was a tyrant."

Smuckers made a small bow as if to apologize for insulting royalty, even if that royalty was long dead and had been a perfect madman while he lived.

"Yes," Violet said softly. "She was very clever. She was learned. A scholar."

"Then you must be very like her," Smuckers said cheerfully. "I know nobody who is such a scholar as Miss Violet Granger."

"But was she pretty?" Violet asked. "I really wonder about that. Was she *only* learned, or did she have other qualities?"

Smuckers had no idea whether Katheryn Parr was pretty. In all truth, the portraits he had seen of renaissance women struck him as ranging from plain to alarmingly ugly. Even the Viscount's ancestors were homely—all high foreheads and pursed lips. However, he thought he could guess where this was going.

"I am certain she was beautiful. Regal-looking, everything a queen should be. For why else would that king marry her? He could choose anybody in England and she was chosen, so of course she was very lovely."

Violet was silent and Smuckers felt that he had somehow failed in his duty. There was something he could not quite work out. "May I enquire, miss, why you wish to know your similarity to Katheryn Parr?"

"Oh," she said, "it was just something Lord Smythesdon said. He said Miss Ravencraft was like pretty Kitty Howard and I was like Katheryn Parr. I just wondered about it."

Smuckers took this to be very good news, indeed. His grasp of Henry Tudor's court was tenuous at best, but he did remember one thing. And that one thing convinced him that Miss Ravencraft had no hold over Lord Smythesdon whatsoever.

"Kitty Howard," he said gravely, "was a chit of a girl, not a woman. I do not say anything against Miss Ravencraft, it not being my place to condemn or raise up your neighbors. I only say I am not surprised by Lord Smythesdon's opinion on the matter."

Violet did not answer and Smuckers began to feel that if he were to be of true assistance in the matter of Lord Smythesdon, he had better dare a great roll of the dice.

"Miss Violet," he said, "if you would permit me to express an opinion entirely out of bounds?"

Violet smiled. "I cannot imagine you ever going out of bounds, Smuckers. You are the essence of decorum. Though I should be very interested in hearing any rogue thoughts that have come upon you."

Smuckers took a deep breath and said, "It is just this—you would be well matched. And I do not mean only in scholarly pursuits. You would make a very handsome pair and your children would be quite comely. I think you know who I am referring to in this. And, I only say, do not allow the circumstances of his arrival to become your next trifle, your next missed dessert. Do not run *from* a thing only because your mother wishes you to run *to* it. She is forceful and you have always had the stern backbone to resist, but do not make resistance itself the point."

"Do not cut off my nose in revenge of my face. Is that it, Smuckers?"

Smuckers, shocked to his bones that he had dared go so far, only said, "God forgive me for a lunatic."

Violet jumped up from her chair and patted Smuckers' cheek. "If you are a lunatic, then you are my own lunatic."

She left the room, leaving Smuckers alone to consider his own special brand of madness.

Lord Smythesdon had sent Jimmy downstairs with a message for Henry Granger. Would Mr. Granger visit him in his sickroom at his earliest convenience.

Henry had received the note with trepidation. Ever since Smythesdon had pronounced them both idiots for choosing The Turk, he had not known on what ground they stood. He could not guess what Smythesdon would do or say once he was not a captive of Chemsworth Hall. Perhaps he was about to discover it.

Smythesdon leaned against his pillows with a glass of port at his side, looking well-satisfied. Perhaps keeping his friend in good supply of port would go some way to encourage friendly feelings for the house.

"Well, old man," Smythesdon said, "now I have my mother and father under the same roof with me, despite my efforts to outrun them. It seems to me that my mother and your mother do quite a lot of scheming together. Oh yes, I have noted them during my brief visits to the drawing room, heads together and plotting like a couple of highwaymen."

Henry did not respond to this description, but felt a cold chill creep up his spine. Smythesdon was a bit too near the truth of why he had been invited to the house.

"If I am to guess," Smythesdon said, "I would say they do their utmost to make a match between myself and Miss Violet Granger. Do you deny it?"

Henry thought for a moment that he *would* deny it. Then he recalled how very intelligent and astute Smythesdon actually was and knew it was hopeless.

"I'll admit it," he said. "I invited you here under false pretenses. My mother made me do it." Henry paused, then said, "Oh, I know it sounds ridiculous. But you do not know my mother! She is like a north wind, nobody can resist her. I suppose you will go back to Oxford and tell everybody how wretched you were treated. How I schemed to get you here to satisfy my mother's demands and how I broke your leg for good measure. I shall be ruined and I deserve it."

Lord Smythesdon took a gulp of port. He had not even suspected Granger of being one of plotters. He said, "I suppose Miss Granger was in on the whole scheme?"

"No," Henry said. "She was told nothing. But dash it, it's Violet. She guessed quick enough. There's not much that can be got by my sister. It was the cause of her rudeness that first evening. She was incensed by the whole thing."

"I see," Smythesdon said. "And here I thought it was only an intense dislike for me."

"Well," Henry said, "you did not help. Learning is a man's purview and why should she know anything about Descartes and why are women riding to the hunt did not help. That was never going to go over well with Violet."

Smythesdon laughed and Henry began to hope that perhaps he would not be ruined at Oxford after all. His friend seemed to view the thing as one big joke.

"No, Granger," Smythesdon said. "That never was going to go over well. I find I cannot regret a broken bone as I believe I have gained a better understanding from it. Now brace yourself, old boy. I'm going to propose to your sister. The question is, how do I do it? You, who know her best, must advise me on the case."

Henry had staggered out of Smythesdon's bedchamber, hardly believing what he had heard. Could it be true? Could his mother's scheme actually have worked, despite Violet's contrariness and despite breaking his friend's leg through his own idiocy? It hardly seemed possible. And yet, Smythesdon swore it *was* possible.

Henry had not understood much of what Smythesdon had told him. He could not fathom what Will Masters had to do with anything. Or why Miss Ravencraft's book had played a part. Or what Smythesdon had meant by Violet pretending to have a broken clock. Or why astrology did not belong in medicine. And especially not what two persons named Katheryn Parr and Kitty Howard had to do with it—he was not even acquainted with those two ladies. Yet, all of those things had somehow added up to a proposal.

He could only account for it by assuming that whatever Lady Mulholland's wishes were, the Gods would move heaven and earth to make it so. There had never been such an ill-conceived plan and yet the lady would come out victorious. It was unfathomable.

That is, his mother would be victorious if Violet would accept. He could not be sure she would. Even if she were inclined favorably to Smythesdon, he could not count on her good sense. He had witnessed, too many times, her habit of seeking out the contrary.

The vision of being related to Smythesdon through marriage was almost too good to be true. His place at Oxford would be assured—the fellow could not disparage him while engaged to his sister. His mother would owe him a debt of gratitude, which was always pleasant and rarely occurred.

If only Violet would accept.

Henry had given his friend his best advice. He had taken all that he knew of Violet Granger and devised a plan. He could only hope the Gods stayed on Lady Mulholland's side and it would work.

Violet had thought to retire early, without tea in her room or Rose and Daisy's company. She had far too much to think about. She had Katheryn Parr to think about. However, her sisters would not be put off. Rose requested tea from Smuckers, Peggy tiptoed up with it and they now sat round Violet's fire.

"You say you are tired," Rose said, "but I do not believe you. I feel there is something momentous occurring and you are keeping it from us."

"Dear Violet," Daisy said. "You cannot keep secrets from us. Do not you remember our oath? Sisters together, our minds and hearts as one?"

"That was sworn upon in the nursery," Violet said drily. "When we figured out that it would be impossible for our governess to determine who had committed a crime if none of us would confess under the duress of missing dinner."

"But I have stuck with it all these years," Daisy said. "I keep no secrets from you."

"Everybody knows my mind at all times," Rose said. "I won't hide what I think and anybody who is horrible had better beware of finding out about it."

"Very well," Violet said, "though it is not at all momentous. Lord Smythesdon compared myself and Miss Ravencraft to the ladies of Henry Tudor's court. She is to be Kitty Howard and I am to be Katherine Parr. *Pretty* Kitty Howard and *scholarly* Katherine Parr. I only wondered about it."

"And you see some insult in being named scholarly?" Daisy asked. "But I would have thought that you would rather like that."

Rose sighed. "Point missed by a mile, Daisy. It is the *pretty* Kitty that irks our sister."

"No Violet!" Daisy cried. "Not really? You are the prettiest of us all."

"Very kind of you to say so, Daisy," Violet said. "But kindness does not make it true."

"The mirror makes it true," Daisy said. "Rose? You can be counted on to speak the hard truth."

"Of course, you are lovely," Rose said. "And I might injure a person to get those curls for my own. The problem with you, Violet, is that you have lived overlong in your head. Now that it is time to come out and have a look around, you are not used to considering your appearance. You are not used to anybody else considering your appearance, though many have considered it all along. Do not you notice when we go to town?"

"Notice what?" Violet asked.

"The stares," Daisy said laughing.

Violet had noticed stares often enough, but had always taken them to be for Rose or Daisy.

"But I wonder, Violet," Daisy said coyly, "why what Lord Smythesdon might think of your looks has such import. We know, of course, that you have revised your opinion of the gentleman. Perhaps we did not know how much?"

Violet was silent for a moment, then she said, "You have insisted on no secrets so I shall tell you. I do not actually know how much."

"Daisy," Rose said, "you see now why our Violet would prefer to be alone? She wishes to determine how much her feelings have changed and we are only a hindrance to it. It is time to say goodnight."

Daisy nodded. "Do think on it, Violet. For myself, I hope your feelings have changed very much."

Daisy kissed Violet's forehead and the two sisters took their tea cups and some biscuits off to Rose's bedchamber.

Violet enjoyed the quiet of her emptied bedchamber for less than five minutes before her door burst open. She would have expected it to be Daisy, having forgotten some item that it was now vitally important to retrieve, but instead it was Poppy and Pansy. They rushed in, their white nightgowns billowing out behind them.

"What on God's green earth has you down here at such an hour?" Violet asked.

"A very dire emergency," Poppy said, her eyes wide.

"It's practically an assault on the kingdom," Pansy breathed.

"There is a plot," Poppy said, dramatically clutching at her chest.

"Sit down this instant and explain yourselves," Violet said, in some amazement at the continued daring of her two youngest sisters. "When you are through, I will scold you terribly and send you back to the nursery."

"She will not, though," Poppy said, throwing herself into the nearest chair.

Pansy nodded and squeezed herself next to Poppy. "Not when she hears it is about her."

Violet folded her arms. "I see," she said. "A plot against me? Am I to be kidnapped by intruders to the Inviolate Kingdom?"

"Practically," Poppy said.

"Essentially," Pansy confirmed.

"Well?" Violet asked. "Out with it."

Poppy and Pansy looked at each other. Poppy pointed at Pansy and Pansy nodded. "It is only this," she said. "We have continued to watch over our kingdom, and that includes the lord's bedchamber since he is our honored guest and must be protected at all costs."

"You did not," Violet said gravely.

"We did," Poppy said, jutting out her chin. "And you shall thank us for it. Henry and the lord conspired together this evening as thick as thieves."

"Thick as thieves," Pansy confirmed. "Even thicker, I thought."

"They talked all about your contrariness, Violet," Poppy said. "How it was to be got around. We were insulted down to our shoes."

"We adore your contrariness," Pansy said. "We did not like to hear it so disparaged."

"Had we been older, and men," Poppy said, "we should have marched in there and demanded a duel. A fight to the death."

Violet worked to piece together the actual facts amongst talk of kidnappings, plots, duels and being insulted down to shoes. "What, precisely, did you hear?" she asked.

"Henry said that if the lord wished you to marry him, then he should try to talk you out of it," Poppy said.

"He should tell you all the reasons why you should *not* marry him, and then you would think of all the reasons why you should," Pansy said. "You would talk yourself into it, you see? With your contrariness."

"And then you would be gone away from us," Poppy said pitifully. "Tricked into going to a foreign county. Our poor papa hates foreign counties."

"If that is not a kidnapping," Pansy said, "then I do not know what is."

Violet hardly knew how to take in the information. Lord Smythesdon planned to propose. Even were she to deny him, a lady finding herself in receipt of a proposal must find it gratifying. All thoughts of pretty Kitty Howard were to be dismissed. But that her own brother had discussed her contrariness and they conspired together to outwit her? That could only be insulting. She had never before felt herself to be so violently pulled in opposite directions. Was she flattered or irate? Happy or unhappy?

She folded her hands together tightly and said, "What else?"

"Oh," Poppy said, "there was all sorts of other nonsense about a book and Katheryn Parr and Merlin and astrology and willow bark and your broken-up clock and Will Masters."

"It was nonsense," Pansy confirmed. "We did not understand a word of it."

"I see," Violet said. "And when is this plot set to unfold?"

"Tomorrow morning," Pansy said.

"In the library," Poppy said.

Violet had fully intended to scold her sisters severely, but she found she could not. Whatever rules they had broken, she would not wish for the world to be unacquainted with the information they had delivered.

She kissed them both, gave them biscuits and hurried them to the stairs, wishing them God speed and good luck getting past Miss Millthorpe and back into their beds.

Violet snuffed the candles and lay in her bed wide-eyed, thinking of Katheryn Parr and contrariness. She did not fall asleep for some hours.

Mr. Smuckers had never felt so certain that he had valiantly defended the interests of the house. He had waited all his career for an opportunity to display his courage under fire and now he had done it.

"I was bold, Mrs. Featherstone. Like a general hemmed in from all sides who must make a decisive move or face certain defeat."

Mrs. Featherstone, having long ago wearied of army talk, said, "Well, Mr. Smuckers? What precisely was this bold thing you carried out?"

"I told Miss Violet that she would be well-suited to Lord Smythesdon. It had to be said by somebody, and I said it."

"And how did she take this bold talk?" Mrs. Featherstone asked, the slightest wish that Miss Granger had not taken it well coming to rest gently upon her shoulders.

"Well," Mr. Smuckers said, not entirely certain how his words had been taken, "after I pronounced myself a lunatic for speaking so plainly, she said I was to be *her* lunatic. That was encouraging, I thought."

Mrs. Featherstone could barely stop herself from rubbing her hands together. It was not every day that the butler was forced to name himself a lunatic. She could hardly sleep for thinking what the morrow might bring. Her old friend disaster was running toward the house hard and fast.

Violet sat composedly in the library. At least, it would appear so to anybody who had been looking. And it would appear so to Smuckers, who had been looking quite a lot. The butler had invented every excuse in the world to come in and out of the room.

Beneath her composed exterior, a whirlwind of thoughts roiled within her. She had devised dozens of reactions. Dozens of clever responses. Dozens of strategies to wrest her dignity back from Lord Smythesdon and her brother. In the end, though, her final decision had been made by the light touch of her fingers to her nose.

The minutes ticked by and Violet had almost the sense of waiting for an execution. As if she were, indeed, poor Kitty Howard or the only very nearly escaped Katheryn Parr. She could not guess exactly when Lord Smythesdon would arrive. There had been no set schedule she was aware of. If she were to go by Smuckers jumpiness, she must think it soon.

The door slowly swung open and Violet raised her eyes to discover if it were the lord or the butler.

It was the lord.

Chapter Twenty

Jimmy and Johnny wheeled Lord Smythesdon into the library. They had seemed to have taken special care with the lord's dress. Violet had not seen his shirt so stiffly starched or his cravat so expertly knotted since his valet had left the house.

"Miss Granger," Lord Smythesdon said, as Jimmy and Johnny rolled his chair to a stop in front of the fire. He motioned to Jimmy to wheel him around directly facing Violet.

"Lord Smythesdon," Violet said. "You are looking well this morning."

Jimmy took this as a direct compliment to himself and said, "Thank you, miss," as he left the room with Johnny. The door quietly closed.

"If you care to tell me what you would wish to read," Violet said, "I am sure I can locate something suitable."

Lord Smythesdon appeared as if the last thought he'd had on his mind was reading upon coming to the library.

"Very kind, Miss Granger," he said hurriedly. "But I wonder if I may discuss a delicate matter with you before proceeding?"

"Of course," Violet said, holding her hands together in her lap. She had not expected that he should go straight to the point.

"This may come as a shock," the lord went on, "and I do not tell you of it to put blame or recriminations against anybody."

"Goodness," Violet said. "This does sound dire."

"Yes, well, it seems there have been those in the house who have conspired. They have conspired to make a match between us."

"Ah," Violet said, not appearing discomposed. "You must point to my mother. She is invariably behind every scheme in the house. Do not begrudge her entertaining herself with her little amusements. They generally hurt nobody."

"It is not only her!" Lord Smythesdon said. "But your brother and my own mother and father."

The lord waited for Violet Granger's outrage. Seeing there was none, he continued.

"Naturally," he said, "*we* understand that there is everything against it. Yes, we have much in common and yes, we certainly are minds evenly matched. And, I will admit, there is nobody more comely than Miss Granger. But none of that could ensure felicity. *We* know it not to be so."

Violet was beyond gratified that nobody, not even little Miss Kitty Howard, was to be more comely than she was. However, she reminded herself to stay the course she had decided upon and not become distracted by compliments.

"Ah," Violet said, "*We* know it not to be so. I see you have been so considerate as to account for *my* thoughts as well as your own."

"Yes," Lord Smythesdon said, "that is exactly what I did. I presumed that you would agree with my superior judgment. I was certain I might speak for you, as women do prefer that sort of thing. Why bother thinking when a man can just as easily tell you what you think?"

Lord Smythesdon paused, then he said, "I certainly would not expect that you might have a differing opinion. Such a thing would not occur to me."

And here it was. The trap that Violet Granger had so often fallen into. He says it is black and so she must say it is white. However, that trap had lost all its trickery. She would not fall into it again. If Lord Smythesdon wished to ask for her hand, he must do so without tricks or guile.

"I will happily defer to your judgment on the matter," she said demurely.

There was a long silence in the library. "You will defer to it?" Lord Smythesdon said softly. "Happily?"

"Indeed."

"But you are not supposed to defer to my judgment," he said in a rush. "Why would you defer to *my* judgment? My judgment, as evidenced by the casted leg you see before you, is terrible! You should never defer to my judgment."

Violet attempted a look of suitable confusion, though thanks to Poppy and Pansy she was not confused in the least. "So you are determined that I *not* defer to your judgment?"

"Precisely," the lord said, nodding.

"Though I respect your opinion on the matter, my lord, I must beg to differ. I am resolute in deferring to your judgment."

Lord Smythesdon was silent for a moment. Then he said, "But what if I were to change my judgment? Would you still have to defer to it?"

Violet bit her lip to stop herself from laughing.

Lord Smythesdon noted her expression. He appeared entirely confused, and then the light began to dawn in his eyes. "Oh, no," he said. "I have attempted something and been entirely caught out. Granger was so certain of it, but I should have known he was off the mark."

"I will certainly defer to *that* judgment," Violet said. "I wonder that you thought to manage me in such a manner."

"I wonder it myself," Lord Smythesdon said quietly.

"I also wonder that you do not begin again without such a doomed stratagem," Violet said quietly.

Lord Smythesdon had turned his head and stared glumly into the fire. At her words, he turned back. "Begin again? Yes! I could begin again," he said, the eagerness in his voice unmistakable to Violet's ears. "Nobody could hold me to such a ridiculous speech. It must be done again. It could be as if nothing were ever said about deferring to anybody's judgment. It could be as if I just now came into the room. It could, yes?"

Violet looked up and said, "Good morning, Lord Smythesdon. You look very well. May I get you a book?"

The lord smiled and made a great effort to wheel himself closer. Noting that he was not likely to make it very far, even were he to take the whole morning at the attempt, Violet casually moved to a chair closer to his.

He said, "I am afraid I have no time for books, Miss Granger, for I have something very important to ask. Seeing as how you are the most beautiful girl in England, and seeing as how your mind is a wonder to behold, and seeing as how I am a better man for knowing you, might you not consent to marry me? Might you not consent to it, even though our respective mothers and fathers are all staunchly in favor of it?"

Violet's thoughts raced to and fro. She had determined that if the lord wished to ask for her hand, he must do so without guile or trickery. Now he had done so and she must answer.

Violet said, "To be sure, the favor of our mothers and fathers *is* an impediment. Especially my mother's approbation—as a rule I would generally go against her wishes. But seeing as how our conversations are so lively and likely to entertain me all my life and seeing as how you are unconscionably handsome, and seeing as how I will never mention white soup again, I will say yes. We will stand together in the face of our parent's approval and weather the blow."

Lord Smythesdon made a great reach with his hand and Violet may have put her own hand in the way of it.

"I believe, Violet Granger," Lord Smythesdon said, "that we are hurrying ourselves toward Euclid's fifth axiom."

"The whole is greater than the parts," Violet said.

"And so we circle back to Euclid, just as we were when we first met in this room."

"Oh, let us not mention *that*," Violet said.

Violet and Lord Smythesdon spent a quiet and happy hour discussing plans. The engagement would necessarily be of some months duration as the lord had no wish to be wheeled down the aisle of a church like a broken old soldier. Violet wondered if she ought to call him Bertie and they agreed it would be so, though only as a strictly private matter. She admitted that she had, at first, disliked the name, but now she had grown rather fond of it. Smythesdon wondered if he should not give up his studies at Oxford, but it was determined that he should take the next term off to allow his leg to heal, and then the couple would take a house in Oxford. Violet might not be permitted to attend lectures, but that would hardly matter. Their home would be the center of Oxford's hive. Anybody with a thinking mind might be admitted to propose their conclusions on any subject. They would host many fine dinners; lively debates would be heard all round. When children came, they would be educated side by side, the girls with the boys. And there was not to be a sidesaddle anywhere. It was agreed that they would be unlikely to secure Smuckers, but Smythesdon thought Jimmy might be tempted away. Violet was agreeable, as long as Jimmy was willing to sneak sweets, and then tea, up the back stairs for any offspring that might be looking for such.

"Oh," Violet said suddenly, "but there is one thing."

"Anything," Lord Smythesdon said.

"All this talk of our parent's approval has reminded me of something. I am afraid we have lumped my father into a league he never joined. I do not think he knows the first thing about it."

"Truly?" Smythesdon said, beginning to look alarmed.

Violet nodded.

"I had best see to that," Lord Smytheson said. "See to that this minute. I have not had a great many conversations with your father. Is there any particular approach you would advise?"

Violet counted on her fingers. "One, do not suppose he is contrary and attempt to argue him out of it. Two, do not mention Hampshire or any other foreign county. Of course, he will know it, but do not encourage him to dwell on it. And three, if he seems a bit misty-eyed and speaks of his many daughters and then seems to trail off—the youngest are Poppy and Pansy. He sometimes forgets their names but will recognize them instantly."

Lord Smythesdon nodded. "Smuckers," he called. "Are you out there?"

The door flew open before the lord had finished his sentence. Violet wondered if Smuckers had not had his ear plastered to the other side of it. "Yes, my lord?"

"Is the Viscount at home just now?"

"Indeed, he is, my lord. He is closeted in his study with the Earl and Mr. Tidewater."

"I require a private interview with him. My father and Mr. Tidewater must go elsewhere. Can you see to it?"

Smuckers stood straighter and thrust his chest forward as if he had been commanded to launch a warship at an enemy's navy. "I can, my lord. I will see to it at once." He snapped his fingers and Jimmy and Johnny came running. "Prepare to wheel Lord Smythesdon to the study."

Smuckers turned on his heel and marched off and Violet had no doubt that Lord Ainsworth and Mr. Tidewater would soon find themselves out on their ears. The only circumstance she did not quite understand was the look of joy that had somehow overtaken Jimmy and Johnny.

Lord Smythesdon's appeal to the Viscount took more twists and turns than he had anticipated. He'd had to confirm that it was Violet, and not another one of the daughters. He'd had to explain away the distance to Hampshire and promise that he must always come to Chemsworth for Christmas as the Viscount could not bear to be parted from his children over the holidays. He'd had to explain that Lady Mulholland would look favorably upon the match, as that was why he was brought here to begin. He'd had to confirm that he would walk again, as the Viscount could not see his way clear otherwise. He'd had to assure the Viscount that Violet was firmly in favor of the idea. He'd had to convince the Viscount that he was not too stupid for Violet Granger. Finally, her father gave his permission, assuming Lady Mulholland really was for it. If she was not, the permission was to be voided as he did not like to cross his lady.

To say that Lady Mulholland was for it was an understatement. However, credit must be given that she did not reveal exactly how much. She knew it cost her daughter some pride to do a thing that she had been nudged to do. Violet had ever been so and her mother had very much feared that though she could not have picked out a more perfect gentleman for her daughter, it might not come off. It had looked hopeless for a time, but then it had suddenly seemed promising. Henry had told her that a great many thanks must go to Will Masters, though neither of them understood why. Lady Mulholland had taken care not to reveal her enthusiasm and it might only be guessed at by how playfully she shook Dandy's paws and plied him with tidbits.

Lord Smythesdon's recovery continued, and much of it continued in the library. There, he and his betrothed spent hours upon hours in conversation. At one moment they were discussing Euclid, and the next they spoke of their preferences in drapes. Over tea they examined the various medical uses of willow bark, and then easily slipped into what size dining room they would require. In the afternoon, they discussed architecture and then slipped into talking of their wedding trip. It was to be a match of intellect and domesticity combined.

Lord and Lady Ainsworth, well-satisfied at the happy turn of events and seeing that their son was no longer in physical danger, departed the house. However, Lady Ainsworth had become very dear to Lady Mulholland. The final seal of approval on the Countess had come from Mrs. Dallway, who pronounced the lady 'full of good sense.' The Viscount had found a kindred spirit in Lord Ainsworth, despite that gentleman's foreign ties to Hampshire. This necessitated that the Earl and his Countess come for regular visits. The Earl remained hopeful that he would one day convince the Viscount to venture out of Oxfordshire and dare the landscapes of Hampshire.

Violet's sisters were of mixed opinion on the match. Rose was delighted for Violet, but had begun narrowing her eyes at Lady Mulholland to attempt to fend off any more of her schemes. Daisy was unreservedly joyful, as she thought the lord the most perfect match for her sister. Marigold was mostly unaffected, though she would admit that the lord had grown more sensible and he must always be respected for not blaming The Turk for his own stupidity. Lily had, at first, fairly hidden from the lord, but he had noted her temperament and spoke to her gently and he gradually drew her out. Poppy and Pansy were distraught that Violet had been kidnapped by Lord Smythesdon. The twins were horrified that Violet had agreed to it and even seemed delighted by the idea. They did not know what to make of it, but Miss Millthorpe insisted that they would understand it better when they were older.

Smuckers, though he would only reveal it to Mrs. Featherstone, took most of the credit for the match. It had been he, and he alone, that had arranged to put Lord Smythesdon in the library in the mornings. It had been he, and he alone, who had dared speak so plainly to Violet Granger. It pleased him to know that he had played matchmaker to an Earl. An Earl was just steps away from royalty and he knew the match to be one more feather in his cap. How many local families with daughters would not dream of securing his services for their own? He was to be eagerly sought. Sought by who and how many, he could not say. To know he was sought was enough.

Now, Lord Smythesdon had regained the use of his leg and the wedding had taken place. Lord and Lady Ainsworth were happily ensconced at Chemsworth Hall and would stay on after the happy couple departed for their wedding tour. The couple were to visit Lord Smythesdon's cousins in Kent before setting off for the continent. Smuckers had taken special care for the wedding breakfast and had even dared to travel to London in pursuit of exotic fruit. He had returned with a pineapple and Mr. Moreau had quickly taken the thing in hand and incorporated it with the cherries into the wedding cake.

Smuckers looked over the table and its diners with a satisfied eye. The party had been constrained to the family, with the only exception being Mrs. Dallway. The butler thought it wise that such an exception had been made by Lady Mulholland, as no doubt Mrs. Dallway would have arrived whether invited or not.

Rose and Daisy sat together near the center of the table. Rose whispered, "I can feel The ODM plotting already."

"Do not be cross, Rose," Daisy said. "She might present you with somebody that you fall violently in love with."

"So you think," Rose said. "However, I would remind you that if she disposes of me, you would be next. How would you like *that*?"

"I shall adore it," Daisy said, "as long as she brings me my poet."

At the end of the table, Lady Mulholland patted her son's hand. "Just six more to go, my darling."

Henry Granger looked around, as if there must be some way to escape. Seeing no clear path, he slumped in his chair. Luring gentlemen to Chemsworth Hall was to be his new career.

"Six more what to go?" the Viscount asked.

"Daughters, my darling," Lady Mulholland said. "Violet has been married and that leaves six."

The Viscount looked round the table, seeming to count them up. Not finding all seven, he said, "Where's the other two?"

"Poppy and Pansy," Lady Mulholland said. "They are still in the nursery."

"That's right, Poppy and Pansy. And that's it then? No more after that?" the Viscount asked.

"I believe that to be the last of them," Lady Mulholland said. "You need not trouble yourself over them, Henry is to get them all married."

The Viscount peered at his son. "Are you? Excellent. I had wondered how I was to go about the thing."

At the other end of the table, Lord Smythesdon leaned close to his bride and said, "We shall be gone a month and by then the house in Oxford should be ready to receive us."

"And then," Violet said, "we shall plan our very first intellectual salon."

"And we shall do our bit for poor old Granger," the lord said.

"Oh, Bertie," Violet said, "you cannot mean that you really intend to join in on the scheme?"

"Why ever not?" he said. "It worked splendidly for me."

Violet smiled. "I will admit that it did. Though I am not certain we should be helping Henry bring more gentlemen to the house."

"If not us, then who?" Lord Smythesdon asked. "You know your sisters better than anybody. Should you not wish to have a hand in who they encounter? You do not wish to leave it all up to your brother?"

Violet considered this. Her husband did have a point.

"Furthermore," the lord said, "I have a splendid idea for Rose. We shall invite the fellow over and see what you think of him."

Violet bit her lip. She could not imagine the gentleman who could hold up against Rose. He would be pronounced horrible as soon as he set foot in the doors.

"I know what you fear," Lord Smythesdon said smiling, "and I have taken it into account."

"She will tell me I am horrible for even thinking of it," Violet said.

"But then she will change her mind," Lord Smythesdon said. "Just as you changed your mind."

"I did change my mind, did I not?" Violet said. "I do so rarely change my mind."

"And I am the lucky fellow you changed it for."

"I did not cut off my nose to revenge my face," Violet said.

"And you bravely went forward, despite your mother's approval," the lord added.

"Heavens," Violet said, "it has just occurred to me that I might produce very contrary children."

"If they are very much like you, I will adore them," Lord Smythesdon said.

And so, the wedding breakfast went on, various members of the family considering what the future might be, what schemes might be enacted and what schemes might be thwarted.

In the end though, Lady Mulholland was confident that she would emerge victorious. She had never lost a battle yet and had no intention of setting a precedent. Rose would be next, as she intended to go in strict order.

The End

More by Perpetua Langley:

The *Chemsworth Hall* series

    Book One, *Violet*

    Book Two, *Rose,* coming soon.

The Sweet Regency Romance Series

    Book One: A Summons to Greystone Hall

    Book Two: The Mysterious Earl

    Book Three: Season of Grace

    Book Four: Return to Hertfordshire

    Book Five: Miss Brookdale's Dowry

    Book Six: The Sweet Regency Romance Box Set #1-5

    Book Seven: Lady Carpathian and the Bennets

    Book Eight: Condescension and Condemnation

    Book Nine: In the Neighborhood of Buckthorn Green

    Book Ten: Blakely Hill

    Book Eleven: Our Particular Friend

    Book Twelve: The Sweet Regency Romance Box set #7-11

    Book Thirteen: The Bennets take on the Tom

    Book Fourteen: Lady Catherine Decamps

    Book Fifteen: The Lady's Jewels

    Book Sixteen: Cousin Emma

Printed in Great Britain
by Amazon